Amethyst Dream

by

Thea Thomas

Books by Thea Thomas

Dark Paranormal
Amethyst Dream
Porcelain Claws

Contemporary Sweet Romance
The Canyon Road Love Stories:
Canyon Road
One Love
Two Weddings

YA Urban
The People in the Mirror

Amethyst Dream

by

Thea Thomas

Amethyst Dream
Thea Thomas

Emerson & Tilman, Publishers
129 Pendleton Way #55
Washougal, WA 98671

Amethyst Dream
Copyright © Emerson & Tilman
Paperback ISBN: 978-1-947151-49-9

BISAC:
[1. FICTION/Occult & Supernatural
2. FICTION/Romance/Paranormal
3. FICTION/Ghost] I. Title.
BIC: FM

DEDICATION:

For all lovely dreamers....

Chapter 1

Elizabeth took the flower wreath down from the front door. The pale pastel roses laced among the stiff black ribbon were a bit wilted but still fragrant. A well-meaning neighbor put it on the door after learning Elizabeth's grandfather had died two days before.

Returning to the kitchen, Elizabeth picked the living flowers from the wreath. They were short stemmed, and she set them afloat in a cut crystal bowl, deciding to leave it on the kitchen table. The flowers looked so friendly in the soft light of the antique 1930s fixtures.

She'd spent much of her time, much more than usual, in the kitchen the last few days. She hadn't realized—until this moment—it was because she could pretend Grandfather sat in the front parlor, watching television as always, as long as she stayed in the kitchen.

Elizabeth climbed the back stairs to her bedroom. The house hovered over her, entirely too huge now that she lived alone. Everywhere she moved, she found the presence of Grandfather—some little item of his, a faint scent of his aftershave, or a note written on the back of an envelope, as was his habit. She'd never before realized how little of herself could be found in this house, even though she'd lived here nearly her whole life.

She sat on her chenille bedspread, white with blue tufts of large, brightly-colored flowers, and looked down at her hands in her lap, her thin fingers intertwined.

Thud-*thud*, came muffled from outside. Ka-ka-ka-*thud*. She stood and moved to the window, pushing it halfway up so she could hear every pop and crackle of the fireworks at Disneyland. She could feel their reverberations through the floor, while the blue, pink, silver and gold sparkling, transient lights poured from the sky.

All her life she'd watched the fireworks from her bedroom window. All her life their beauty and freedom had made her sad and lonely. Now the sadness mingled with the sadness of the loss of her grandfather. The colors in the sky streaked and ran together and rained with her tears.

As she stared at the fireworks through her reflection in the dark glass of the window, her face appeared to change—it became more full, her hair darker and straight. She couldn't even see her eyes for the glinting of dark-rimmed glasses, though she'd never worn glasses in her life.

Startled, she stepped back from the window. The strangest sensation ran through her body from head to toes. A muscle in her forearm began to jump. Elizabeth moved to the bed and hugged herself. "I—must be too exhausted. I've got to get some good sleep."

She turned on all the lights in her room and slipped into a nightgown. But she couldn't shake the image of that face—that was *not* her face—reflected in the window.

2 ~ Thea Thomas

Chapter II

The next morning, Elizabeth opened the front door with her little push cart in hand. An errant stiff breeze caught at the door and the skirt of her house dress. While she struggled with the heavy door, her skirt, and her cart, all at the same time, she happened to look across the street and saw Mrs. Wilmer doing precisely the same—attempting to grab onto the front door, her push cart, and the skirt of her tiny-print house dress at the same time.

Except Mrs. Wilmer was seventy-five years old. Elizabeth stopped. She let the wind fling the door open against the house and her push cart escaped like a puppy, scampering to the corner of the porch while her skirt buffeted about her knees.

Everything—the door, my cart, even my *clothes*— everything is trying to get free, she thought.

Ignoring the push cart, she went back into the house, pulling the door shut. Then she tip-toed into Grandfather's somber study and stole to the serious, dark monolith of his desk. Even though Grandfather would not come in and ask her what she was doing at his desk, her stomach clinched, her hand shook as she slid open the middle drawer and picked up the car keys.

She left the study, continuing resolutely out the back door, then into the garage, trying not to think about the last time she'd driven. But she couldn't help it—she saw herself two months ago driving into the garage, the last time she brought Grandfather home from the hospital.

She refused to linger on that memory, turning her thoughts to the fact that she'd almost never driven anywhere alone in her life, and she'd certainly never driven Grandfather's car without him present. She put the key in the ignition, turned it. The engine kicked over a couple times, then fell silent.

"What's wrong with you, old timer?" She tried again. Again it ground and quit.

Elizabeth got out of the car, pacing around it. Then she climbed back in, staring at the steering wheel, thinking. "Ah-ha, the battery! The car's been sitting a long time." She waited a couple minutes, then turned the key again. It kicked over three times instead of twice.

She got out of the car again and strolled around the garage, contemplating the tools hung neatly on the walls. Two Saturdays every month, Ralph-the-gardener came and clipped and snipped and mowed the front yard, the back yard and the side yards to neat and trim perfection.

Although he had a truck full of his own equipment, from time to time Elizabeth had seen him sharpening and tending to Grandfather's tools. Suddenly she understood Ralph's affection for these antique tools. Even though she couldn't guess the function of half of them, they were beautiful, each hanging in silent repose, waiting to do its job. How much more beautiful they must be to Ralph, she thought, who knew which chore each one made easier in a time before noisy riding mowers, blowers and weed whackers.

Elizabeth got back into the car again and turned the key. The engine kicked and started. "What a clever car!" She patted the dash, feeling very accomplished.

Then she drove the two-and-a-half blocks to the store. Yes, she told herself, it was silly to drive two-and-a-half blocks. But this particular drive, the first of her independent life, had nothing to do with the two-and-a-half blocks, or the groceries.

As she pushed a grocery cart up and down the aisles, she noticed other young women about her age. Most of them wore T-shirts and shorts. Their hair shone bright with natural colors, and quite a few unnatural colors, long and straight or short-short exotic cuts. And they wore make-up.

She looked into the mirror overhead at the end of the aisle and saw herself, a virtual recluse, and a stranger in this sea of modern chic at the local grocery store. She studied her reflection, bemused—dressed in an over-sized small-print house dress, hair in stiff little curls. She didn't even know when she'd last seen her lipstick—the sum total of her cosmetics—a sample left by an Avon lady.

As she pushed her cart past the paperbacks and periodicals she stopped before *Mademoiselle.* She'd always wondered what might be secreted between its covers. If ever Grandfather's disapproving spirit intended to make itself known, this had to be the moment. But she didn't feel him over her shoulder as she picked up the magazine and put it in her cart. She moved purposefully to the packaged cosmetics and added a compact, mascara, and a lipstick, 'Mauve's Twilight,' to the *Mademoiselle*.

Feeling guilty and tremendously pleased, she continued her circuit around the store, gathering breakfast cereal, vegetables, bread, almond milk, some peanut butter, jelly, cans of soup. In the last month of being alone she'd discovered that she didn't like to cook. Now, once in a while she'd make herself a sandwich and maybe open a can of soup, but she'd decided that cooking for herself, alone, was boring.

Indulging in one last whim, she grabbed up a two-liter bottle of Dr. Pepper, her special secret. She loved Dr. Pepper. Back at the car she stowed the groceries on the floor behind the driver's seat. Then, because only the milk was perishable, she decided to go all out with this freedom idea and go for a drive.

Driving up Tustin Avenue and then down Main Street without goal, she became aware that men were looking at her. It didn't make sense, she thought, who cared about a mousy woman in an old car? Ridiculous! But as she paused at a red light, two cute young men a couple lanes over were unquestionably looking right at her, nodding and talking animatedly.

She glanced down self-consciously and discovered to her horror that her gas tank registered below empty. She pulled into the first filling station she came to, got out of the car and went into the Quik-Mart-Gas-Up.

"Forty dollars on number five, please." She handed cash to the boy behind the counter.

"That your fifty-six?" the boy asked.

"My what?" Elizabeth asked.

"The fifty-six, the mint condition fifty-six."

Elizabeth continued to stand with her hand extended, wondering what the boy was talking about.

The big man with the beer belly and a six-pack in line behind her spoke up. "Yeah. It's a beaut, huh?"

"What?" Elizabeth tried again to dispel her confusion.

"The fifty-six," the boy said again, "the one with the wide white walls."

"Ha-*HA!*" the big man behind her seemed almost to explode. "Funny, kid! The one with the wide white walls. *HA-ha-ha.*"

Elizabeth turned and looked at him as if he were speaking a foreign language. "Your Chevy, lady," the big man gestured toward her car. "The one with the wide white walls ... get it?"

Elizabeth shook her head slightly.

"A car like that, you know, it's like, if you had an elephant out there and someone asked, is that your elephant, the one with the tusks ... you know. Like as if there's a lot of elephants ... see?"

"Oh," Elizabeth said. "Well, yes, that's my car." She hated getting gas, she decided. "That's my elephant," she added, walking out the door.

As she returned to the car, she replayed the conversation, then she put it together with all the men who seemed to be looking at her as she drove around. Well, that explained *that!* But she still didn't understand if the attention was because the car was admirable or ... a white and turquoise elephant in the street.

"'Scuse me," the beer-bellied man said, deferential, approaching Elizabeth as she struggled with the gas cap.

"Yes?" she said, wrenching the gas cap off. She did *not* want him to ask her if she needed help.

"I'm wondering if—if your car might be for sale?"

"You *like* it?" Elizabeth asked.

"I just said it's a beaut, didn't I?"

"I didn't know if you were serious, or ...."

"Serious, of course. A refurbished fifty-six in mint condition. Yeah. Absolutely serious."

"Well, I'm sorry," Elizabeth said, "it's not refurbished."

"No?" The man's expression took on disbelief.

"No. This is its original condition."

"Wow," he said reverently. "That's amazing. Would you be interested in selling it?"

"Oh, I don't think so."

"No? Too bad. Would you mind—could I just peek at the interior?"

"Well, I suppose," Elizabeth said, not knowing what else to say.

He poked his head in the door. Elizabeth replaced the gas nozzle and screwed the gas cap back on. She came around to the driver's side of the car, trying hard not to think about how embarrassed she felt. His muffled voice came back out to her.

"Wow ... 's great. Lookit ... no holes ... clean's ... whistle." He backed out of the car and turned to

Elizabeth. "I suppose you're going to tell me that's actual mileage?"

"Well, everything on the gauges is just ... what is."

A car behind them honked. Elizabeth jumped. "Oh, goodness," she said, "how *rude* of me." She worked her way around the large man, slunk into the driver's seat and started the car. As she pulled away she nodded with a small polite smile at him.

He nodded back, grinning, holding a thumb up.

At home she put the groceries away, alternately feeling embarrassment for herself and laughing at herself. "Serves me right for thinking men were paying attention to me!" she scolded while putting the broccoli and carrots in the refrigerator vegetable bin. "First of all, vanity is a dangerous emotion, or so I've been told. Secondly, you have to have something to be vain about."

The *Mademoiselle* and cosmetics were in two small plastic bags at the bottom of the big one. Elizabeth had forgotten that she'd even bought them.

"Speaking of vanity!" She tried to keep her disapproving tone of voice, but excitement won over. She took her treasures to the second floor bathroom, battled them out of their packaging and finally applied them. The lipstick was too dark and the powder too light, but she didn't care. Maybe it's a little sad, she thought, to be experiencing at twenty-eight a thrill over cosmetics that I might have experienced years ago.

She smiled at the small heart-shaped face in the mirror. "At least I'm willing to admit I'm acting out my arrested growth. Grandfather raised me to the

best of his ability, even if outmoded by a century."
She had a wild and absent mother to thank for that.

The dark lipstick made her mouth appear too tiny, and the powder made her already white skin pallid. But the mascara transformed her eyes! Curling and defining her thick eyelashes made her big brown eyes sparkle. She'd never dare say, or even *think* herself beautiful, but she considered that she could possibly pass for—rather pretty.

She took the *Mademoiselle* to her room and sprawled out on the bed, studying the women in the ads, and lost heart.

"I'm just a pale frump, and there's no point in trying to tell myself otherwise."

Chapter III

The next morning Elizabeth woke up when she realized that the annoying noise was the telephone ringing. The ogreish troll behind her in a Mack truck, honking his horn, fell back into the abyss of dream.

As she stumbled sleepily out of her room she noticed the *Mademoiselle* in the trash. That's strange, she thought, it's four feet from the bed, it couldn't have slipped there. The telephone kept ringing and she couldn't give the magazine more thought. She ran downstairs to the only telephone in the house, in Grandfather's study.

"Hello?" she answered breathlessly.

"Well, hello yourself, where were you?"

"Martha!" Elizabeth exclaimed, delighted to hear her friend's voice. "I was sleeping. I had to run from my room to the phone in Grandfather's study."

"Well, for pity's sake, girl, get a cell phone!"

"Oh!" Elizabeth couldn't imagine it. "I don't think I can afford it."

"Oh, please, Elizabeth, you can afford it."

"Really?" Elizabeth hadn't spent money on anything beyond subsistence since her grandfather had passed, until last night when she bought the magazine and cosmetics. She'd broken two appointments to talk about finances with Grandfather's attorney. She couldn't bring herself to discuss Grandfather's 'estate,' which would make his passing so final, even though he *was* gone. And she also didn't want to find out she had no money to live on. "Do you think Grandfather left me anything besides this big old house?"

"My goodness, you're naive," Martha said.

"Yes," Elizabeth agreed, "I am."

"Your grandfather had a highly successful men's clothing store for fifty years. When he sold both the property and the business he *must* have seen a small fortune, not to mention what your 'big old' house is worth. You could probably sell the house, buy a condo and live comfortably on the profit alone." Martha paused, then continued, "your Grandfather only had you, an obedient granddaughter with straight teeth and perfect health, to spend money on. And I don't think he made a vice of spending money on you."

"No, not much, he didn't."

"So, get some phones already! Anyway," Martha continued without missing a beat, "I called to tell you about a rug and fiber arts wall hanging exhibit at the Bower's Museum. Do you want to go with me?"

"I'd love to. But aren't you afraid I'll bore you, droning on about stitches and styles?"

"That's precisely my point, dear girl. I want to learn, and you're my valued resource." Elizabeth could hear

Martha tapping her iPad. "Let's see, today's pretty booked. How's your tomorrow?"

"All my tomorrows are un-booked," Elizabeth answered.

"Agh! Deplorable, Lizzie, that's got to change! I'll pick you up at eleven-thirty in the morning and take part of the afternoon off. Maybe I'll get crazy and take the whole afternoon off."

"We could wait until Saturday."

"No way," Martha returned emphatically. "You miss my point, I *want* to take some time off. Besides, the exhibit will be crowded on Saturday. Don't start that 'oh no, I'm in the way,' routine of yours. Now I mean it, no guilt, just fun."

"Yes Martha. Okay Martha," Elizabeth recited, "no guilt, just fun. See you tomorrow!"

Elizabeth went back upstairs, passed her bedroom and continued down the long dark hall to the end room, the room that long ago had been her mother's. Elizabeth had taken it over for her workroom when her mother gallivanted off to who-knew-where the last time Elizabeth saw her, twelve years previous.

She opened the door. Her rug-making paraphernalia, several projects in mid-development, arrayed throughout the room.

She remembered how Grandfather used to call to her from downstairs, "Rapunzel, Rapunzel, let down your golden yarn." She smiled.

All her love for the soft wool and the solid feel of the weft growing in the warp underhand, even the smell of the wood frames, and wool and jute and raw silk—the gorgeous, sensual sight of the hanks of pure

colors, waiting to be knotted or woven or stitched—
flooded over her when she opened the door, with a
nostalgia as strong as if remembering a person.

In the middle of the room stood the biggest project she'd ever undertaken, a nine-by-twelve-foot
latch-hooked rug with a Samarkand-styled pattern
of her own design, two-thirds complete.

She went over to it and began working as if she'd
only interrupted herself for a few moments instead
of more than a year.

Chapter IV

Elizabeth managed to wake at nine-thirty the next morning, even after working on the rug fifteen hours, non-stop. Her shoulders and hands were sore and she had a nasty blister on her right forefinger, but it wouldn't be long and the Samarkand would be finished. She had to admit she savored the aches and pains. Battle wounds! She couldn't wait to put the rug on the floor at the foot of her bed where its reds and blues would complement the hardwood.

She jumped in the shower to get ready for her day with Martha. When Elizabeth was nine or ten, her mother had met Martha in a ballroom dance class. They soon discovered that they had much in common, and became dedicated to the search of more interesting dance partners than the class afforded.

Although Elizabeth's mother, Gloria, was ten years older than Martha, she didn't look it, and the two of them, to hear Martha tell it, had the guys lined up.

"And why not?" Elizabeth thought, "they're two gorgeous, flirty women."

However, the result of the flirtation with night clubs led Gloria off to some more exotic spot on earth. Or so she would have everyone believe. Since then, Martha had befriended Elizabeth, and every now and then she escaped her frenetic schedule and came up with something for the two of them to do.

Elizabeth stepped into her gold satin-finish cotton dress with fitted bodice and full skirt. Except, she noticed, it was not as fitted as it used to be, hanging loose and looking almost like one of her shapeless house dresses. She'd lost weight since Grandfather became ill, and she didn't even know it.

She brushed her hair hard, trying to relax the awkward curls from the last home permanent she'd given herself. Then she applied mascara and a bit of powder. She looked around for the lipstick, but couldn't find it.

"Strange ..." She peered into the nearly empty medicine chest. "Where could it have gotten to?" As she looked around on the floor, a prickly sensation crawled up her forearms and down the back of her neck.

She turned quickly, feeling watched. "What ...?" She rubbed the prickles away from her neck, "you're rattling around too much in this cavern of a house, and now you're talking out loud to yourself."

As she looked around the bathroom one more time for the lipstick, the front doorbell rang. Hurrying to her room, she grabbed a small clutch purse, a note pad and pencil, then ran down the winding front stairs to open the door. There Martha stood, wearing designer sunglasses, a mauve business suit complemented by a gorgeous white silk blouse and simple black patent heels. Cool and sophisticated.

Elizabeth wanted to run back to her room and never come out again.

"Ready?" Martha asked.

"Sure." Elizabeth nodded. She screwed up her courage, stepped through the door and locked it behind her.

Martha chatted non-stop on the ride to the museum. But Elizabeth hardly heard a word of it, answering in monosyllables. She recounted to herself the odd events: today, the *Mademoiselle* in the trash, the vanished lipstick. Last night, the strange woman's reflection in the window ....

"What are you studying out?" Martha finally asked bluntly.

"Pardon me?"

"You're like on some other planet." Martha pulled down her sunglasses to give Elizabeth a pointed look.

"Yikes, Martha, eyes on the road!" Elizabeth squealed as the car drifted into the other lane.

Martha refocused on her driving. "*What* is on your mind? You haven't heard a word I've said."

"I *do* have a lot on my mind," Elizabeth agreed. "With Grandfather ... gone, I've been—I have a lot to think about." Elizabeth was about to share with Martha the weird events, but Martha reached over and squeezed her hand.

"I know kiddo, of course. Sorry, sometimes I forget that some things are about other people. Sometimes." She laughed. "It seems it'd be *easier* all around if everything was always about me, but such is not the case."

Elizabeth giggled. Martha had a way of always shifting her mood to something better. And the bright sunny day was so real and normal, that the weird events faded away.

Martha started struggling with flinging her heels into the back seat and pulling on Reeboks at the stop lights. "I hope you don't mind," she said to Elizabeth. "I don't imagine there'll be anyone at this exhibit I want to impress."

"I don't care what you wear on your feet, just as long as you stay in our lane." In truth, Elizabeth loved the incongruity of the Reeboks with the designer suit.

She sighed in relief as they pulled into the museum parking lot. "We made it!"

"Of course we made it, you silly girl. I've never had an accident."

"*There's* a miracle," Elizabeth breathed as she got out of the car.

"I heard that," Martha called back to her, already halfway to the museum entrance.

That was the one thing about Martha that disconcerted Elizabeth—always in such a rush, as if she simply had to get to the next thing. She hoped Martha wouldn't ruin the exhibit by flying through it, dragging Elizabeth along behind like a trailing kite.

Then Elizabeth had the most delightful realization. She could come again! She could come alone, she could stay all day. She could take notes and make sketches. She wouldn't have to ask Grandfather's permission, or risk his disapproval. And so, smiling, she hurried to catch up to Martha.

In the museum Elizabeth trotted alongside Martha, nodding in agreement to her intermittent, "oh, pretty, look at that."

The exhibit, primarily nineteenth century American hooked and woven rugs, also had a few remarkable Persian, Turkish, and Indian carpets, displayed in showcases on frames allowing their backs to show as well as their fronts. If Elizabeth had her way, she would study each one to the extent of counting knots. And she *would*, she told herself, when she returned on her own.

"Where's your running commentary, Elizabeth?" Martha suddenly asked.

"Running commentary? I don't want to bore you ...."

"I'll let you know if you're boring me. You must know more than these terse little notes: 'probable construction between 18-something and 18-something.' "

"Well, yes, I do," Elizabeth agreed. "For instance, did you know that the Persians make a small copy of the carpet for the weavers to follow, while the Chinese draw a full-sized replica of the rug design on paper and put it beside the loom for the weavers to copy?

"But the east Indians have a very interesting system called *ta'lem*. The *ta'lem* writer records the color of every knot, row by row and then a *ta'lem* reader reads this list to a roomful of weavers. Wouldn't that be a remarkable thing to see and hear? A room full of artisans, hands flying, creating one of these magnificent works of art to the mantra of a list of colors being recited. I can see the sun slanting in on piles of colored wool ..." Elizabeth gestured to show the angle of the sunlight, "and the carpet frames and the people sitting side by side, but each in their own sort of transfixed, meditative space, listening to the incantation, obeying it, trusting that every tiny knot will produce a complete and beautiful image."

Elizabeth caught Martha's study of her. "I did it, didn't I? I bored you."

"No, Elizabeth, you—you amaze me. I never knew you had so much poetry in you. I *really* see your room of weavers. This display is like a spiritual experience for you, isn't it?" Martha asked.

"What an uncanny word choice. Whenever I go into an oriental carpet store, or even into my own rug-making room, I've always thought the carpets are like church stained glass windows, only opaque."

"So they are!" Martha exclaimed.

After that they took a more leisurely, attentive, stroll through the exhibit. Elizabeth was amazed to see that Martha listened carefully to every bit of information she shared. Whenever she and Martha had been together before, Martha talked and Elizabeth listened.

In fact, Elizabeth thought with life-changing insight, everyone has always talked and I have always listened. Now, I begin to talk, and I am listened to.

Afterwards they went to Chez Cafe for a late lunch.

"Are you losing weight?" Martha asked when they were seated.

"Apparently. This dress used to fit better, anyway. I haven't had much interest in food lately. I'm home alone, no one to cook for, so I don't cook, no one to eat with, so I don't often eat."

"I see," Martha said. "I thought you were on a diet."

"Why would I go on a diet? I'm not fat."

"That's what I was about to say. There's something else different about you too ... what is it?"

"Well, I, I bought some mascara a couple days ago."

"Ah, yes," Martha said. "I guess that, and the weight you've lost, accounts for your huge, waif-like eyes."

"Waif-like?"

"I mean that as a compliment. The wise-yet-innocent look."

"Wise-yet-innocent. But—plain."

"Are you nuts? You're darling. I wish to goodness I looked half as pretty as you do with so little make-up."

"You're just saying that."

"I am *not*. I've never said any such thing to any woman in my life!"

The waitress brought their salads. When she left Martha continued, "my dear girl, get some confidence! I don't know where it's supposed to come from after a lifetime of Miss House Mouse, but work on it."

Elizabeth nodded. "I know. I'm pathetic. I don't have a clue about anything!" She then launched into telling Martha about driving around in her grandfather's car, and the attention she thought she was getting, which had her so mystified. "But all they were all interested in was that old car of Grandfather's!"

Martha laughed so hard she had to put her fork down and wipe her eyes. "Oh, geez, Lizzie, what a picture, you cowering in the shadow of the giant beer-belly. And he was only after your fifty-six."

"Well, I'm relieved to learn that it's a funny story. I thought it was rather sad."

"No, sweetie. Loosen up! Some things are simply *so ridiculous*."

Elizabeth scowled.

"Isn't it funny?" Martha insisted. "Come on now ...."

"And you call that car a 'fifty-six' too! There's a whole language out here in the—*world*—that I don't know anything about. I'm an alien in my own culture."

Martha shook her head. "It just so happens that your car's a classic, it also happens that you didn't know it. But now you do. Now you can join the rest of 'civilization' out here." Martha's tone was droll. "You're free now, honey, so take advantage of it and grow!"

Elizabeth suddenly started to cry. Shocked, she grabbed the napkin out of her lap and dabbed at her eyes. "I'm *sorry!*" she whispered to Martha. "I *have* been realizing I'm free and I can do things. If you only knew the emotions I went through the other night when I bought a *Mademoiselle* and Dr. Pepper! I felt as wild as if I'd held up a convenience store. I felt guilty doing things Grandfather disapproved of, I felt happy to have things I've always wanted, I felt angry at not having been allowed to have that freedom before. And then I felt guilty again.

"And now you say—you say exactly that." Elizabeth pulled herself together, and sat up straight. "I want to sell the so-called *'fifty-six.'* I want to get something ordinary and new."

Martha reached over and patted Elizabeth's hand. "You can sell it or trade it, you can get something snazzy or plain, you can buy any magazine or beverage. Even wine. In fact, let's have a glass right now. Let's celebrate your coming of age."

"Yes, let's," Elizabeth agreed, smiling. "Almost a decade late."

"Or perhaps it's right on time." Martha flagged the waitress, chatted with her about wines and ordered something while Elizabeth sat feeling very much like a ten-year-old out to lunch with someone who knew what she was doing.

When the waitress went scurrying off, Martha turned back to Elizabeth. "Get out that pad and pencil of yours," she ordered, retrieving her iphone, "here's my car dealer's number. Tell him I sent you and he'll make you a deal."

"He will?"

"Of course! He owes me. I gave him the best three months of his life. He's dying to do me a favor."

"Oh!" Elizabeth said, embarrassed.

"Now, Elizabeth," Martha said, "don't get all weird. Another thing you'll have to learn to take in stride is that sex is a part of life too."

"Yes, yes, I know it is," Elizabeth agreed, "I just don't want any details."

23 ~ Amethyst Dream

"Then, I'll keep the details to myself." Martha smiled slyly, raising an eyebrow. "The point here is business. My friend, Edward, will help you unload the fifty-six, he'll help you figure out what you'd like instead, and then he'd better give you a good deal, or I'll want to know the reason why!"

The waitress returned with a couple of glasses and a bottle of wine.

"Drink your wine," Martha ordered.

Elizabeth drank her wine. A feeling of lightness rose right to the top of her head, and blossomed all through her, right to her toes, totally dispelling her brooding, dark, mood.

For the first time in her life Elizabeth became inebriated, or at least she thought she must be, as everything Martha said after the first glass of wine seemed ridiculously funny. She giggled until she thought her teeth would fall out. But Martha was giggling too, so, Elizabeth decided, even if she was making a spectacle of herself, at least she wasn't alone. She wasn't too sure how much wine she had, but she did notice that Martha had only poured herself one glass.

And then, some time later, Martha drove Elizabeth home.

Chapter V

lose to dawn, Elizabeth heard her grandfather's
voice. It came through her sleep, urgent and
insistent. She wanted very much to understand what
he was trying to tell her—he said *something* about an
amethyst. She became wide awake in the effort of trying to understand him. In that first instant between
sleep and wakefulness, she could have sworn the
shadow of her grandfather stood at the end of her
bed, but at that same instant, a ray of sun peeked
through the blinds and he disappeared.

It was then that she realized the percussion sec-
tion of a marching band stomped through her head.
So! This was a hangover.

She longed for a glass of orange juice. Dragging
herself down the back stairs into the kitchen, she
coaxed what little juice she could from two sad and
wizened-looking oranges she found in the bottom of
the refrigerator, well on their way to making a wine
of their own.

As she sat at the kitchen table, head in hand, she
tried to shake the intense, strange dream that had

awakened her. "I think I must move out of this house." She looked at her clutch purse on the kitchen table where she'd flung it when she came in last night. What was she supposed to do? She picked up the purse, and under it she saw the note pad she'd carried around yesterday. Oh! The car dealer.

Well, first she'd have to see what condition her finances were in. Still wobbly and deciding that wine was perhaps not the best beverage of choice for her, she went into Grandfather's study, where she called the bank and asked the teller the balance of her personal savings account. As she recalled, she had around a thousand dollars. She hoped that her savings in combination with Grandfather's car would make a down payment on a new, small car.

"Thirty-one thousand, two-hundred-thirty-three dollars and seventy-two cents," the teller told Elizabeth a few moments later.

Elizabeth forgot her headache. "Excuse me?" she said, "I asked for the balance of the savings account of Elizabeth Morris."

"Yes. That's it—barring any activity yesterday or today."

"The last I knew, I had about a thousand dollars."

The teller giggled. "Well, you do, plus over thirty more to keep it company. Would you like to speak with the manager?"

Bemused, Elizabeth paused, then said, "Yes, I think I need to."

"Of course. Hold, please."

A few moments later another woman came on the phone. "Good morning, Miss Morris. I'm sorry if there's some confusion. I thought you were aware of the financial arrangements since your grandfather passed."

"No. I'm supposed to talk with his attorney, but I haven't yet. I've been—I haven't been in the mood."

"I understand. To clarify, your grandfather had thirty-thousand dollars put in your passbook savings. Then you have your trust of three-hundred-thousand per year in an easy-to-access money market account. And, of course, there are the long term accounts now in your name, as well as a few other financial instruments. If you'd like to make an appointment to come in and talk, I'd be happy to discuss the details with you."

Stunned, Elizabeth, stared at the black Bakelite base of the old rotary dial telephone. "Yes, I'll do that. Monday morning, about ten?"

"That'll be fine," the manager said.

"So I can buy a car?" Elizabeth asked.

"I would say yes," the bank manager answered. "You could buy any reasonably priced car you fancy."

"Well, thank you," Elizabeth said.

"Always our pleasure, Miss Morris."

After she hung up, she hurried upstairs to shower and dress. "Any car I fancy. Hmmm. I'll be happy with something plain and easy to handle. You're right again, Martha!"

*   *

Elizabeth pulled onto the I-5 freeway south, headed for the Irvine Auto Complex. When she arrived, she

27 – Amethyst Dream

walked shyly into a pristine showroom, surrounded by the shining hides of new cars like a herd of quiet, immaculate livestock, waiting to be lassoed and ridden to their new homes.

Elizabeth went to the back of the showroom behind a plate glass wall and approached the Barbie Doll-looking receptionist sitting behind a metal desk, seriously engrossed in a magazine.

"Excuse me," Elizabeth said.

"Yes?" the young woman gave Elizabeth a superficial glance.

"Is Edward Vance here?"

"He's out back with a customer." She returned her attention to the magazine.

"I see," Elizabeth said. "Is there ... should I ... I need to talk with him."

"Who may I say is here?"

"He doesn't know me. I'm a friend of a friend of his. My name is Elizabeth Morris."

The receptionist picked up a mic. "Edward, Elizabeth Morris is here to see you," blasted, Elizabeth was certain, over a mile radius.

"He doesn't know me," Elizabeth reiterated after the walls stopped echoing.

The receptionist shrugged.

Elizabeth wandered among the new cars, trying to visualize owning any one of them. They all looked so flamboyant in their showy spotlights.

A young mother came through the front door, pushing a baby stroller. The pretty baby immediately caught Elizabeth's attention. Elizabeth smiled at the baby and the baby smiled back. The mother caught the interchange and smiled too. She ambled toward Elizabeth.

"Goodness," she said confidentially, "my husband told me to look for a car I like? But I don't know, look at all of them!"

"I'm having the same problem," Elizabeth said. "I mean, not that my husband—that is, I'm not married. I mean, I'm trying to decide what I like, but I don't know. Everything looks so flashy."

The young mother nodded.

"You have a beautiful baby," Elizabeth said, finding the little girl with the golden brown curls and the sea green eyes far more attractive and interesting than the cars.

"Well, *we* think so," the mother agreed. "But then there's nothing less objective than a mother's opinion of her child."

"Oh no!" Elizabeth protested. "She really is beautiful and so *still*, as if she's having very deep thoughts."

The mother laughed. "I thought it was just me, but I guess if someone else sees it—she *does* seem to be deep, or very sober. She's only a little over a year old, but she seems as if, I don't know, as if her last life taught her patience, as if she's a very old soul."

"Yes," Elizabeth agreed. She kneeled down in front of the baby and looked deep into her round eyes. The baby looked back steadily. "You probably still remember a lot of things from the other side, don't you, pretty little baby?" Elizabeth wanted to touch the baby's soft white hand, but restrained herself.

29 ~ Amethyst Dream

"Elizabeth Morris?" a man asked behind her.

Elizabeth stood and looked around, refocusing. "Yes," she extended her hand. "Edward Vance?"

"That's me. Pretty little girl you have there," he said, smiling down at the baby.

"Oh!" Elizabeth looked behind her. The baby's mother had her head in the window of the sedan behind them. "She's not my baby, she's this woman's baby."

The woman pulled her torso out of the car window, turned and put her hand possessively on the stroller and smiled. "Yes, she's mine, warts and all!"

They all chuckled, but Elizabeth couldn't imagine being so casual about the beautiful child. Well, she thought, I guess if one has a remarkable baby like that, day in and day out, at some point it seems ordinary.

"What can I do to help you?" Edward asked Elizabeth.

"Martha suggested I talk with you."

"Martha! Martha West? How is she?" His attention suddenly focused on Elizabeth.

"She's fine. She's excellent, in fact. We spent the day together yesterday."

"Really? I'll have to give her a call. *So!* What can I do for you?"

"I have a nineteen-fifty-six Chevy and I was wondering if I could trade it in on ... one of these." She looked around the showroom.

"A fifty-six? Goodness. You don't hear that every day. Do you have the car with you?"

"Yes. Out on the curb."

They went outside and stood in front of the car. Then Edward started poking and prodding every nook and cranny of the car, saying *"hmmm,"* repeatedly, after which he led Elizabeth back inside to a desk at the opposite end of the office from the receptionist.

"Well!" Edward began. "Let me tell you, just between the two of us. That car is a find. I honestly couldn't give you in trade what you could get for it from the right person."

"But I don't know the right person," Elizabeth pointed out.

"I do!" Edward crowed triumphantly. "I know this guy, he's kind of eccentric but he's all right. Anyway, he's into vintage stuff. I'm sure I remember him saying once he'd really like to get his hands on a mint condition fifty-six. Want me to give him a call?"

Disappointed, Elizabeth felt Edward was politely trying to get rid of her. "But what about my new car?"

"Hey, Miss Morris, I'm here to sell cars, right? And you're a friend of Martha's, I'm going to take care of you."

Well, Elizabeth thought, I trust Martha, so I guess I'll have to trust her friend. "Okay," she said.

Edward scrolled through a list on his computer, then dialed a number. "This guy's a writer, Peter Shamus. You ever hear of him?"

Elizabeth started to say, "No ...."

"Peter!" Edward said heartily into the receiver. "Hey, guy, you still in the market for a mint condition fifty-six? ... yeah? I got one. Ya gotta see it ... You're on deadline? Okay guy. But ya interested in this five-six or not? Deadlines come and go, buddy, but a car like this ... yeah, well, I don't see why not. Let me ask." He looked over at Elizabeth. "Can you go by his place? He lives right here, it's not three miles. At *The Lakes*. You know *The Lakes*?"

Elizabeth shook her head.

"You don't know *The Lakes* or you don't want to drive over?"

"I don't know *The Lakes*," she said. And I don't want to drive over, she thought.

"Yeah, Peter, she'll be right over." He hung up and gave Elizabeth explicit directions to Peter's house, drawing a little map. "Okay, Miss Morris, are you good with that?"

"Yes, I believe so. But I can't help but wonder what's in it for you?"

"Oh, I'm hurt," Edward said, not seeming the least bit pained. "Really! *Wounded!* But frankly, I expect to sell a car. Am I right or am I right? You're going to come back here and buy a car, right?"

"Well, yes. That is, you're right, but I was going to buy a car anyway."

"Right. But look, you'll buy a car, I'll make a few bucks, you'll make Peter happy with that car, he'll make you happy by giving you a fair price, you'll have more money to spend on a beautiful new car. And, bonus, You'll tell Martha I'm wonderful—huh? Huh? Am I right or am I right?"

"Well, right again, I suppose, Mr. Vance."

"Eddy, please! Call me Eddy. Any friend of Martha's I hope will be a friend of mine."

"Thanks ... Eddy," Elizabeth said awkwardly,

shaking his hand then leaving his plate glass office.

She got in her car and started to follow Eddy's hand-drawn map. But as she drove, the beautiful baby girl came back into her mind. She became shocked to discover a pining, an ache, for a child like that—she'd never known such a feeling until this very moment.

Curious and distracted by this deep feeling of discovering something entirely new within herself, this notion of motherhood, she soon realized she'd become lost. She pulled over and studied the map, only to see that she sat right in front of Peter Shamus' house, situated on the charming lake.

She gathered her courage—yet another new person!—got out of the car and walked up to the front door, which she found slightly ajar. She knocked on the door jamb.

"It's open," someone shouted from upstairs.

She stepped into the entry way, keeping her hand on the open door. "Hello?" she called cautiously. She felt immensely ill-at-ease in a strange man's house—a strange man she'd been *told* was strange. "Hello?" she called again. "I'm Elizabeth Morris? Eddy sent me? I have my car, the fifty-six Chevy?"

"I'm upstairs."

"Well," she answered back, "I'll wait here."

"I'll be right down, just gotta finish a thought."

Elizabeth waited by the door in view of the stairwell. A few minutes later a thin, youthful-looking man came bounding down the stairs in red shorts and a black tee-shirt. His sandy hair tousled over his forehead and he had a scraggly growth of beard. His pale eyes were deep set and intelligent in a thin, angular face.

"Hi," he extended his hand, "I'm Peter."

Elizabeth let go of the door and took his hand, his long, thin fingers were warm. "Elizabeth," she answered. This man, even in his casual attire and ill-kept appearance had so much presence, Elizabeth was taken aback.

"I ... I ... the car is outside."

"Good," Peter said, clearly distracted.

"I guess this is a bad time for you," Elizabeth asked, "with a deadline?"

Peter finally looked at her, and his study made her feel like stone one moment and butter the next.

"Thanks for coming," he finally said, apropos of nothing.

Elizabeth nodded, then went through the front door.

"Wow!" Peter said, following her. "Hey, that's a *beaut!*"

"So I've been told," Elizabeth answered, confused by Peter's sudden change in character.

"Where'd you get it?"

"My grandfather. My grandfather bought it new."

"Really!"

They walked up to the car and Elizabeth handed Peter the keys. "Thanks," he said taking them, but walking completely around the car before getting in. Elizabeth got in the passenger side. "Look at this interior," he said when he got in, running a hand over the upholstery. "You don't mind if I drive?" he asked.

"Mind if you drive? I want you to buy it—I want you to *always* drive it."

"Yeah, me too!" Peter said, starting the engine.

Elizabeth relaxed as Peter drove around the lake. She couldn't remember when she enjoyed herself more, even if it wasn't really what it looked like. But she let herself pretend that it *was* what it looked like—like she was going for a drive with an interesting, and yes, attractive, man around a beautiful lake.

Neither of them spoke. They both seemed very comfortable with that too. Elizabeth stole a glance at Peter, at his artistic long-fingered hands on the wheel. She noticed that his nose had a decided bump, and she found herself liking that imperfection, as well.

She sadly released the illusion when he pulled into his driveway. "Handles like a dream," he said. Then he chuckled. "I'm known for my clichés. Come on in."

They went through the garage, into the kitchen. The east wall of the kitchen was entirely glass and faced the lake.

"How wonderful!" Elizabeth exclaimed. "What a view!"

"Um?" Peter said. "Oh, I guess so. I'm used to it. Make yourself comfortable." He gestured to a small dinette. Elizabeth sat and looked out at the lake. It was very still, with only a few white ducks bobbing gently on its surface.

"Tea?" he asked.

"Oh, yes, please."

"Strawberry or Earl Grey?"

"Strawberry sounds nice."

35 ~ Amethyst Dream

Peter put on the tea kettle, then came over and joined Elizabeth at the dinette.

"I love this house!" Elizabeth murmured. "Open and light and modern." She started to say, just this morning I was thinking about moving into a place like this, but she held the thought, deciding it sounded forward. Then, strangely, the dream of Grandfather—which she didn't want to think about at all—came to mind.

Instead she said, "I've never been to *The Lakes*. I've lived all my life in Orange County and I only vaguely knew these lakes were here—but it's *so charming*."

"It's nice," Peter agreed, but not very firmly. "I suppose. However, I'm sort of tired of it. You know what I'd like?"

The kettle started whistling, Peter got up and attended to making tea.

"No," Elizabeth said, "what would you like?" She really wanted to know.

Peter brought back tea mugs effusing warm strawberries, and sugar and spoons. "I'd like some big, old, early nineteen-hundreds place, with the parlor and drawing room and music room, antique light fixtures, and maybe even back stairs and front stairs. I really love period stuff, it has so much character. But ... do you know the kind of place I mean?"

Elizabeth sat stunned, her eyebrows raised. "But ...."

"I didn't think that was shocking," Peter said.

"No, not shocking," Elizabeth replied. "Amazing and well, *yes, shocking*. You've just described my home exactly. *Exactly!*"

"You're kidding." Peter's eyebrows rose to match Elizabeth's.

"I am not!"

"Look, woman, you have my car, you have my house—why have you been keeping them from me?"

Elizabeth giggled. "Well, you have *my* house!"

"Maybe we should trade," Peter said.

Elizabeth looked at him with an intensity she rarely dared to look at anyone. "Maybe we should."

"Wow," Peter said. "When I came down the stairs, I wanted to thank you for providing me with the face I've been searching for. A character in the book I'm working on hasn't quite gelled yet, and I came down the stairs, and there was my face. I mean *your* face. But I'm going to borrow it, hope you don't mind. And then you have the car I've been trying to find, and, drum roll, please, the house I've fantasized."

Elizabeth felt embarrassment and shyness rolling over her—everything suddenly so *personal*. What was it about her *face* that caught his attention? She didn't know what to say, so she changed the subject.

"What do you write?"

"Westerns and science fiction."

"Oh," Elizabeth said, nodding. "Westerns and science fiction. I can see the connection."

"How so?"

"No. That's my sum total ability to be, ahm, funny."

Peter laughed right out loud. "Now *that's* funny. I assume you don't read either genre."

Elizabeth shook her head, feeling strangely rude to have never read either a western or a science fiction book, much less having read a book by this man, Peter Shamus.

He appeared to read *her* like a book. "That's okay. You wouldn't have known if you'd read one of my books anyway, since I almost always write under pseudonyms.

"But," he went on, "the book I'm working on now, the one your face is going to help me finish, this book is, I dare to say, literary. I'm actually using my real name."

"What's it about?" Elizabeth asked.

"Oh, boy, please don't be offended if I don't talk about it. It's one of my many quirks not to discuss a work in progress. Books I've finished I don't mind talking about. Except I usually can't remember them." Peter laughed.

Elizabeth liked his pretty teeth and she liked how the angles of his face softened when he laughed.

"Anyway," he continued, "tell me more about your house. Is it haunted like old houses supposedly are?"

Elizabeth stiffened. "No, it's not haunted," she answered brusquely.

"What a pity. Ghosts lend so much character to a place." Peter picked up his tea mug and gave Elizabeth a look over it in mid-sip. "I ... somehow, made you uncomfortable."

"A little, yes."

"What did I say?"

Elizabeth shrugged. "I ... never mind me, I'm just ... strange. My grandfather passed recently. I've lived in that house with him all my life, and now I'm alone. Which is why I'm thinking of moving. So I can figure out what 'a life of my own' means, without the constant reminder of my grandfather all around me."

Peter nodded to everything Elizabeth said. "I'm sorry about your loss, Elizabeth, and I'm sorry I made you uncomfortable."

"Don't apologize, please!"

They sipped their tea and slipped back into the comradely silence they'd shared in the car. A quiet happiness stole over Elizabeth like nothing she'd ever known as she watched the cheerful little ducks on the lake.

"*Soooo*, anyhow," Peter finally said, "your car, what are you asking for it?"

"Oh!—I don't know. I have absolutely no idea. And I mean, *no* idea."

Peter nodded thoughtfully. "What if I call Eddy and let him give us his opinion of what it's top value might be, and, if we're agreed, I'll write you a check."

"You'll, just, write a check?" Elizabeth asked, surprised. Strange world where money appears in her bank account and people casually wrote checks for large amounts of money.

"Sure. I got some funds earmarked for, well, a vintage car. And, there it sits, in my driveway!" He reached for his phone and called Eddy. After a brief conversation the three of them came to an agreement, Elizabeth a bit stunned at the matter-of-fact, rather large sounding, numbers being bandied about between.

Peter hung up and grabbed his checkbook, but stopped in mid-signature. "Wait. We should just go to the bank and cash this, then we can take the pink slip to Eddy and have him notarize it. You can get your new car—and I can have your old one, and the business will be done. If that sounds okay to you, and if we can manage to pull off the business so smoothly."

"Okay," Elizabeth nodded to everything he said, assuming it made perfect sense, as that's how it sounded. She gave Peter the keys again, and they went out and got back in the car.

"On the subject of your house ...." Peter said as he drove to the bank.

"Yes?"

"I'm beginning to feel like I'm twisting your arm, but if you are actually interested in selling, I mean, seriously, I hope you'll let me be the first to know."

They pulled into the bank parking lot. Elizabeth got out a pencil and a slip of paper. "Here's my address. Come by some time and take a look at the house. At the very least, with your appreciation of the antique, I think you'll enjoy a, ahm, tour. It's sort of a museum."

Peter took the slip of paper Elizabeth handed him and carefully put it in his wallet. "I warn you, I *will* take you up on this invitation."

In less than two hours Elizabeth had sold the Chevy, waving bye to Peter as he hurried back to his deadline, and then she decided to buy a shiny, new, black Prius.

She was so excited, she didn't even mind driving home in the rush hour traffic. She took turns wishing everyone would look at her new car, and feeling relieved when they didn't.

Chapter VI

Elizabeth hadn't awakened with such feelings of anticipation since childhood birthdays when her mother was still around.

The last couple of days were like a new kind of birthday. She loathed to let the mood go. Although all the empty spaces where her beloved Grandfather used to be left a hole in her heart, she at least started to feel alive again. She began to see that she could make decisions and even be pleased with the results.

For example, the beautiful new car.

"All your life you've been a—a *wimp!*" she told herself as she leapt out of bed. "But no more. Today I'll get a real estate agent to give me an appraisal on this place. And I'm going to check out what's available at *The Lakes*."

There was a real estate agency only two blocks away and, although she wanted to drive her new car, she restrained herself and walked.

As Elizabeth passed through the doors of Ocean State Realtors, she tried to get her eyes to adjust to the near darkness. She squinted at the person sitting at the reception desk.

"May I help you?"

"Yes, I'd like to talk with someone about listing my home. That is, if I can find a home that I like better."

"You've come to the right place," the woman said. Elizabeth could barely make out a smile—at least she could see teeth. "Mr. Antonella will be happy to discuss your options with you."

She stood and Elizabeth followed. It wasn't just her eyes adjusting, she realized. It was *decidedly dark* in here.

The woman led Elizabeth into a small cubicle. "Mr. Antonella, Miss, oh, I'm sorry, I forgot to get your name."

"No, ahm, I didn't say, I mean, you didn't ask .... ahm, Morris, Elizabeth Morris," Elizabeth said, feeling unnerved by the darkness and confusion.

"Please, sit," Mr. Antonella gestured to an overstuffed chair on the opposite side of his desk.

Elizabeth sat and the receptionist left. She looked at the man on the other side of the desk. Her eyes finally adjusted to the dim lighting and she saw before her the most physically gorgeous man she'd ever been this close to in her life. His large dark eyes were complimented by black sweeping eyebrows, so precise they were almost too perfect.

A few locks of dark, thick, shining hair spilled over his high, smooth forehead. His chiseled cheekbones and jaw were a perfect setting for his full-lipped mouth, his aquiline nose, and those incredible eyes. Even his after-shave was evocative—of what, Elizabeth wasn't quite certain. But it made her strangely, and even more uncomfortably, self-conscious.

What was someone who looked—and smelled—like this doing in a little, nondescript, neighborhood real estate office? she wondered. Probably making a lot more money than waiting to become famous in Hollywood, she answered her own unspoken question.

"What can I do for you, Miss Morris?" His intense dark eyes looked her over as if he found her very interesting. Which she doubted.

"I—I have a home—nearby ..." she stuttered shyly. "I'd like to get an estimate on its value. And I'd like to see what's available at *The Lakes*. I'd like to find a place right on the lake."

"We can do that," he leaned back and steepled his fingers. "But if you have a house in *this* neighborhood and you want to move to *The Lakes*—how much equity do you have in your place?"

"Equity? I ... I own it, it's mine."

"It's paid off?"

"Yes."

He leaned forward, interested again. "Well, then, maybe we've got something we can work with."

"Oh, yes, I think so," Elizabeth answered. She hadn't been prepared for this stranger's preconceived prejudice about the 'neighborhood.'

"I'm not particularly busy right now," Mr Antonella said, shuffling papers together. "Shall we go check your place out?"

"Well ..." Elizabeth hesitated. "I'd really prefer to have an idea about what's available before I start thinking about selling my place. After all, if I can't find something I like more, I'll stay put."

"Oh, there's always something available." He held up the massive multiple listing. "In all these thousands of listings there's got to be something you'll just love." There was an odd flatness to his tone. He'd clearly said this many, many, *too many*, times.

"No," Elizabeth answered firmly, standing her ground, "not if there isn't anything on the lake in *The Lakes*."

A tight look came around the agent's eyes. "First things first, Miss Morris. Okay? I need to see what kind of buying power we're talking about before I spend time going through the multiple. Okay?"

Elizabeth did not like his tone. She almost got up and walked out. She gave him a studied look, and, as she watched, a whole softening, chameleon change came over his features. "Shall we go?"

Elizabeth stood and walked out of the office wondering why she felt as though she was working for this man instead of the other way around. Wondering why she let him lead her out of his office.

Mr. Antonella led Elizabeth out the back door to a red Corvette in the parking lot. He opened the passenger door and she folded herself into the seat.

He got in and started the car. "Hope you don't mind if I take my Vette, I don't very often get a chance to drive it during the day."

"Oh. No, that's fine."

"Do you like it?"

"What?" Elizabeth asked.

"My car."

"Oh. Well, it's flashy, Mr. Antonella," Elizabeth answered. She couldn't very well say what she felt, which was that, in fact, it didn't strike her as an adult car. "Turn left at the corner," is what she did say. "On the right, in the next block, the corner house."

"The corner house! The Morris estate? You're *that* Morris?"

"Well, my grandfather was 'that Morris.'"

His attitude changed immediately. "Well, I'm impressed," he said, turning and giving her that appraising eye again. "I *am* impressed! You walk in off the street ...."

"I didn't see much point in driving two blocks," Elizabeth said, not entirely comfortable with the extreme proximity of his over-bearing beauty and perfume and ... interest.

"Ha, ha!" Mr. Antonella laughed. "That's very amusing. Ha, ha. Sit right there." He leapt out of the car and ran around and opened her door, offering her his hand. They walked up the path to the house, and Elizabeth let them in the front door.

"Um-hum," he said, standing in the pools of stained glass light.

"This room, Mr. Antonella, to our left ...."

"Please, please call me Marsalis. If we're to do business together, I'll feel more comfortable if you call me Marsalis. And I hope you'll let me call you ... I'm sorry, what was your first name again?"

"Elizabeth."

"Liz, that's great."

"Well, actually, I'm not a Liz," Elizabeth protested.

"Of course you are. You just haven't let it out yet."

Elizabeth wondered what that meant, but she let it pass. "Anyway, as I was saying, the first room to our left has always been Grandfather's study, technically it's the parlor." She led him into the room. "The pocket doors work perfectly." She demonstrated. "The next room is the music room," she said, leading him into the neighboring room, where loomed a grand piano.

"Do you play?" Marsalis asked perfunctorily, peering at the hardwood flooring.

"Not really. I took lessons in grade school, but my artistic inclinations took another direction."

She led him through the music room to the next room, dominated by a large four poster bed. "This was originally the back parlor, but Grandfather moved in here oh, about five years ago when the stairs got to be too much for him."

The front doorbell rang.

"Who could that be?" Elizabeth said, surprised. She'd paid the paperboy last week. "I'll be right back."

She peeked through the front door window and saw Peter wandering around the porch, dressed in jeans and a green turtle neck pullover the color of his eyes, surprised at her immediate reaction of delight to see him.

"Hello!" she called to him through the screen door.

He turned abruptly. "Hi! Are you busy? Is *that* what you bought?" he asked, jerking a thumb over his shoulder at the Corvette.

Elizabeth giggled and the preposterous notion. "Oh, heavens, no! It's the real estate agent's."

"The agent? Oh!" Peter said, clearly disappointed. "Should I go?"

"No, of course not!" Elizabeth hurried to cover her embarrassment. Yes, they'd talked of trading homes, but she thought it only friendly banter. "I—

wanted to get a notion of what this place is worth, not wanting to be caught again as unprepared as I was yesterday when I didn't know what the car was worth." She opened the screen door wide Come on in," she urged.

"I shouldn't interfere while you're trying to conduct business," Peter protested.

"Nonsense! I might as well show the house to everyone at once!"

Peter stepped into the entry way bringing the fresh scent of spring with him. "Well, all right, but only because I'm dying to see it." Elizabeth watched him take in the stained glass window panes around the front door, the antique light fixture overhead and the beamed ceilings, soaking it up as if it were a particular work of art worthy of minute attention. "Oh, yes. This is *exactly* it!" Peter whispered.

"Don't use up all your awe in the entry way," Elizabeth laughed. "The house is big."

Peter turned his serious gaze on her. "I'll try to conserve my energy."

Elizabeth led him into Grandfather's study and began her litany again. "This was originally the parlor, but it's been Grandfather's study for years. Then the next room is the music room ..." She urged Peter along as he lingered, obviously savoring every inch.

"The next room was the back parlor, but we turned it into Grandfather's bedroom about five years ago."

Marsalis stepped into the music room.

Somewhat awkwardly, Elizabeth introduced them— such a strange position she'd never been in, in her life! "Marsalis Antonella, this is an acquaintance of mine, Peter Shamus."

The two men shook hands.

"Peter is curious to look at the house, so I figure I may as well give a group tour," Elizabeth said smiling, and watched as Peter returned her smile, while Marsalis's features became stormy.

She turned from them both and continued her museum tour recitation. "If we walk through the bathroom, we come into the kitchen," Elizabeth continued. "The pantry is here by the back door. Grandfather 'updated' the fixtures in the kitchen in the 1940's.

"A couple years ago one of them developed a short, and he was furious that the new lights weren't any more reliable than that. Ah, well, that was Grandfather." She chuckled softly at the memory.

Peter nodded with empathy, while Marsalis, in the far corner of the room, scratched down notes, oblivious to Elizabeth's reminiscence.

"This is the back stairway." She flipped on the light switch in the stairwell and the three of them ascended silently upstairs.

"There are five bedrooms, although only one bathroom up here. The rooms and closets are large enough that it wouldn't be difficult for another bath to be put in."

She walked down the hall and opened the first door. "This is an empty room and the next one is very similar." She opened the second bedroom and they peeked in.

"*Tall ceilings!*" Peter exclaimed.

"Oh, yes, I guess so," Elizabeth agreed. "I'm so used to them, I don't even think about it." She moved across the hall. "This is my room." Her door stood open. Again she felt a slight rush of shyness to have two strange men looking into her bedroom, although relieved that she'd perfunctorily made the bed and nothing of note was in disarray.

In fact, she thought, attempting to look at her room through other eyes, it was quite charming. The cheerful sunlight poured in, happily inhabiting the pale yellow walls, dancing across her white and blue bedspread, and sinking into the rich, dark wood of the doors and windows and floor.

"*Sweet space*," Peter whispered, and seeming, to Elizabeth, to be taking down mental notes, though quite different from Marsalis's. Ah, not only her face, but her own room would find its way into his writing, she suspected.

"Next, the bathroom, then another empty bedroom. And, last but not least, the room at the end of the hall. This is where I keep my work." She opened the door to her rug room.

"*Oh! Wow!*" Peter exclaimed in awe. He wandered into the room among the waiting-to-be-completed carpets, then turned to Elizabeth with a reverent expression. "You do this?"

"I do," Elizabeth said. Suddenly her heart began to race. No one besides Grandfather and Martha had ever been in this room where she captured her visions in wool and silk. This was, strangely, even more intimate than her bedroom.

"What incredible talent!" Peter sighed, turning his attention back to her work.

Elizabeth glanced at Marsalis. He was looking her up and down, unabashedly.

"I'm very impressed with your art, Elizabeth," Peter said.

"Personally," Marsalis said, "I'm impressed with the woman."

Direly afraid that she was about to begin blushing—and once that started, she'd never get it under control—she begged, "gentlemen, please!" and walked out of the room, leaving the two men no choice but to follow.

"This is the grand front stairway, which returns us to the dining room." They meandered down the elegant winding mahogany stairs and came into the massive dining room.

"The wainscoting is mahogany and the built-in breakfront has all of its original bevelled glass." Elizabeth pointed across the room. "That swinging door takes you back into the kitchen and pantry. And that's the house!"

"Quite the place, quite the place," Marsalis started enthusiastically. "Of course it needs a lot of updating. But I can see potential!"

"What do you think it's worth, roughly?" Elizabeth asked.

"Well, it's not the usual thing. You know, we really need to call an appraiser in on this. This place has just been sitting here for years, appreciating."

"But surely you can give me a ballpark notion," Elizabeth persisted.

"Well," Marsalis hesitated, "strictly off the record, I wouldn't want to stake my professional reputation on what I say ...."

"Of course not," Elizabeth said.

"But very rough ballpark, a couple million."

"Really?" Elizabeth said. "Well, I guess Martha knows what she's talking about."

"Who's Martha?" Marsalis asked suspiciously.

"A friend."

"Tell me I'm interfering if I'm interfering," Peter said. "But that talk we had yesterday? About trading? Could we pursue that conversation further?"

"Seriously?" Elizabeth asked.

"Very."

"I'd love to continue that conversation—seriously." Stealing herself for the worst, she turned to Marsalis. "I'm very sorry Mr. Antonella, but Peter was first."

"Using what for collateral?" Marsalis asked Peter in a less than polite tone.

"He likes that question," Elizabeth interceded, trying to lighten the tone.

"A lake front property at *The Lakes*."

"It's very unlikely your place is equivalent to *this* property."

"Of course not," Peter agreed, remaining polite.

"You wouldn't want to downscale," Marsalis said to Elizabeth.

"That's *exactly* what I want to do."

Marsalis nodded curtly, looking from Elizabeth to Peter. "Well," he said, "well then, you want me to start drawing up papers?"

"Ah ... ahm ... you're going a little *too* fast, Mr. Antonella," Elizabeth answered.

Marsalis whipped out his business card and handed it to her. "Well, give me a call if you need my services."

Elizabeth took the card, while Marsalis turned and stalked out the front door without further word.

51 ~ Amethyst Dream

A moment later, they heard the Corvette door slam and the engine roar to life.

"Kind of a moody guy, huh?" Peter asked.

"Seems so, doesn't he?"

They wandered into the music room. "Anyway," she looked at Peter, again drinking in his surroundings. "How shall we work this trade out, if you're serious?"

"I'm *serious*, and I'm willing to work it out almost any way you say," he answered.

Elizabeth took a deep breath. "Things are moving fast, faster than I've ever had things move in my life."

Peter shrugged, smiling. "No rush. None. We'll slow down. You're the boss, *no pressure!*"

"That's okay, pressure me. Just keep pushing, it's what I need. All I have to think of is that view from the kitchen at your place, and I wonder why I'm dragging my feet. Now I guess I'll *have* to have that talk with Grandfather's attorney. I'll ask him to draw up some paperwork. I don't think we need to pay Mr. Antonella when I have grandfather's attorney on retainer. But ... I hope you'll forgive me for asking, do writers really make so much money? Did you have some blockbuster that I probably wouldn't know about anyway?"

"No, you're right. I don't make millions writing westerns. I got involved in a speculative deal and it has made me very comfortable. Which is one of the reasons I'm eager to move. I'd like to invest that money in the home of my dreams before someone persuades me to speculate again, and I lose it."

"I see," Elizabeth said. "Well then, full steam ahead! Shall we say we'll move the end of the month?"

"Let's say it," Peter agreed happily.

They shook hands, binding a lady and gentlemen's agreement, then planned to meet again two days later, after Elizabeth had talked with Grandfather's attorney.

* *

Shortly after Peter left, the telephone rang.

"Hi, Marsalis here," he said when she answered, his voice cheery and bright.

"Mr. Antonella?" She paused, confused. "How did you get my number?"

"Oh, there isn't anything I can't get if I decide it's important for me to have it. Listen, the reason I'm calling ...."

"I hope you're not angry," Elizabeth interrupted. "I'm sorry to have bothered you today. I really didn't think Peter was serious when the suggestion came up to trade."

"No, no, I'm not angry, that's business. I assure you I've been in much worse situations and with intent of malice on the part of the client. I'd hardly be justified in wasting my energy on being angry with you. You meant me no harm."

"That's absolutely true, and I'm glad to hear you say it."

"However," Marsalis went on, "if you'd like to make me feel better, why not go out to dinner with me?"

"Out to dinner?" Elizabeth asked.

"Yes. To eat. You do eat?"

"Not much, lately." Elizabeth's confusion mounted. A drop-dead gorgeous man had just invited her to go out to dinner. Grandfather was not standing in the back of the room, disapproving. She had no reason to say no. And she wanted to say yes. She'd wanted to say yes to going out to dinner with a man for quite a few years.

But now the word wouldn't come.

"Are you still there?" Marsalis asked. "I know we just met, but how can I get to know you if I don't spend time with you?"

"Yes," Elizabeth finally said.

"You'll go to dinner with me?"

"Yes, I'll go to dinner with you."

"Great! I'll pick you up about seven?"

"Okay," Elizabeth said. "Seven."

"Bye-by," Marsalis said.

"Good-by."

Elizabeth hung up the telephone and stood staring at it for several moments. Then she walked to the mirror over the fireplace and peered at her reflection.

"I don't know," Elizabeth told the woman who looked back at her, "you look very plain to me. Why would this gorgeous man want to go out with you? He could go out with *any* one."

But I don't care, her thoughts replied. I want to go out with this gorgeous man. Even if it's only once, it beats *never*.

Chapter VII

Elizabeth had no idea where Marsalis would take her for dinner but it was Saturday and she decided to dress up as much as her wardrobe allowed.

In her room she opened closet door all the way and flipped on its light, then studied what she saw—pastels, small prints, cottons, double knits, mid-calf length.

"Granny dresses! Granny dresses. Every, single one of them! Your moment comes, and you're unprepared."

But then she thought about her mother's closet-full of clothes, so old they might be new again.

She hurried down the hall to her rug room and flung open the closet door. There hung a raft of silk and crepe and velvet outfits, muted solid colors, wild bright large prints, lots of black and bright red, fitted bodices, flared skirts and straight skirts, knee-length and floor length, daring necklines, little jackets and shawls, all wrapped up in clear plastic from the dry cleaners, just as her mother had left them.

They were fabulous! Elizabeth had forgotten what fantastic, dramatic, taste her mother had. Or maybe, she thought, she hadn't paid much attention to her mother's clothes, when looking at them only reminded her of her absent mother. But now she refused to dwell on that.

"Thank you, Mother! It took a lifetime, but you've finally done something for me. If I can just find something that more or less fits ... on the list of things you didn't share with me include 'voluptuous body.'"

Elizabeth eliminated the black dresses and the red dresses and the floor-length dresses and the dresses with so little fabric she wondered how Gloria managed to stay in them.

She was still left with five very likable options. Of these her eye went to a pale turquoise crepe dress of a 1940s cut. Fitted bodice, lowered waist, cap sleeves, slightly padded shoulders, straight skirt with a peplum trimmed in a wide, antique white lace, and a little matching lace bolero. No plunging necklines, no slits up the skirt.

"I couldn't have found something I like more if I'd shopped for a week," Elizabeth muttered, taking the dress to her room. She held it up to herself before the full-length mirror. It suited her very well, from this perspective.

She took off her house dress and slipped the crepe dress on. She was afraid to look in the mirror. She looked down at the dress. It seemed to fit. Finally she raised her eyes to the mirror, and what she saw made her utter a small gasp—nothing short of a miracle! Thin. Chic. Sophisticated.

"Wow, Elizabeth," she whispered. "Maybe there's more of your mother in you than you realized."

She took the dress off and put it back on its hanger. "Two interesting men in two short days, Lizzie, you wild thing." She giggled. She decided to take the entire afternoon getting ready, starting with a long, hot bubble bath.

Everything was wonderful! She was going on a real date with an incredibly good-looking man, never mind his mood swings—no one was perfect. She would soon move into a house that fulfilled dreams she hadn't even had yet, and she owned a new car that granted her freedom. What more could she want?

"Well," she said, putting the plug in the claw foot tub and turning on the tap full blast, pouring in bubble bath, "I could want a child. In fact I *do* want a child. However, dear girl, you may be able to buy a house and a car and get a date in two days. But babies still take longer."

She let herself melt in the bath as if she was maple sap and the warm water was a spring thaw. She indulged in a romantic fantasy with Marsalis as the star. But in her fantasy, he was sweet and intelligent like Peter—and, interestingly, she discovered, he had a smile very much like Peter's as well.

57 ~ Amethyst Dream

Half-an-hour later Elizabeth somewhat reluctantly climbed out of the now-chilly water and wrapped a big, fluffy towel around herself. As she reached for her toothbrush, she saw her new compact in the sink. It was open, face down. She picked it up, bits of shattered mirror fell clinking into the sink.

She stood, mystified, peering down at the broken mirror. "This was *not* in the sink when we walked through the house."

She thought back to yesterday when Peter asked her if the house was haunted. If there was ever a man Grandfather would disapprove of her going out with, it would be Marsalis. She added the mystery of the teleporting and broken compact to the teleporting *Mademoiselle* in the trash, and the still-missing lipstick.

Frowning, she cleaned up the shards of mirror. "I'm not stopping now. I have to live my life, and, haunted house or not, I intend to."

*   *

Marsalis came at seven-thirty instead of seven, and for half-an-hour Elizabeth had worked herself into a tizzy, pacing up and down Grandfather's study.

When he finally arrived, he gave s soft wolf-whistle when she opened the door, but said nothing about being late. Discombobulated by his wordless appreciation, she debated if she should or shouldn't mention his tardiness. He then pulled a little bouquet of pink tea roses and baby's breath out from behind his back.

"These remind me of you," he said, "delicate and shy."

"Thank you," Elizabeth said, breathing in the flowers, forgoing further thought of mentioning the time. "Let me put them in water." She moved toward the kitchen. "Thank you," she said again. So! Men really did bring flowers! Se looked over her shoulder, "do you want to sit for awhile?"

"No, thanks. I've got an eight o'clock reservation at Orange Hill. You ever been there?"

"Yes, but not since I was about twelve," Elizabeth called from the kitchen. She returned with the flowers in a vase and set them on the piano. "My mother and one of her boyfriends took me there a couple of times."

Marsalis nodded.

"It has a beautiful view," they both said together, and laughed.

*   *

At Orange Hill they were seated by the panoramic window—Orange County spread out below them as if they were on a throne and the lights below were a diamond-studded foot stool.

"You look beautiful," Marsalis said to her. "I find a woman who can look a lot of different ways very enticing."

59 ~ Amethyst Dream

"Oh? Am I that sort of woman?" Elizabeth asked, curious, surprised.

"I've seen you look like two completely different women in only one day, so I would say yes."

Silenced to thought by the Marsalis's observation, she smiled at him sweetly, but said nothing, returning her attention to the stunning view. The waiter soon came up, taking their orders, after which she led the conversation into lighter terrain.

But, Elizabeth silently admonished herself, she'd better hang onto her heart as, otherwise, she feared she might be in danger of falling in love with this, in all probability inaccessible, man.

"What are you going do with yourself now?" Marsalis innocently enough over their salad.

"I don't know. I'd like to get a job, I'd like to be meaningfully engaged, but I have no training, no skills." She paused, reflecting on her next comment, then decided to go with it, just to see how it sounded out loud. "I learned quite a bit about nursing, taking care of my grandfather for the last five years when he's been so ill. But I would not care to go into nursing. I'm just ...."

"You're not cut out for it. You're sensitive. You need to be helping people fulfill their dreams."

Genuinely surprised, by his insight, Elizabeth replied, "Why, yes, Marsalis, you're right. That's very well expressed."

"Why not go into real estate?" he suggested.

"Oh, I don't know about that," Elizabeth answered. "My biggest problem, I guess, is that I'm very shy."

"It's the best way to get over shyness," Marsalis pointed out. "You tell yourself it's simply your job, and the first thing you know, you're not so shy."

"Sounds like a testimonial," Elizabeth observed.

"It is. *I* was shy. "

Elizabeth made a soft, disbelieving, sputtering sound.

"It's true, Elizabeth. But having to work with people got me over the worst of it. You could come and work in my office. You could study for your real estate license at the same time." He paused. "I know you don't *have* to work, what with your grandfather's estate, but everybody needs to be occupied, don't you think?"

"Yes, I agree," Elizabeth nodded. "But I doubt I'd be of much use to you, honestly."

"Let's try it and see. Can't hurt anything." He continued with his dinner as though the entire thing was resolved. Elizabeth decided to go along with him.

What could it hurt?

And so a within the week, Elizabeth enrolled in real estate school, was given a desk in Marsalis's real estate office. But she didn't stop there. She called Martha to ask her who she ought to go to, to have a professional face and hair make-over. She bought herself a new wardrobe, including two pairs of designer jeans.

61 ~ Amethyst Dream

And when she went to the grocery store and looked up at the mirrors, she didn't see a frumpy housewife from out of the past. She saw a pretty, trim, self-confident, contemporary-looking young woman.

Chapter VIII

Elizabeth tore the last day of May off her desk calendar—unbelievably, another month had disappeared. Since she'd moved to *The Lakes* and started working at Ocean State Real Estate, the weeks flew by like days.

She wasn't sure which she enjoyed more, getting up in the morning, excited about going to work, or the pleasure she felt in the evening driving to her new home, anticipating the cool lake, and, lately, with the days growing longer, the beautiful dusky sunsets reflecting cinnabar and pink off the surface of the cobalt blue water.

A client was coming into the office in a few minutes and Marsalis was not back yet. She checked the mirror in her desk drawer, always surprised anew by the cute pixie hair cut hair, and the transformation brought about by the right makeup. She could hardly remember what she used to look like.

She took to studying for her real estate license with delight and zeal, and, although not yet licensed, she discovered she learned quickly. Marsalis frequently left the lion's share of the work to her, but it didn't bother her. As he said, it was good training.

But she did still dislike the cavern darkness of the work environment. "Edna," Elizabeth called to the secretary, "I wonder if there's something we can do about the lighting in here?"

"What's wrong with it?"

"It's so dark!"

"I'm good with that," Edna answered. "The place doesn't have to be dusted so often."

Elizabeth shrugged. She didn't care for Edna's attitude, but she was in no position to argue. At that moment, Marsalis's clients came through the front door.

"We have an appointment with Mr. Antonella," the man said to Edna.

"Mr. Antonella is unexpectedly detained. He asked me to refer you to Miss Morris." Edna waved back at Elizabeth.

"Hmm," he said hesitantly. "Okay, thanks." He and his wife came up to Elizabeth's desk.

She stood and smiled, gesturing to be seated. "Mr. Antonella told me you'd be coming by. Let's talk about the home you're hoping to find."

Elizabeth spent the afternoon showing the couple eight properties, none of which seemed quite this or quite that for them.

On the drive home, Elizabeth pieced together some random facts and came up with the realization that Marsalis was pawning off his difficult clients on her.

People who were not buyers. He had a keen sense of who those people were likely to be, and an equally keen sense of recruiting Elizabeth to attend to them. It was disappointing to never have a win. But she reminded herself that that was part of the job, too.

When she got home, she found herself facing that odd empty feeling she'd been experiencing lately. After making a cup of tea, she went up to her new rug room. Since she'd moved, she hadn't touched anything.

She smiled remembering the weekend she and Peter traded homes. They rented a truck and first took her personal things and put them in his garage. Then they filled up the truck with his things and piled them up in the front parlor. They'd even ended up trading most of their furniture on a friendly long term basis as they agreed that each home was already suitably furnished.

On Elizabeth's second load, the only thing left was the contents of her rug room. She'd finished the six-by-nine Samarkand the night before. She hadn't wanted to move the loom, rug and all.

The night before the move she stood proudly surveying her handiwork, then felt a pang as she realized the carpet would not live on these dark hardwood floors, among the antique surroundings, which had been her intention since she'd conceived it.

So the next day she presented the carpet to Peter. Stunned, he tried to refuse it, but she wouldn't let him. "This carpet belongs to the house," she insisted. "Please, enjoy it."

"Enjoy it? I'll *treasure* it." He ran his hand over the carpet reverently.

Elizabeth brought herself back to the present moment. That was then, and this was now. What she needed *now*, she decided, was to get involved in a new carpet-making project. She went back down to her kitchen, got out some graph paper and her set of "Fifty-Eight Wonderful Colors Felt Tip Drawing Pens" and began sketching a design.

Two hours later, she sat back to appraise her creation. And there revealed was the clue to what *really* bothered her. The graph paper had been transformed into a darling pastel forest, with a Hansel and Gretel cottage in the center, puffy pink and white clouds in a pale blue sky around the border.

A rug for a baby's room.

Because what Elizabeth wanted more than anything, as happy as she was with her new life, was a sweet, soft little person to love. But how could that come to be? She and Marsalis had been dating, but her "Victorian morals" as he put it, prevented her from letting the relationship progress beyond affectionate-yet-platonic. She was at least smart enough, she told herself, to realize that Marsalis was not the marrying sort.

But that didn't mean she didn't wish he was. Or that *something* might happen in her life with the promise of maternal fulfillment. She decided she would begin to create the baby carpet, enjoying the belief that it would draw her closer to her heart's desire.

* *

The following Sunday Elizabeth took Martha to brunch. After they'd filled their plates to embarrassing heights, they sat by a window overlooking the bay.

"You look gorgeous!" Martha said as the waitress poured champagne into their plastic champagne glasses.

"Thanks to your suggestion that I put myself in Shauna's hands for a make over. I was this a lump of clay upon which she defined my features."

"You were most certainly not a lump of clay, but she did do an excellent job of emphasizing your beauty."

'That's sweet of you to say, Martha. And you sound sincere."

"Of course I'm sincere! Why would you even say such a thing?"

Why indeed? She asked herself. Marsalis was always saying she was gorgeous—right before he asked her to do "a little favor." "In the real estate business you get used to a song-and-dance routine," she finally answered.

Martha nodded. She understood. "But with me, my friend, what you see is what you get. No song and dance. You can let your hair down. That is, what little bit of it you have left!"

67 – Amethyst Dream

Elizabeth reached up and tugged on one of the spikes of hair framing her face. "Not good?"

"Very good! Just, you know, very very short. But, anyway, what's new with you? We never get to talk!"

"True. But if you heard all the times I've talked to you in my head, you'd ask me to kindly please hang up.""So it's you buzzing in my brain!" Martha exclaimed. "Have I given you good advice lately?"

Elizabeth fell silent, but fidgeted.

"I thought you were 'happy, happy, happy,'" Martha continued, studying Elizabeth's discomfort. "Isn't that what you said?"

Elizabeth nodded. "I *am* happy. And I'm grateful too, to be so content. Even though Grandfather is gone and I miss him terribly, I have my new home, which I love, and my new job, which is interesting. It helps take me out of myself. I'm finally growing up, Martha. I didn't know life could feel so full or be so interesting. But still there's some perverse creature in me who, with all I've got, wants more."

"Sure. We're all that way. What more are you after?"

"Specifically, ahhh—a baby." Elizabeth shocked herself, it was the first time she'd said it out loud.

Martha nodded.

"What do you mean by nodding?" Elizabeth asked. "Aren't you surprised?"

"Not in the least tiny little bit," Martha answered. "Not at all. Why should that surprise me? More to the point, why should it surprise you? If you hadn't been so preoccupied with your grandfather all these years, it likely would have come to you long ago."

"Maybe," Elizabeth said. "It's hard to hypothesize about that now. But what should I do?"

"How about this?" Martha leaned forward as if she was about to impart a secret, magic formula. Elizabeth leaned toward her. "Date—fall in love—get married—have a baby."

Elizabeth leaned back with a wry grin. "Sounds like a good plan, Martha, but I'm hung up on the first point."

"How so? Look at you! You're adorable, sweet, fun, kind, polite, and financially independent. With the possible exception of needing to be more sure of yourself, I can't imagine why you don't have the guys lined up."

"Oh, sure," Elizabeth agreed, "I anticipate *that* in the near future. No, Martha, I'm not the gregarious young woman you portray. First of all, I'm not made of stuff that dates more than one person at a time. What am I saying? One man is one-hundred percent more than I've dated all my life!"

"Silly girl."

"Maybe so, but that's me. And I'm dating Marsalis now."

"Yes? And?"

"And, well, and I'm certain he's not the marrying type."

Martha tsk-ed. "Look, dear girl, why put yourself at cross purposes? Don't mark time with someone who's goals are opposed to yours. I shouldn't even have to tell you that."

Elizabeth felt a tiny wall of defensiveness welling up. "I suppose you've *never* dated anyone who had goals different from yours?"

"Goodness, Elizabeth, in my case, dating has *been* the goal. I've never wanted children or a husband. Of course I've had to let a few good ones go when they started out fun but developed an urge to make me the centerpiece for home and hearth. But I believe I've stood pretty much by my own standards. That needn't make you angry, Lizzie."

"No, it doesn't. It *doesn't.* But be honest Martha, you've seen Marsalis. What woman would voluntarily stop dating him?"

"I'll grant you he's very good looking, physically. But beauty's only skin deep. I didn't just make that up, by the way." Martha chuckled, then hesitated. She looked out at the bay. "I don't want to alienate you by criticizing him, but I feel I have to tell you that there's something about that guy I don't trust. Personally, I wouldn't go out with him once. He has a quiet anger that makes me very uncomfortable."

"Oh, pooh!" Elizabeth said. "He's kind of quiet, and the two minutes you saw him, he'd just had an unpleasant altercation with a client."

Martha nodded. "I was only voicing an opinion, but I hope you'll give it some consideration. Anyway, let's get back to this motherhood thing. Let's say you're a one-guy sort of gal with mommy-ing in mind." Martha went on, "Let's say the guy doesn't have daddy-ing in mind. Let's say further, that the woman is financially solvent, a responsible person, in good health. Now, all I wonder is, why you don't just go ahead and make a baby."

Elizabeth's fork clattered to her plate.

"Don't freak out. Look, my point is, you think Marsalis's gorgeous, so why not increase your odds of making a gorgeous baby? There's no one in your life to go tsk-tsk. If you do it of your own free will, plan it out and so forth ... well, it seems perfect to me."

Elizabeth shook her head. "Maybe I don't have anyone in my life to go tsk-tsk at me, but *I'd* be tsk-ing. Anyway, if I did that, Marsalis would be out the door so fast, I'd be knocked over by the gale. He'd never believe that I 'made a baby' as you so casually put it, for any reason other than to trick or trap him."

"Okay." Martha shoved her plate away. "Here's what I really believe you should do. I think you should become a foster parent. Although you're not married and have never had any children, you were a wonderful nurse to your grandfather and you certainly have the skills to take care of a child, and you can certainly afford to hire a nanny." Martha paused and leaned back, studying Elizabeth, then threw up her hands. "I suppose you have all kinds of objections to that suggestion too."

"Noooo ..." Elizabeth said thoughtfully, then broke into smiles. "I love it! Why didn't I think of that myself? Thank you, Martha, you are the rudder in my life. Fantastic idea!"

"Well, that was easy!" Martha raised her champagne glass. "To the mommy-to-be."

Chapter IX

Elizabeth tried to still the bundle of nerves she'd become—Mrs. Vargas, the social worker assigned to her after an extensive telephone interview, was on her way to conduct the in-home interview.

Elizabeth was sure there was something she should have bothered to study or learn, that there were probably *lists* of things she should know, but didn't. She hated the thought of being quizzed and even worse, of appearing stupid. And even *much* worse, of losing her chance to be a foster parent.

But when Mrs. Vargas came to the door, Elizabeth calmed immediately. The woman had such a kind face, Elizabeth couldn't imagine that she had anything but kindness in her whole being.

"Come in, please," she said, opening the door wider.

"Thank you." Mrs Vargas followed Elizabeth into the living room. After they were seated she took in her surroundings. "Very nice home, Miss Morris."

"Thank you," Elizabeth answered. "May I get you some tea or coffee?"

"Tea would be lovely."

It didn't look as though Mrs. Vargas had moved a muscle when Elizabeth brought the tea tray back into the living room, and yet Elizabeth sensed there was nothing in eyesight that she hadn't evaluated.

"Suppose you tell me why you want to be a foster parent," Mrs. Vargas said as Elizabeth poured the tea.

After handing her a cup of tea, Elizabeth sat in the overstuffed chair across from Mrs. Vargas, studying her for a moment, wanting to organize in her mind what to say. But she was so taken with the appearance of the woman that she was speechless for a moment. Her pale brown skin caught the back lit rays of the sun from the window behind her, and it appeared to Elizabeth that she radiated a warm yellow light. The impression that Mrs. Vargas poured forth her own unique light was vivid.

Her expressive-yet-calm dark brown eyes were surely a refuge for the lost and the lonely, and her long-fingered hands gently cradling the china cup had, without a doubt, cradled many a homeless child, more fragile than china.

"I ... I don't know where to begin, exactly," Elizabeth breathed. "Although I have everything in my life that one could want—money, a job I like, a beautiful home, my health, and people who care about me, there's something missing. I'm always brought up short by this hollow feeling. What's wrong? I ask myself. Oh, yes, the answer comes back, you want to be loving a child."

Elizabeth fell silent.

Mrs. Vargas nodded, calmly. "Is it possible that you have a need to continue caring for someone, to carry on where you left off after your grandfather died?"

Surprised that Mrs. Vargas would candidly bring up such a sensitive subject, Elizabeth was also surprised that she didn't feel uncomfortable about it. "Perhaps, but I don't think that's a bad thing. I spent years learning how to take care of someone who needs care. I *think*, if I was only missing a habit, I'd volunteer to work in a retirement home. But I have this desire to nurture an infant.

"You might be wondering," Elizabeth continued, "like a friend of mine does, why I don't get married and have a child of my own. But, quite frankly, I'd rather be nurturing a child than pursuing a marriage relationship. I don't know why my priorities are sort of backwards, but they are."

"Don't be too quick to judge yourself," Mrs. Vargas said. "You're not alone. A lot of single people make wonderful foster parents, which is why the foster care program became open to singles. Some of our singles environments are the best foster homes we have. Do you mind if I look around?"

"Not at all, please do."

Elizabeth took Mrs. Vargas on a tour of the house. When they returned to the living room, Mrs. Vargas sat and made notes for a few moments while Elizabeth tried not to fidget. Finally Mrs. Vargas closed her notebook and looked at Elizabeth. "You know, your house is not very childproofed."

"Oh?" Elizabeth asked, dismayed. Of all the things she had prepared herself to hear, this was not one of them. She had worked hard to make her home attractive, and meticulously clean.

"No," Mrs. Vargas answered. "That is to say, it's a beautiful, but adult, home. All the crystal knickknacks and the easily knocked over little tables and the open stairway and the open space from the patio to the lake are not a baby environment. I think, although I can tell you're very sincere, and you have a good and generous heart, I think you don't realize what the day to day business of caring for a child entails."

Elizabeth swallowed hard. She had thought, until this moment, that the interview was going well. Even so, she knew she had nothing to gain if she became emotional.

"Of course I intend to hire a nanny," she answered as calmly as she could muster. "I guess that goes without saying, since I'm working. I wouldn't hire anyone without your approval. I'd like to say, too, that I wonder if any first time mother happens to know everything she needs to know about caring for a baby. Most women have a mother to help give her direction. But I don't. I suppose some basic instincts evolve during pregnancy, and I don't have that either.

"I assure you," Elizabeth went on, putting her tea cup on the coffee table, "I don't consider moving a few glass items, putting baby gates on the stairway and building a wall around the patio too much to expect. On the contrary, I'd enjoy it immensely. Anything that has to do with being a good parent, I would love to do."

Mrs. Vargas nodded in her soothing manner. "Well, that's good." She gathered her things and put them in her briefcase. "Thank you for the tea, Miss Morris, and for letting me see your lovely home." She stood and extended her hand. "I'll take a few days to evaluate the interview—and I trust you will do the same."

Elizabeth followed Mrs. Vargas to the door, thanked her for coming and closed the door behind her. But her movements were robotic. She felt sure she'd been given an extremely polite "no." And she failed at convincing herself it was not something to cry over.

Chapter X

Three weeks later, after Elizabeth had tried hard to give up the idea of becoming a foster parent—three weeks of not entering her carpet room because she didn't want to look at the pastel baby carpet she'd begun on the loom—she came home from work to find a message on her landline answering machine from Mrs. Vargas asking Elizabeth to return her call.

She dialed the number Mrs. Vargas had left as her home telephone number before she even took her purse off her shoulder.

"Hello?" Mrs. Vargas' calm voice answered.

"Hello, Mrs. Vargas, this is Elizabeth Morris. I just got your message."

"Oh, Miss Morris, I'm glad to hear from you. I have some news. We have a baby girl who needs a foster home."

Elizabeth caught her breath.

"Before you say anything," Mrs. Vargas went on, "there are details you must know, that you have to consider. The baby is nine months old, she is very sweet-natured, but she was born with talipes."

Talipes?" Elizabeth asked.

"Yes. Clubfooted, in lay language. Because of the complications in her very young life, she's not gotten the daily treatments she needed, and she'll have to have surgery in the near future."

"Oh, goodness," Elizabeth said, taken aback.

"The poor baby has become orphaned since you and I last spoke," Mrs. Vargas went on. "Would you like to see her?"

Elizabeth hesitated, and the silence seemed to roar. "Do you think I'm capable of being effective with these special circumstances?"

"Miss Morris, you were the one who implied you'd do anything to be a foster parent."

"I *would,*" Elizabeth said emphatically. "But I'm thinking of the baby ...."

"I appreciate your caution Miss Morris," Mrs. Vargas said agreeably. "But the reason the board and I decided to give you a try with this particular case is because of your experience and background in caring for your grandfather."

"I see," Elizabeth said. They were "giving her a try." It was an audition, with a child's life as a stage prop. This would not be the moment to tell Mrs. Vargas about her loathing of hospitals—that just to drive by UCI Medical Center on the freeway gave her a rush of nausea.

"Additionally," Mrs. Vargas went on, "there happens to be a nanny available who couldn't come more highly recommended. I know her personally and her record is excellent. She's worked with handicapped children before. She's a resourceful, hardworking, reliable person." Mrs. Vargas paused for a moment. "Of course the foster care program will not cover the expenses of the nanny ...."

"I don't care about that!" Elizabeth burst out, incensed. "Goodness!"

"That's what I thought," Mrs. Vargas said. "Anyway, I know this is a lot to throw at you all at once, but it came up suddenly. Gail, the nanny, returned my call today to let me know she's available."

"I see," Elizabeth said, at a loss for words. At a loss for *thoughts*.

"Do you want to see the baby? Or not?"

Elizabeth looked around the living room from which she'd removed her occasional tables and all the fragile knickknacks within baby reach, even as she had been certain that she'd never hear from Mrs. Vargas again. "Yes," she answered. "Of course."

Mrs. Vargas suggested coming over with the baby in two hours and Elizabeth agreed.

After she hung up, she looked around in stunned silence. Her shoulder bag slipped from her shoulder, bringing her back to reality.

She checked herself in a mirror. She looked harried and nervous after a particularly stressful day at work. Not an appropriate picture, she told herself.

She went upstairs and indulged in an Epsom salt bath. Then she put on a pale green lounge suit.

While she wolfed down some salad, the doorbell rang.

Elizabeth opened the door. There stood a smiling Mrs. Vargas, her mother-earth eyes soft and compassionate, her arms full of lavender blanket.

"Come in," Elizabeth said, feeling breathless.

Mrs. Vargas stepped through the doorway. Elizabeth led her into the living room and Mrs. Vargas sat on the sofa. Elizabeth hovered around her unable to decide if she should sit near or far.

"Amethyst, this is Miss Morris' home," Mrs. Vargas said in a mellifluous and soft voice. "She wants to meet you, pretty baby." Mrs. Vargas shifted the blanket and two round-as-quarters dark blue eyes looked up at Elizabeth, a look that plunged straight into her heart.

"Oh!" Elizabeth breathed. "Oh, how—*precious!*" Elizabeth reached for the baby without knowing it, and when the realization of her incredible attraction to the little girl hit her, her hands stopped in mid-air, unable to move forward or to drop.

"You can hold her," Mrs. Vargas said, handing the bundle to Elizabeth.

Elizabeth took the baby and looked down at her remarkable face, the huge unflinching eyes, the black ringlets of hair, the delicate cameo skin.

"Oh my! Oh my goodness, Mrs. Vargas, you didn't tell me she was so beautiful."

The fresh scent of baby powder wafted up around Elizabeth and she felt herself relax. "Pretty baby," Elizabeth cooed, hugging her. Something jabbed her through the blanket. Elizabeth frowned.

"The brace," Mrs. Vargas said.

"Oh! Poor baby," Why would such an innocent and fragile being have to endure any sort of hardship? Elizabeth wondered. "Poor baby," Elizabeth cooed, rocking her gently.

Mrs. Vargas stood and walked around the room, looking at the art on the walls, saying nothing. Elizabeth had the impression Mrs. Vargas was allowing Elizabeth and the baby a moment to bond. Even though it was obvious, Elizabeth was grateful. She wanted to return the unabashed stare of the baby.

She felt that haunting, hollow emotion abate.

Mrs. Vargas turned to Elizabeth, and Elizabeth looked up at her. "You called her ...."

"Amethyst. It was her mother's favorite gem."

"Amethyst." Elizabeth looked back at the quiet, serious baby, who still had not taken her eyes off her. "What a pretty name you have, baby." Elizabeth smiled at Mrs. Vargas. "You have excellent instincts, I'm completely head-over-heels from now and forever in love with little Amy."

"And she seems to like you. Since her mother died, I'm the only person she doesn't cry around—until now. Here, I'll write Gail's number down for you. And then, I'm afraid Amethyst and I must be going."

Mrs. Vargas wrote down the nanny's telephone number, then Elizabeth reluctantly handed the baby back to her. "By-bye, Amy-baby. See you soon, I hope!"

"I hope so too," Mrs. Vargas agreed, smiling.

After Mrs. Vargas left, Elizabeth wandered about the house with a pencil and note pad, making a list of all the things she had to get and all the things she had to change. The downstairs study she'd turn into the nanny's room. She'd hire someone to build a latticework wall around the patio, which would, in any case, make the space prettier, and perhaps that same someone could put baby gates at the top and the bottom of the stairs.

She needed to get a crib, a play pen, some toys. She'd have to discuss with Mrs. Vargas or Gail, if she agreed to be Amy's nanny, about essentials for the baby. What did she know about diapers and baby food? All she knew about baby clothes was that they were very small.

She went to the telephone to call Martha, but ten stopped with the number half dialed. No, she decided. She wanted to keep this moment to herself. There would be numerous times to share her new happiness with her friends after Amy had moved in.

She retrieved the phone number Mrs. Vargas had written down, and called Gail, instead.

Chapter XI

Gail, who had been completely apprised of the situation by Mrs. Vargas, agreed to come over the next afternoon. Elizabeth liked Gail's voice and manner on the telephone and hoped that impression would carry over in the face-to-face meeting as well. If they were about to live together, they'd must have pleasant chemistry between them.

When she got to work, she bounced into Marsalis's office. He was on the telephone and he held his hand up with his "I'm busy" gesture without looking at her. She continued to stand in the doorway.

Finally Marsalis hung up. "Good grief, Elizabeth, can't you tell I'm busy?"

"And can't you tell I have some business to discuss?" Elizabeth returned. Wow, she thought, she could never have talked to Marsalis like this before yesterday. Before Amy.

Marsalis leaned back slowly in his black velvet swivel chair, fingers steepled. "My, my! We ate our Wheaties this morning, didn't we?"

Elizabeth shrugged. "I just wanted to tell you that I'm taking the afternoon off."

Marsalis leaned forward again. "Why?"

"I have some personal business."

"You haven't ever taken one minute off."

"I know," Elizabeth answered. "In fact, I've often worked through lunch. And now, today, I'm taking the afternoon off."

"Mighty short notice," Marsalis sounded tough. "I was going to have you take the Watsons around."

"Well, I won't be able to." Elizabeth was curious about this new person in her who could so readily be assertive with Marsalis.

"I've never seen you like this."

"I've never been like this," Elizabeth turned to leave his office.

"Wait," Marsalis's voice shifted into a big cat-purr.

It caught Elizabeth by surprise. She stopped with her hand on the door frame, looking over her shoulder. "Yes?"

Marsalis stood and moved toward her. As always, whenever he came near her, his musky fragrance and powerful eyes made her heart jump. He leaned up against the wall close by her.

"Does my girl have a date?" he asked, holding her gaze.

Elizabeth laughed. "A *date*, in the *afternoon*? For pity's sake, Marsalis, I just have an appointment. It's personal. That is, for the moment I don't want to talk about it." She moved away from him toward her desk, then turned and gave him a big smile. "You flatter me though."

Marsalis shrugged. "I'm just trying to figure out why you're acting so strange."

"You mean, as if I have a life of my own? Hmmm ... I might be acting a lot more 'strange' from now on." Elizabeth sat at her desk and busied herself with the pile of listings requiring attention.

A short while later Marsalis, frowning, passed her desk. "I've got to get some things done if I have to take the Watsons around this afternoon."

Elizabeth nodded.

At noon she tidied her desk and picked up her purse. "See you tomorrow, Edna," she called as she passed through the door.

"Huh?" Puzzled, Edna looked up as her from her computer screen.

"I said, 'see you tomorrow,'" Elizabeth repeated. "I'm taking the afternoon off."

Edna's confusion morphed to a schoolmarm look of disapproval. "Really?"

"Did I forget to ask your permission?" Elizabeth's sarcasm was lost on Edna.

Edna harrumphed. "Wish I could go gallivantin' off at will!"

"It's none of my business what you do, Edna, but in the three months I've been here, you've quite a few afternoons off," Elizabeth observed.

"That's different," Edna sniffed. "That was business."

"Even I have responsibilities. Bye now." Elizabeth went to her car, determined not to let Edna get to her.

But she found herself thinking about Edna as she pulled out of the parking lot. Why did she have to always be so unpleasant? Because, Elizabeth realized, Edna believed herself to be in love with Marsalis, and she didn't need Elizabeth in the way.

She thought of Edna's dumpy, frumpy style and the fifteen years she had on Marsalis. Marsalis and Edna? Not likely. Even with her lack of experience, Elizabeth could see that Marsalis played Edna like a violin.

And he's probably doing the same with me, Elizabeth thought, with sudden insight, reflecting on the character change in him that morning from bile to honey when he didn't get his way. It wasn't the first time she'd witnessed his mood swings, but it was one of the strangest. Sometimes he seemed almost robotic.

Setting those thoughts aside, she stopped at her favorite Lebanese bakery to pick up some freshly baked baklava to serve when Gail came over. *Oh!* She didn't feel *anything* like a potential employer about to interview a potential employee. No, she felt like a supplicant, praying that this woman would fill all the gaps she, herself, didn't even know how to anticipate in her pending role of motherhood.

When she arrived home, she went into the barren downstairs study to sense what kind of first impression it might give Gail. She wished she had at least put something on the floor and the walls so that it didn't look quite so empty and unfriendly.

She lugged a chintz print overstuffed chair into the study and stole one of the floor lamps from the living room to make a soft light beside the chair, which, other than a stark little desk, was the only furniture in the room.

Then she went upstairs and put on jeans. No, she decided, that made her look too young and not serious. Opening her closet door all the way, she spied her "previous-self" print house dresses. She tried one on, and decided to go with it, even though it looked a bit incongruous with her pixie hair and contemporary make-up. The doorbell rang and she ran downstairs, flustered.

Elizabeth opened the door and greeted a woman with a face very much like the moon, with long, dark hair to her waist, tied back with a scarf of many colors, dressed in a black sweater, a crazy quilt jacket, and what appeared to be layers of skirts, all surrounded by the essence of patchouli. She grinned and extended her hand to Elizabeth. "Hi! I'm Gail Wanaski."

Elizabeth took Gail's soft, warm hand, delighted with her, on sight. "Hi, Gail, I'm *so* happy to meet you. Please, come in." A sense of *déjà vu* flowed over Elizabeth as Gail stepped into her house. Even as they walked into the living room, Elizabeth could not shake the feeling they had done this before.

"Make yourself comfortable while I get some refreshments," Elizabeth said. "I'm not quite organized yet, I hope you don't mind."

"No, no, doesn't phase me in the least," Gail said, following Elizabeth into the kitchen, friendly and familiar. "What a great spot!" She sat at the breakfast table, looking out at the lake. "A real artist's place, isn't it?"

"Why, yes," Elizabeth agreed. "In fact, I bought it from a writer."

"No kidding? Right again! Who?"

"Peter Shamus. But he usually writes under some pseudo ...."

"No kidding! Peter Shamus, alias Kim McCorky, alias D. Daniels."

"You know him?" Elizabeth asked surprised.

"Oh no! I don't *know* him, I just worship him from afar, so to speak, at the altar of his tomes."

"You've read his books?"

"Sure. Everything. Even his westerns. The man's got style. And sensitivity. And, here's the important part—he writes likable, intelligent, *real* women characters."

"Hmmm," Elizabeth used as the kettle started to whistle. She filled a diffuser with Earl Grey tea and placed it in a little teapot the poured boiling water over it. She recalled how Peter had said he was going to borrow her face for a character in his current book.

The aroma of bergamot floated up around her.

"You haven't read him?" Gail asked, incredulous.

"I'm afraid I haven't. You see, I didn't know his pseudonyms." Boy-oh-boy! Elizabeth thought, that sounds really lame. She brought the teapot to the table and let it steep.

"And you didn't, for instance," Gail suggested, "ask what name he wrote under?"

Elizabeth shook her head, feeling really, *really* stupid. What an odd turn this 'interview' had taken. She couldn't keep from breaking out into a nervous giggle.

"I'm sorry, Gail—this is *not* the conversation I'd envisioned! I feel like I need to say, 'does this mean you don't get the job?'"

Gail broke out in a robust, alehouse laughter, her round green eyes closed up into little half moons in her round pink cheek, moon face. "I don't mean to scare you. You're supposed to try to do that to me! Although I don't scare easy."

"So I see! But I *do* scare easily," Elizabeth confided. "Oh, the pastries! I picked up some baklava on the way home." She looked around the kitchen. "I wonder where I put them?"

"Are they in that box on that little table behind the sofa in the living room?" Gail asked.

Now *that* was an eye for detail, Elizabeth thought. She scurried into the other room to retrieve the pastries. "You're very observant," she said, returning with the box.

"Oh, I have a knack for things out of place. You also recently moved a chair and a lamp or a small round table."

"Amazing, Sherlock!" Elizabeth giggled, surprised.

"Naa, nothing amazing. There's marks on the carpet."

Elizabeth placed the baklava on a plate, brought it to the breakfast table, then sat across from Gail and poured two mugs of tea. She couldn't remember a single thing she'd earlier thought would be absolutely essential to ask.

"I hope I haven't put you off," Gail said, biting into a piece of baklava. "Yummy! I love baklava! I know I can have that effect. But I'm strong of mind, character, and body. Also I have a résumé as long as your arm."

"It seems very odd," Elizabeth replied. "I have the strongest feeling I know you already. Even though I'm sort of intimidated by you, it doesn't really bother me. It seems as if we've already covered that ground, and now it's time for us to make a home for Amy."

"I'll drink to that," Gail said, holding her tea mug aloft.

Elizabeth clinked her mug to Gail's.

The telephone rang.

"Excuse me," Elizabeth went into the living room to answer it.

"How'd it go?" Marsalis said without preamble.

Elizabeth turned her back to the kitchen. "How did what go?"

"Your appointment."

"Well, it's not over yet, but it's going quite well." Elizabeth wanted to feel defensive about his invasion of her privacy. But, for some odd reason, she felt flattered.

"Not over yet," Marsalis repeated. "Do you suppose it'll get over in time for me to take you to dinner?"

"Tonight?" Elizabeth asked, surprised.

"Sure, tonight. Or will your 'appointment' last all night?"

"Look, Marsalis," Elizabeth felt her temper rising after all, "you know better than anyone that I don't ..." It dawned on her that Gail could hear her every word.

"Don't?" Marsalis teased.

"Yes, don't!"

"Okay, okay, Liz, don't get excited. I'll pick you up at seven-thirty."

"I think not, Marsalis. Thanks, but I have a lot on my mind, and I'm exhausted." Elizabeth suddenly realized the truth of her words. "Let me take a rain check, when I'm more relaxed."

"Huh! Rain check. You're treating me pretty casually." He sounded truly surprised.

"I'm sorry, but I need to get back to business."

"No, no. *I'm* sorry," Marsalis said curtly.

"That's okay. See you tomorrow."

"Right." He cut the connection with a noisy click.

Elizabeth slowly hung up. She was nothing short of amazed how he could stir her up. Was this love? If so, it was a fundamentally annoying emotion. She ran her fingers through her hair and returned to the kitchen.

"More tea?" she asked, filling the kettle with water.

"If you do," Gail answered. "Men! Ain't they exasperating?"

"Well ... I don't really know," Elizabeth answered, returning to the table. "I've lived an extremely sheltered life. That is, up until a few months ago when my grandfather passed away. I date Marsalis occasionally, but not much lately because I, well, I guess Marsalis's right when he calls me a prude ...."

"Malarkey," Gail exclaimed, patting Elizabeth's hand. "Male malarkey, and don't let him try to convince you otherwise."

Elizabeth could hardly believe the sense of relief she felt hearing someone else support her stance. "Thank you, Gail," she said simply.

The kettle began whistling and Elizabeth got up to steep more tea. "But he *is* incredibly good looking."

"Hmmm," Gail said.

"No, really. He should be a model—or something."

"Oh, I'm not doubting it," Gail said. "That was just my 'the gorgeous-guy-syndrome' hmmm."

"If anyone deserves that 'hmm,' it's Marsalis." Elizabeth returned with the teapot. "What's funny, though, is, he never really seems to care much about me." Elizabeth stared out at the lake and let her thoughts reflect off its surface. "He seems to be enjoying our time together sometimes, then he has a mood swing, and ... everything makes him sarcastic."

"Hormones," Gail pronounced. "Raging hormones."

Elizabeth turned to Gail. "I guess that explains it. But what I'm saying is, he never seemed to care about me until just today, when I told him I was taking the afternoon off."

"You work together," Gail observed.

"Yes. And this morning, when I told him I was taking the afternoon off, he got all jealous, asking me if I had a date. And just now on the phone he was trying to get me to go out with him tonight. He's never wanted to go out in the middle of the week." Elizabeth sipped her tea. "He's checking up on me. Strange."

"Not the least bit strange," Gail said. "The rooster never worries about the hens *in* the pen. But you're suddenly doing new things and it looks to him like you're out of the pen. He figures he has to put in extra effort."

"You think so?" Elizabeth asked. "If I was doing anything for him to be at all, the tiniest bit suspicious about—but in fact, with a baby, I'll be tied down, not 'loose.'"

"You haven't told him about the baby?"

"No, because ..." Elizabeth stopped short. "Well, I didn't know why, but now I see it's because I don't want to meet with his disapproval—if he disapproves. And he always disapproves of anything that's not his own idea."

"Are you afraid he'll dissuade you?" Gail picked out another pastry.

"No way! But I don't want negative energy of any sort. I feel so private about Amy. As if I'm going through a of mental gestation. I'm so-o-o happy. I haven't been able to get Amy out of my mind for a minute. Not for a single moment. I woke up twice last night feeling excited, and both times I'd been dreaming about her. Lovely dreams.

"I didn't know I could be so strong-willed, but I won't let anything interfere with my making Amy happy and healthy." Elizabeth paused. "And having

you here, and happy with us too, Gail, if you want to
be a part of our family."

"I'd love to be part of your family!" Gail answered
with a huge, warm, round grin.

Chapter XII

Gail planned to move in Thursday night and Mrs. Vargas was bringing Amy over Friday evening.

Thursday afternoon Marsalis called Elizabeth into his office.

"Have a seat," he ordered. He stood over her, studying her for a long moment before saying, "You're just—glowing."

"Oh?" She looked down at her hands and fussed with the pleats in her skirt.

He remained silent for another long moment, then sat on the corner of his desk and folded his arms. Elizabeth glanced up at him, unnerved by his beauty and disapproval.

"Anyway," he said, relaxing, pasting on a smile, "I wanted to make sure you remembered our dinner tomorrow night."

"Dinner? Tomorrow?"

"Yes. Don't tell me you've forgotten?"

"Yes—no—I mean ...." What *do* I mean? Elizabeth wondered. "Nothing was definite."

"Well, it's definite." Marsalis walked around his desk and settled in his chair, looking down at his work. "I'll pick you up about six-thirty."

"But—I'm—n-not free," Elizabeth stammered.

The vein in Marsalis's left temple pulsed. "You're n-not free?" he mimicked with cruel precision.

"That's right." *Why don't I tell him about Amy? All I'm doing is raising his ire.* "Look, Marsalis," she screwed up her courage, "the thing is, I I don't feel close enough to you to share what's going on in my life. And browbeating won't get it out of me."

"*Browbeating!*" Marsalis shook his head in disgusted disbelief. "Good grief, Elizabeth, melodrama isn't necessary."

At that moment his phone rang and Elizabeth took the opportunity to return to her desk, feeling shaky. *I have too much to look forward to,* she reminded herself, *to let a man's jealousy interfere with the beautiful picture developing in my life.*

Marsalis didn't talk with her the rest of the day. And for the rest of the day, she told herself she didn't care. But in her heart of hearts, she knew she would miss their once or twice a week dates, if that's what he decided.

I have Amy now, and Gail. Marsalis may be gorgeous, and he sometimes makes me feel gorgeous ... but so what!?! I have a wonderful life without trying to jump through his hoops.

She turned her mind away from him and concentrated on her work.

*   *

After Gail moved in that night, Elizabeth made a small cozy fire in the fireplace and the two of them settled in front of it with hot cocoa and note pads to make lists of things Amy might need, and a list of things Elizabeth felt she needed to learn, which grew longer and ever longer.

Finally Gail put down her pen. "Don't worry yourself sick, girl! You'll be surprised how much instinct will kick in."

Elizabeth nodded. "I believe you—I'm not really worrying, I just have all this energy! I only have one, huge worry, and that is taking Amy to the hospital, taking her to surgery. She's so tiny, so helpless. It breaks my heart."

"I'm here," Gail said softly. "I've been through much unhappier and much less promising scenarios."

Elizabeth studied Gail. "Really?"

"Yes. But I won't go into details on this, the eve of your motherhood. I just want you to know you can count on me."

Elizabeth nodded thoughtfully. She got lost in wondering if she could ever become strong and wise like Gail.

"Are you having a nice trip?" Gail asked.

Elizabeth chuckled self-consciously. "I was just hoping I'll grow up to be like you!"

Gail laughed, her plump cheeks ballooning. "Well, thank you, Liz-girl. I hope you grow up to be like me too!"

97 - Amethyst Dream

They laughed, then decided they'd better retire.
Tomorrow would be a big day.

*　　*

Marsalis avoided Elizabeth all the next day. Fascinated,
she observed her own emotions—it didn't bother her
in the least. More to the point, she wished she didn't
have to be at work today at all. How often would she
have *that* feeling after Amy became a part of her life?

Maybe she'd start working part-time. She didn't
need the money, she needed to be with her new family.

As she thumbed through the multiple listing,
she reflected on her surprising metamorphosis. A
mere month ago it would have been hard to imagine
choosing not to go out with Marsalis. Now the emotional entanglement with him seemed insubstantial
and adolescent compared with her deepening feelings for Amy and the companionable relationship
with Gail.

Marsalis left the office at three, and Elizabeth left
soon after—she had more important things to attend
to than selling houses to strangers. She had to make a
home for her own foster daughter.

As she came through the garage into the kitchen,
she was delighted by the sight of Gail standing by
the stove, hair piled on her head, gathered up by one
of her wildly colorful scarves. A delicious aroma per-
meated the air. The house felt warm and cozy, welcoming her home.

98 ~ Thea Thomas

"What smells so *fantastic*?" Elizabeth asked.

Gail brushed a wayward tendril of hair off her forehead, which immediately plopped back again. "Quinoa, broccoli, basil and garlic casserole."

Elizabeth kicked off her heels, plopped her purse and briefcase on the sofa in the living room then came back into the kitchen. "But, Gail, cooking is not part of your job description."

"You don't want me to cook?" Gail asked.

"Are you kidding? I *love* you to cook. But you don't have to."

"If you think I'm about to eat those frozen what-ever-they-are you have in the freezer," Gail pointed her wooden spoon at the offending appliance, "you're much mistaken. Plus, I can't sit around all day, I need to keep busy. And third and finally, I love my own cooking."

"I must have done something very right to deserve the miracle of you," Elizabeth stood by Gail and inhaled deeply. "Oh, yum. I think I've never smelled an aroma so tantalizing in my life. Would I be a terrible person if I went up and took a hot bath for a few minutes while you slave away in the galley? I'd just love to shake this day off."

Gail shook her head. "Dear heart, this is hardly a feast, it's a modest but healthy meal. Go take a bath, you look like you need to get rid of tension. Put some Epsom salts in the water."

"Okay, Mom," Elizabeth teased.

After Elizabeth had taken a bath in water as hot as she could tolerate, she threw on a pair of soft cords and an oversized man's plaid flannel shirt she'd found in the back of a closet that Peter had apparently overlooked. She'd been meaning to ask him if he missed it, but she kept forgetting and now she'd grown attached to it.

She padded barefoot into the kitchen.

"That's more like it," Gail said approvingly.

"Are you *still* in the kitchen?" Elizabeth asked.

"I got up to put the tea kettle on when I heard the bathtub draining. But after you went up, I whipped up a strawberry mousse for dessert. Low calorie, and tasty."

"I *hope* it's low calorie. Are you sure you aren't trying to fatten me up?" Elizabeth accused.

"You probably don't put on weight no matter what you eat," Gail said. "But not to worry, I have an associate's degree in nutrition."

Elizabeth shook her head in disbelief. "Incredible. Is there anything you can't do or don't know?"

Gail shrugged as if to say, whatever-I-don't-know-isn't-worth-knowing. "If what's around here exemplifies your diet, your nutrition is not balanced."

"Guilty," Elizabeth confessed.

"Motherhood requires energy, you know."

The doorbell rang and Elizabeth excitedly scurried to the front door, Gail close behind. Mrs. Vargas held Amy, all in pink, with a pink baby duffel bag over her shoulder. Elizabeth and Gail emptied her arms.

"Thanks," Mrs. Vargas said. "Excuse me for a moment, Amy has some more things." She turned and hurried back to her car in the driveway.

Elizabeth, holding Amy, went into the living room. She sat, staring down at the precious baby, forgetting everyone and everything. Amy studied Elizabeth in return with that strange little lonely-yet-trusting look of hers.

Soon Gail and Mrs. Vargas came in, arms loaded.

Elizabeth finally looked up. "My goodness!" she exclaimed, "Gail and I discussed some of the things we might have to get for Amy—it didn't even cross my mind she'd already have things."

"Let me get dinner on the table." Gail emptied her arms and went back into the kitchen.

"How can you leave Amy?" Elizabeth called after her.

Gail came back to the doorway. "It isn't easy. But you're the mommy. I'll be with her all the time you're at work."

"Ugh! Don't remind me!"

Elizabeth turned to Mrs. Vargas. "I've been thinking how difficult it'll be for me to work full-time with Amy in my life now. How can I possibly leave her? I might start working part-time. I took the job because I wanted to be occupied. But now," she hugged Amy yet closer, "I have so much to occupy my time."

Mrs. Vargas smiled at Elizabeth as she organized Amy's belongings. "I'm certain you'll make the right decisions. And I trust Gail completely."

"Gail is amazing!" She looked down at Amy's beautiful, sad face. There, in that little face, were all her own dreams of the future. She wanted nothing more. She looked up at Mrs. Vargas, tears in her eyes.

"I'm sorry," she said. "I'm *just so happy!*"

Mrs. Vargas nodded. "I understand. Completely."

Suddenly, a loud knock resounded at the door.

Gail came into the living room. "Expecting company?"

"No," Elizabeth answered, "I'm not. Could you see who it is, please?"

Mrs. Vargas and Elizabeth were quiet while Gail answered the door.

"Yes?" Gail said.

There was a long pause, then Elizabeth heard Marsalis's voice. "Ahm, who are you?"

Gail answered cooly, "I could ask as much of you, but I suspect you're Marsalis."

Elizabeth stood and went into the foyer. "Marsalis! What are you doing here?"

"I—what's that?" he quizzed, pointing at Amy.

"It's a baby, Marsalis," Elizabeth answered. "What are you doing here?" she repeated.

"Why are you crying?" Marsalis asked back.

"Because I'm happy. Now, it's definitely your turn to answer a question. Why are you here?"

Marsalis cast a glance at Gail, then returned his attention to Elizabeth. "I decided to drive by, since you've been acting so weird lately. And I saw a strange car in your driveway." He glanced at Gail again. "I guess you're just having some girl friends over. I don't know why you couldn't have just told me that. Unless .... "

"Unless what?" Elizabeth asked.

"Unless you were trying to make me jealous."

Gail snorted.

Marsalis and Elizabeth turned and looked at her.

"Sorry," Gail said. "Excuse me." She let go of the door handle and returned to the kitchen.

"I didn't tell you because I didn't feel like it," Elizabeth said to Marsalis. "But now that you're here, you might as well come in a get introduced."

Elizabeth led Marsalis into the living room. "Mrs. Vargas, this is my boss, Marsalis Antonella. Marsalis, this is Mrs. Vargas, a social worker. Gail, you just met. She's the nanny I hired to help me take care of my foster daughter, Amy. Isn't she beautiful?"

"Foster daughter? What do you mean, foster daughter?"

"Just that."

"I don't understand." Marsalis's expression was genuinely puzzled. Elizabeth had never seen him so confused. She watched as he looked around and suddenly took it all in. Then he went through one of his chameleon changes. "But, Elizabeth, this is big news. This is great! I had no idea! If it's what you want, wonderful. When you decide to go for something, nothing stops you, does it?"

"No," Elizabeth said. "At least not when it comes to the really big things."

Marsalis looked at Amy. "My goodness, she *is* a pretty little thing, isn't she?"

"Soups on," Gail said, and, to prove the point, carrying a soup tureen to the dining table.

"Gail's very literal," Elizabeth laughed. She turned to Marsalis. "Would you care to join us?"

"Oh, no. I wouldn't think of intruding any more than I already have." He flashed his big screen smile to all three women. "I'm just happy to see you don't have another *man,* Elizabeth." He said it in a teasing tone, but Gail and Mrs. Vargas exchanged a look that Elizabeth read as, "Who does he think he's kidding?"

"I'll see you to the door," Elizabeth said, relieved that he volunteered to leave.

"No–no, no, no. I'll let myself out. I'll call you later this weekend, and you can tell me how this little beauty," he winked at Amy, "is doing."

"All right," Elizabeth said.

He reached out and lightly touched Elizabeth's cheek. "Motherhood looks good on you." He turned and no one moved until they heard the door close.

"Okay!" Gail said. "Let's eat!"

Elizabeth put Amy in the new play pen and covered her with her fluffy pink blanket, then she and Mrs. Vargas sat at the dining room table, while Gail ran back and forth between the kitchen and the table, bringing in her delicious meal.

"I insist you join us," Elizabeth said to her, trying to sound stern.

"I will, I will, but don't stand on ceremony. Go ahead and start."

"Not without you," Elizabeth asserted.

"Okay, I'm here." Gail brought in a steaming bowl of green beans and tomatoes. She started passing the food around.

"Boy, you're right, he's a looker. But a little odd, huh?" Gail said casually.

"Marsalis? He's just spoiled," Elizabeth answered.

The talk shifted to care of Amy, and after dinner Mrs. Vargas showed Elizabeth and Gail Amy's physical therapy routines, then the three of them went upstairs and put her to bed in her new crib in Elizabeth's room. It was nearly eleven when Mrs. Vargas finally gathered her belongings to leave.

"You have my telephone numbers," she said, "don't hesitate to call me. Otherwise, I'll call you in a few days."

"Thanks, Mrs. Vargas, thank you. We'll talk soon," Elizabeth said.

*   *

Elizabeth, Amy, and Gail settled into a happy matriarchal routine. Elizabeth worked one more week full-time, then changed her schedule to every other weekend and the alternate Monday through Wednesday.

Much to her surprise, Marsalis took her much-reduced schedule in stride, and was altogether supportive of her new-found motherhood.

Maybe, she thought, he's more sensitive than I thought. If only he didn't have those dramatic and unprovoked mood swings! He seemed to her so preoccupied with his facade that whatever might be inside never truly developed.

Elizabeth recalled a cicada she'd seen a few years previous that had just emerged from its cocoon, glistening, perched on a branch. It stretched its raw new legs and body and wings and looked at her as if to say, "Aren't I pretty?"

105 ~ Amethyst Dream

She'd chuckled at its odd anthropomorphic behavior.

That's how Marsalis seemed—as though he felt everyone should be taken with his beauty, while not knowing for himself if he was beautiful. Oddly, this trait endeared him to her. His facade was bravado, but underneath he was a lonely, fragile and unsure little boy. She had an urge to protect him.

Chapter XIII

Elizabeth looked up from her desk at work to see Peter jogging by the office in green and white shorts and a green T-shirt. He stopped and peered into the dark office. She waved to him. He turned around, came in, and jogged up to her desk. By then Elizabeth was giggling—Peter always made her feel so happy!

"What've you been doing?" they asked each other in tandem. They burst into giggles.

"You first," Elizabeth said, catching her breath.

"No, you!" Peter grabbed a chair and straddled it backwards, tipping the back until it rested against Elizabeth's desk, balanced. "I haven't seen you in here for so long, I thought you quit."

"No, but a lot's been happening." Elizabeth moved a stack of papers aside, and schooched closer to Peter.

"Such as?"

"I started working part time because I became a foster parent."

Peter bolted his chair upright. "Seriously?"

Elizabeth beamed. "Yes. Absolutely seriously. I have the most beautiful little foster daughter in the world, her name is Amy. And I have a nanny, Gail." Elizabeth almost launched into Gail's admiration of Peter, but she decided to hold off.

"Amazing, Elizabeth. Wow! You're—*wow*—I'm thunderstruck!" Peter tilted his chair against her desk again. Elizabeth liked how cozy that felt. "So—when do I get to meet the family?"

"Any time, of course. *Me casa es su casa.*"

"That's true," Peter observed. They laughed again.

"Why don't you come over for dinner Friday night? Gail and I'll cook up a feast—we love excuses to do that."

"I'll be there!"

"By the way," Elizabeth asked, "do you like fans?"

"Fans?"

"Yes. Of yours. Of your books."

"It sort of depends," Peter said cautiously.

"On?"

"Some fans are—kinda—scary."

"What if they're not scary. What if they're lovable, intelligent, and well-read?"

"Then they're my very favorite person."

"In that case, be prepared." Elizabeth gave Peter a stagy cryptic look.

"Oh-oh—what do you mean?"

"Mystery is the best part of anticipation," Elizabeth said, refusing to say more.

Gail and Amy were playing splashy bath when Elizabeth came home that evening. "Guess who's coming to dinner Friday night," Elizabeth asked, rolling up her sleeves and joining in the play.

"Umm, Marsalis," Gail guessed. "What do you think baby?" Gail said in a squeaky-toy voice to Amy. "Is Marsalis coming to dinner Friday?"

"Na-na-na!" Amy said, slapping both plump little hands down on the water.

How is it possible that everything Amy does is the absolutely cutest thing on earth? Elizabeth wondered while the surge of adoration in her chest calmed.

"Well, she's right! It's not Marsalis. It's Peter."

"Peter?" Gail turned away from the bathtub and faced Elizabeth. "Here? For dinner? Just like that?"

"Here!" Elizabeth said. "For Dinner. Just like that!"

"What should I wear? What should I cook? What time is he coming? Do you think I could ask him to sign one of his books for me?"

Elizabeth laughed. "The unflappable Gail flaps! My goodness, Gail's got a crush on Peter!" she said to Amy, wrapping a big fluffy towel around her. She sat on the bathroom rug beside Gail and dried Amy.

"I do!" Gail said. "I don't care who knows it! It's a simple fact!"

"Do you want me to ask him to bring a couple of his books?" Elizabeth asked.

"I have everything he's ever written. I'd love for him to sign my beloved and dog-eared copy of *After the Year Before the Millennium*."

"If anything ever touched an author's heart," Elizabeth observed, "I suppose showing him a copy of one of his books that's the adult equivalent of a teddy bear would do it."

Elizabeth kissed Amy and fussed with her adorable black curls while Gail put her leg brace back on. Amy took the attention quietly, wearing a sober expression.

"Now I know what 'this is going to hurt me more than it hurts you' really means," Elizabeth said softly to Gail.

Gail nodded. Then the two of them put a cute little rabbits and kittens print playsuit on Amy.

"There's our baby, There's our little girl!" Gail said. "You want to play in your play pen, Pussy Willow?"

"Pay-pay-pu," Amy imitated.

Elizabeth and Gail laughed, while Elizabeth picked up Amy and the three of them went downstairs.

"I suppose I should be sort of embarrassed about how little I know about Peter as a writer," Elizabeth said.

"Yes, you should!" Gail agreed. "But I'm glad you know Peter as a person. He has a following, and we're always sort of surmising what he's like. Do you want to read one of his books?"

"Well, sure."

Gail started toward her room.

"I mean, not right now, but eventually. When Amy isn't taking so much of my attention. Anyway, wouldn't it seem sort of funny if I just happened to read one of his books a day or two before he comes over for dinner?"

Gail shook her head. "What's strange is that you'd just about have to go out of your way *not* to have read Peter by now. I know you like to read, the house is full of books. I'd say you're afraid of something."

"Am I afraid?" Elizabeth asked Amy in a falsetto.

"Bingo!" Gail exclaimed. "You're afraid to read Peter. You're afraid you might not understand it, or something like that. Hey! As long as you don't read him, you don't have to be responsible for what you don't know."

"Interesting extrapolation, my dear Watson, but inaccurate. I hesitate to read him because—because I have such a huge respect for him now, and science fiction and westerns are not my thing, and I'm afraid, you know, that I'll *lose* ...."

"Oh!" Gail nodded, insight dawning, "I was wrong, for once."

"Yup."

"But," Gail defended, "the reason he has such a following is because he doesn't write genre hack at all. He's witty and droll. He invents wonderful things. You should at least read some of his science fiction. *After the Year Before the Millennium* is great. Did he tell you that five of his science fiction novels are being brought out again, in hardback, under his real name?"

"No. He doesn't talk to me about his work."

"Well, no wonder!" Gail got up and went into the kitchen, Elizabeth, carrying Amy, trailed after her.

"Geez, Gail, are you his agent or his public relations person?"

"I'd be either, happily."

Elizabeth looked deep into Amy's dark blue eyes. "I'll read him. But I reserve the right to my opinion."

Gail was digging around in the freezer. "Well, of course!" her muted voice agreed.

"You can't blame me for thinking that he might be writing at a level of escapism that I wasn't interested in escaping to. Anyway, what should we feed this illustrious, this renowned author?" Elizabeth asked, pulling the play pen to the kitchen table and putting Amy down among her toys.

While Gail made dinner, the two of them came up with a menu that Elizabeth wrote down on the back of an envelope.

"You have to make your amazing oat bran dinner rolls, and your fabulous strawberry mousse, Gail, if you want him to completely fall in love with you."

"Done and done," Gail said.

Elizabeth found herself looking forward to Friday night with happier anticipation that she would have imagined. It was an entirely different feeling from the one she had when she was about to go out with Marsalis.

Until this insight came upon her, she hadn't consciously known going out with Marsalis made her nervous and ill-at-ease.

What does that say about me, she wondered. On the one hand, there's Peter, a world famous author and I feel a bit shy around him, but I'm really looking forward to it. On the other hand Marsalis, a less-than-mediocre real estate salesman, and I feel like a mouse trapped in a tiger cage.

On a third hand, she continued arguing with herself, even though I'm physically platonic with both Peter and Marsalis, my relationship with Marsalis is psychologically romantic. So, it's not Marsalis that makes me nervous, she reasoned, it's this whole in-love-with-love thing.

In the meantime, Gail behaved like a teenager before going to a concert of a rock-hero. Elizabeth delighted in seeing the usually cucumber-cool Gail all aflutter.

"I was thinking of my Gypsy look, lots of scarves and skirts and colors," Gail said. "And then I thought, no, too eccentric. So I thought, the navy blue suit, have you seen it? But then I thought, no, too severe. So then I thought .... "

"I'm wearing that big old plaid flannel shirt Peter left here and blue jeans," Elizabeth put in.

"Really?!"

"Really. But only because I'm curious to see if Peter recognizes the shirt. Don't worry, Gail, Peter is a regular guy. He's a very accessible, down-to-earth, nice guy. Just be comfortable."

"If you say so." Gail sounded unwilling to let go of her apparel planning.

"Let's go check out your wardrobe and see what you look special in," Elizabeth suggested.

"Let's!"

They went into Gail's room and an hour later, after all her clothes were piled everywhere, they decided on a lacy lavender pullover and a full, floor-length, multi-print skirt.

"You look great, Gail," Elizabeth said. "A little bit Gypsy, a little bit reserved."

Chapter XIV

When Elizabeth opened the door Friday night, Peter was laden with gifts of fruit and wine.

"Oh, Peter, you didn't have to bring anything."

"Couldn't come empty-handed." He gave her an appraising look. "What looks familiar?"

She pirouetted slowly.

"That shirt! It's uncanny, I used to have one just like it, that is, not me, but ...."

"This is it. You left it in the back of one of the closets. I meant to ask you if you missed it, but I kept forgetting. It's so huge, I decided it wasn't yours."

"You're right, it's not mine, but it seems strange that I'd overlook it. I guess you're supposed to have it. It was my father's favorite shirt. When he died, my mother gave it to me. It looks great on you."

Elizabeth's smile fled from her face. "Oh, Peter, I'm sorry!" Elizabeth couldn't remember when she'd embarrassed herself so completely.

"Don't be, Elizabeth. I love seeing you in it. It's getting some use, instead of mouldering in the back of a closet."

"I'm going to change immediately. I had no intention of keeping it, I just wanted to tease you," Elizabeth insisted.

Peter shook his head firmly. "I refuse to take it. It's a gift from me to you. Or perhaps from my dad to you. Even if you don't like it, you'd better keep it or you'll hurt my feelings."

"But I *do* like it. I love it. I was attracted to it the moment I saw it, and I've never worn men's plaid shirts in my life."

"See? It belongs to you. Now then," Peter changed the subject, "let's see what you've done to the old fort."

Elizabeth studied Peter for a moment and decided he was sincerely untroubled about giving her the shirt. She turned and waved at the living room. "I haven't done anything really. Except add population. Come and meet Gail. She's creating culinary wonders you will never forget."

"Ah!" Peter said, won over. "Take me to her!"

They went into the kitchen where Gail was busily putting the final touches on the meal.

"Gail, I'd like you to meet my friend, Peter Shamus. Peter, Gail Wanaski, my right hand, and, I might add, an admirer of your work."

Gail wiped her hands on her apron, her color high. "I hope you don't mind a damp hand," she said, extending it. "It's a great pleasure to meet you, Mr. Shamus. It's true, I'm one of your biggest fans."

Peter shook her hand heartily. "Happy to meet you. Judging from the perfumes in this kitchen, I'm about to become one of *your* greatest fans. By the way, don't you dare call me Mr. Shamus again!"

Oh! What should I call you?"

Then Gail and Peter exchanged a confidential look. "Mr. Big Hand!" they said in unison, and broke into laughter.

Still laughing, they turned to Elizabeth. She looked at them blankly.

"Mr. Big Hand is a character in one of Peter's stories," Gail clarified. "He's an imaginary friend of a little boy. At least that's what everyone thinks. You see, the big hand comes flying off this kid's clock and it, like, stalks the kid. It's real spooky. Finally the kid confronts it and says, 'what should I call you?' and it answers ...."

"Mr. Big Hand," Elizabeth guessed, monotone.

Peter and Gail started giggling again.

"Well," Gail gasped, "you had to be there. I mean, the story, the way Peter writes it, it's terrifying! It's great!"

If the evening was about to become one literary allusion after another, Elizabeth told herself, I should have taken Gail's advice and read some of Peter's work.

"Enough hilarity," Peter said. "Let me see the beautiful baby."

"You'll have to wait a bit, she's sound asleep right now." Elizabeth noticed that this was the second time in only a few minutes Peter responded with sensitivity to her discomfort. She'd never in her life had a man come to her emotional defense, and for a new and strange feeling, it was very comfortable. "She'll wake up pretty soon, but if you want, we can go take a peek at her."

"Of course I want!"

Peter and Elizabeth went upstairs and tip-toed into the bedroom.

They stole up to the crib where Amy slept on her tummy with her cherubic little face toward them. Elizabeth watched Peter look down at Amy, his angular face becoming soft. He studied Amy's face as if it was the first time in his life he'd gotten close to an original da Vinci.

Finally Peter gave Elizabeth a soft smile and took her hand. They tip-toed back out of the bedroom.

"Aren't babies miraculous?" Peter asked as they went back downstairs.

Elizabeth nodded.

"Amy's beautiful, Elizabeth. She's perfect."

"Yes," Elizabeth said quietly. "She *is* beautiful. And she's perfect. Although she was born with a club foot."

Peter stopped at the bottom of the stairs. "Oh, Elizabeth, I'm sorry to hear that. How severe?"

"Well, it's only her left leg, but it's fairly severe. She has to have surgery and I'm dreading it. I don't know what I'd do without Gail. She promises it will be smooth sailing. Of course, it'll ultimately be wonderful for Amy. But I think about the surgery and just about go nuts."

"Well, don't go nuts, dear," Peter patted her shoulder. "You've been entrusted with a special gift and I know you'll be strong. You have what it takes to go through this experience, which will add to your prodigious store of empathy and wisdom."

Elizabeth felt herself close to tears. Peter didn't have a way with words only on paper, she thought. "I've gotten so involved in what's going on right now, that I forgot about the greater design. I don't know what I've done to deserve such wonderful people as you and Gail and Amy."

"The privilege is mutual," Peter answered.

"Are you two going to stand around praising each other all night," Gail called from the dining room, "or can we eat now?"

"We're coming."

"What do you think of our little darlin'?" Gail asked Peter as they sat at the dining table.

"She's remarkable," he said. "I can't wait until she wakes up, I want to see that pretty little face animated."

"Yes, indeed!" Gail nodded.

The dinner conversation revolved around Amy and Gail and Elizabeth's new life without further allusions to Peter's writing. Elizabeth, fully aware that Peter and Gail were being thoughtful of not leaving her out of the conversation, resolved to begin to rectify the gap in her education the next day.

As Elizabeth watched Gail and Peter banter, it became clear that they were two passengers on the same trip, intelligent and sensitive, sharing the same offbeat sense of humor, that, even without cryptic literary references, Elizabeth didn't quite follow.

"I'll go get Amy," Elizabeth said when she heard her during dessert. "Prepare yourself, Peter, for a second sweet treat."

"Don't wake her on my account," Peter protested.

"She's awake," Gail and Elizabeth said together.

"She doesn't have to worry about being ignored around here!" he observed. "I didn't hear a peep."

"She hardly ever peeps," Elizabeth said, laughing. "She rocks her crib when she wants attention. Didn't you hear that '*squee-squee*' sound?"

Peter shrugged. "Sorry."

Upstairs, Elizabeth could see Amy in the glow of the night-light, sitting up, playing with a stuffed giraffe.

"Hello, baby," she said softly. Amy looked up and smiled. She had five teeth now.

"Bet!" she said, her name for Elizabeth as Gail was always calling her 'Pet.' She held the giraffe up for Elizabeth to admire.

"Pretty giraffe!" Elizabeth took Amy's baby brush and perked up her black curls. "Pretty toy. Shall we go downstairs and see the new person?"

Peter and Gail had moved to the fireplace in the living room. Peter sat on the sofa, facing the stairs, waiting for Elizabeth and Amy to return.

"There she is!" he said as they came into the room. "Look at that beautiful little girl!"

Elizabeth took Amy up to Peter. "Amy, this is Peter."

Peter held out his arms and Elizabeth surrendered her, slowly. "I don't know how she'll react to a man. I don't think there've been many in her short life."

Amy looked up at Peter's face with surprise, her eyes opened wider and rounder and wider and rounder, and her mouth turned down into a tiny 'n'. Very quietly she looked around, saw Gail and Elizabeth smiling at her. She looked back at Peter. The downward turn of her mouth neutralized some, and then she seemed to relax.

"I guess she trusts you," Elizabeth said.

"I'm privileged," Peter answered quietly.

Gail nodded. "Babies know the good guys from the bad guys, you can't fool them."

"Aren't you sweet?" Peter asked Amy. "Beautiful black curls and huge blue eyes!" He inhaled deeply. "*Ohh,* and you smell as if you've come straight from heaven!" He beamed at everything and everyone. "I want to join your matriarchy!"

Elizabeth and Gail laughed.

"If you did," Elizabeth pointed out, "it wouldn't be a matriarchy anymore."

"No, no!" Peter protested, "I wouldn't be an official member, I'd be a slave. Just call me Egor. I'll fetch water and, I don't know, wash your cars. In exchange for getting to bask in your gentility."

"You haven't seen the whole picture, Peter. Sometimes we get pretty rowdy."

"All the better!"

"He's not easily dissuaded, is he?" Gail asked Elizabeth.

"Seriously," Peter said, "I don't know how I can repay your wonderful hospitality."

"Well," Elizabeth said, "there are two things you *could* do."

"Gladly! What are they?"

"First of all, I wanted to ask if I could hire Ralph away from you for a few days to install baby gates and build a fence around the patio before Amy starts toddling around."

"Done! You don't even need to ask me, just ask Ralph, I'm sure he'll be delighted to do it. What's the second thing I can do for you? The first one doesn't count, because I'm not doing anything."

"I believe it would make Gail happy if you signed one of your books."

"That's too easy," Peter said.

"But she's right," Gail put in. "It would mean an awful lot to me."

"Bring it on. I'll give you a copy of the anthology when it comes out."

"Oh no," Gail protested. "That's too much!"

"Not in the least. When have I had an evening as special as this?" Peter hugged Amy close to him. "Never! That's when," he went on, answering his own question.

"I'll go get the book," Gail said, jumping up.

Elizabeth thought Peter suddenly looked sad. "Well, it's not the last night like this."

"You read my mind," Peter said, surprised.

"You looked so sad all of a sudden."

"I didn't know I was that transparent."

"You're not, as a rule. Usually I find you enigmatic. I guess there're no secrets with a baby on your lap." Elizabeth plumped up a pillow on the couch, "Anyway, you have to invite us over now."

Gail came sailing back to the fireplace. She took Amy from Peter, handed her to Elizabeth, gave Peter the book, then put another log on the fire.

"You really will be calling me Egor if you're unfortunate enough to be trapped with my cooking," Peter protested. "Especially when compared with Gail's talents."

"As if we'd leave all the cooking to you!" Gail said.

"That's right!" Elizabeth agreed. "Remember, we know where you live. Either you invite us, or we'll invade."

"*Descend,*" Gail interjected.

"Without warning, like locusts, laden with pots and pans."

"And make you eat every single bite!" Gail insisted.

"Oh, to be so lucky!" Peter rolled his eyes. "Okay then, let's say next Friday. I'll cook a main course and, I don't know, grill some vegetables."

"Sounds great!" Gail said.

Elizabeth nodded. "I have next weekend off, so I won't have to worry about waking up early Saturday morning."

"Do you have to work tomorrow?" Peter asked.

"Afraid so." Elizabeth wrinkled her nose.

"Then I guess I'd better get out of here."

"You don't have to leave! I think I'll laze around for a few more minutes, then Amy and I'll sneak off to bed. I bet you and Gail have a lot to talk about. Don't let me poop the party."

Peter opened the cover of the book Gail had handed him and scrawled a paragraph or two.

"Writing another book?" Elizabeth teased.

Peter closed the cover and handed the book back to Gail. "I got inspired. I almost can't believe I just met you tonight, Gail, I feel like I've known you for ages."

"It was like that for me too when I first met her!" Elizabeth said, recalling the strong sense of *déjà vu* she had when Gail first walked into her home.

"And *you've* stolen my heart," Peter said to Amy, giving her a hug. "If we really are getting together next week, I can stand to leave to your delightful domicile now." He handed Amy to Gail and stood. They all meandered to the front door and Peter took his leave with a poof of chill night air.

Elizabeth and Gail wandered wordlessly back to the fireplace, even though Elizabeth knew she should go up to bed.

"So—is he everything you ever fantasized?" Elizabeth asked.

"He's quite a bit more, isn't he? You didn't tell me he was so attractive. I didn't expect that. I mean, I've seen pictures of him on his books and on the web, but they don't do him justice, do they?"

"Do you think he's attractive?"

"My goodness. How can you ask?"

"I remember when I first saw him I found him both homely and attractive, if that makes sense.

As I got to know him better I found—find him—more and more just, you know, *attractive*, like magnetic."

"Yes," Gail agreed, "exactly! Magnetic. Spiritually, emotionally and psychically. You just want to be close to him and talk with him."

"*You* just want to," Elizabeth clarified.

"Yes, me, I mean me. Don't you too?"

"Well, sure. But I met him at a difficult time, and all those things happened, switching houses and selling him the car. Nothing has been usual around him. I haven't been able to separate the person from the events."

"People bring events to themselves," Gail said.

"There's a frightening thought! It's enough for me to sort out the events I'm consciously trying to deal with, without being responsible for what I might unwittingly produce."

"Even so, my dear Liz-girl, it is as I say."

"Anyway," Elizabeth changed the subject, unable to contemplate Gail's belief at the moment. "I think the two of you make a great couple."

"Peter and me?" Gail burst out. "Oh, no, it's not Peter and me. I think he's wonderful, but it's a brother-sister thing. No, dear heart. The couple is *Peter and you.*"

Elizabeth burst out laughing. "Oh, Gail, please. I'm not Peter's sort. He's too—everything. Wise, intelligent, worldly, clever. Well-read. I mean, I act like a pal around him, but the truth of the matter is that I'm awestruck. Intimidated."

Gail said nothing more, and they lazily watched the fire.

"It was a wonderful evening," Elizabeth said.

"A wonderful evening," Gail agreed.

Elizabeth stood, cuddling Amy. "Nighty-nite, Gail."

"Nite-nite, my two pets."

Chapter XV

The next Friday, Elizabeth, Gail and Amy came in through Peter's back door like family.

"Smells good!" Gail proclaimed.

"I've made a vegetable bake-feast," Peter said.

"What's that?" Elizabeth turned Amy around so Peter could give the baby a little kiss. "A huge breakfast, only later in the day?"

"No, I baked everything, whole and in its natural state. Potatoes, carrots, big red onions, tomatoes, bell peppers, broccoli."

He turned on the oven light and they all peeked in at the phalanx of beautiful, whole vegetables.

"It looks like you know what you're doing," Gail said.

"*Hah!*" Amy exclaimed.

They all laughed. "You're not about to be left out, are you, baby cakes?" Elizabeth said, hugging her. "So, Peter, show us what you've done to the homestead."

"I haven't done anything down here except in the front room."

They all trouped through the dining room, then the foyer. They came to the front room that had been Grandfather's study. Peter had turned it into his library and books were shelved from floor to ceiling.

"Wow! I didn't realize you had such a library," Elizabeth said in awe.

"Most of the books were in storage. I've been planning my library in my mind's eye since long before I saw this house." He gestured through the other door of the library and they could see the length of that side of the house. "As you can see, I haven't done anything to those rooms. Apart from setting up the library, I've been concentrating on the upstairs."

Elizabeth hadn't thought about what it would feel like to be in her lifelong home the first time since she'd moved out, until this moment, crossing the threshold into Grandfather's study. Even though it looked entirely different, she had a nearly palpable sense of Grandfather's presence.

Elizabeth shifted Amy from one hip to the other. "Do you have the heat shut off in here? It's kind of cold."

Gail had been standing quietly in the doorway of the room. She came and took Amy from Elizabeth. Elizabeth pulled her cardigan tight around her, leaning close to Gail.

"Ah, well," Peter hesitated, "I had the room closed off most of today."

"Oh," Elizabeth said. She looked around the room, hoping for any little nook of warmth. But there was none. She studied Peter, who was eying his books as if they seemed strange to him. "You don't like this room very much, do you?"

"Quite frankly, no. It's disappointing, I had hoped to spend most of my time writing in here. But, I have to tell you, the room is always sort of cold ...."

"That's strange because it always used to get too hot," Elizabeth said. "If we turned up the heat so that the rest of the house was comfortable, this room would be so hot, you couldn't stand to stay in it."

"I'll have Ralph give the ductwork a going over." Peter led them out of the library back into the foyer. "By the way, he said he's available next Wednesday, ready to begin on your projects, if you want him."

"Fantastic! I want him," Elizabeth answered cheerfully, relieved to leave the library.

"He's amazing," Peter went on as they climbed the front stairs. "He takes care of things I wouldn't even think to tell him to take care of. And he does superior work."

"I'm glad you decided to keep him on," Elizabeth said. "He belongs here."

Peter nodded. "He does. More than I do."

As they toured the upstairs, it turned out that Peter had taken over Elizabeth's bedroom for his own. Elizabeth observed that her Samarkand carpet looked even more stunning with Peter's masculine furniture than it would have with hers.

"Look at the workmanship," Peter raved. He pulled up a corner of the carpet to show Gail the reverse side. "Flawless!"

"Hon, that's beautiful," Gail said to Elizabeth. "I wonder if I'll ever be lucky enough to see such magnificence on the floor where I live?"

Elizabeth felt shy. "Oh, come on you guys, it's not that remarkable."

"Yes," Gail said in her not-to-be-contradicted voice. "It is."

"Well, I did start that one for the baby's room—before there was a baby. I guess I should get back to it. It doesn't set a very good example to start and not finish a project, does it, Amy?" Elizabeth shyly hoped to redirect the focus of attention away from her and onto Amy.

Amy looked at Elizabeth from the billowy cradle of Gail's arms, seeming to understand that her opinion had been solicited. "Arr–Bet!" She squiggled and clapped, and smiled her bitsy, self-satisfied smile.

Elizabeth looked at Peter, staring at Amy in awe. "She has so much personality."

Elizabeth and Gail both laughed. "That's because she has such personable role models," Gail said, imitating Amy's little self-satisfied smile with amusing accuracy.

They moved out of Peter's bedroom and down the hall to what had previously been Elizabeth's rug making room. It was plain to see that this was where Peter did his work. He'd constructed built-in desk along three walls, with cork board above. Colored notes by the hundreds were stabbed into the cork board with colored push pins, and piles of paper were stacked everywhere.

"I guess this is my favorite room in the house," Peter confessed. "Out this window on a clear day, I can see the mountains in the distance. And there are all kinds of birds living in these trees. With three walls of desk, I work on three books at a time. This is the most productive I've ever been."

"Wonderful," Gail exulted. "That's all I want to hear. If you wrote a book a day, that'd be about right for me!"

Peter chuckled, "The probability of developing that skill seems fairly remote. But I bet I know what we can accomplish in one evening."

"What?" Gail and Elizabeth chorused.

"Demolish an oven-full of food."

"I'll bet you're right," Gail agreed as they hustled down the back stairs into the kitchen.

They had dinner in the dining room, all the aromas of the baked foods and Gail's warm dinner rolls and sweet cherry cobbler filling the air right up to the antique chandelier. The light glowed off the red mahogany wainscoting, reflecting a rubescence on their faces, and not a niche of darkness was allowed among the happy banter.

"Isn't Peter a good cook?" Gail asked Amy, as Amy downed more mashed carrots.

Amy looked right at Peter and cried,"Beetie!"

"Wow! You're *in* 'Beetie!'" Gail laughed.

Peter glowed. "I've been knighted!"

Gail, Peter and Amy laughed, while Elizabeth smiled serenely, warmer in her heart than she had ever been in her life.

A while later Elizabeth excused herself. She left the dining room in the direction of the kitchen, then crept quietly through the rooms until she came to Peter's library.

What was this hollow sensation?

She turned away from the walls of books and went into the foyer to continue her circuit back to the dining room. Out of the corner of her eye she sensed—or did she really *see?*—movement on the dark winding stairway.

She held her breath. An amorphous light shadow hovered on the stairs, then it disappeared. Elizabeth could have perhaps convinced herself it was a stray beam of light through the stained glass windows, if not for its trailing movement and the strong scent of liniment. How well she knew that odor that had resided for years in a little jar on Grandfather's bedside table.

Elizabeth waited for several moments, trying to dissuade herself of the unnatural sensory impressions, but she couldn't. She returned to the dining room, to the wonderful tangible realities of Amy's soft, sweet-scented skin, Gail's pleasant boisterous laughter, and Peter's quiet study of her.

She kept the intangible event—the presence of her grandfather—to herself.

Chapter XVI

Ralph came over the following Wednesday with tool box in hand. He installed baby gates at the top and bottom of the stairs. Then he, Elizabeth, and Gail sat at the kitchen table and designed a fence for the patio. Ralph sketched Elizabeth's and Gail's numerous suggestions and they finally came up with a sturdy redwood lattice fence, three-and-a-half feet high, with a gate to the lake shore. Ralph showed them the baby-safe latch he'd bought for the gate.

Elizabeth hadn't thought of having a gate in the fence, and she was touched when she realized that Ralph had been ahead of her in the planning of 'Project: Baby-Safe' before he even came over.

Ralph and Gail got along fabulously. Elizabeth had never seen Ralph smile except shyly and deferentially. And, although his demeanor was still shy and deferential, he laughed at Gail's jokes. Elizabeth had never heard Ralph laugh, either. But then, Grandfather never joked with the "help."

Ralph had started working for Grandfather when Elizabeth was only ten, and all she'd noticed at that time was that when he was with Grandfather, Grandfather was too busy for her.

She'd learned to stay out of their way.

Since she'd only seen Ralph with Grandfather, she had it in her mind that Ralph was much older than, in fact, he was. Now she saw that he was a youthful and energetic man, in his forties, good-looking, lean and silver-haired. For the first time in her life she watched him work. He made an art of it, handling his tools as if they were extensions of his mind and hands. Which, she realized, they were.

It was apparent that it didn't hurt Gail's eyes to watch him, either, Elizabeth noticed. She came up beside Gail, who had stopped her chores to watch Ralph constructing the fence.

"Interesting?" Elizabeth whispered.

Gail nodded. "He's a good worker, isn't he?"

"I mean ...." Elizabeth hinted.

"Oh, Lizzie!" Gail protested. "Will you stop matching me with every man you see me talk to?"

"It's only been Peter and Ralph," Elizabeth pointed out. "And only because they seem to like you and you seem to like them."

"Oh, well, men always like Gail," Gail said, continuing into the kitchen.

Elizabeth nodded. Indeed, she was sure that was true—any intelligent man would certainly find Gail most attractive.

*   *

As Amy's surgery drew nearer, Elizabeth became ever more nervous. She found it difficult to go to work and almost impossible to sleep.

"I don't know what I'm going to do with you!" Gail finally said. "I thought we agreed that you would *not* upset yourself about this routine surgery."

"I'm hopeless, I know!" Elizabeth acquiesced. "If you knew everything I'm thinking, you probably wouldn't like me very much."

"What are you thinking?"

Elizabeth sat at the kitchen table and watched Gail knead bread, the kitchen rich with the scent of yeast.

"What would it be like if you weren't here," Elizabeth began quietly.

"Why would you go and think a thing like that? I couldn't be happier, I'm not about to leave." Gail didn't miss a beat of her bread dough slapping against the bread board.

"No? Why would you stay if I didn't have Amy?"

Gail stopped her rhythmic kneading. "What *ever* are you thinking?"

"I'm thinking—ooh! I feel so torn, so guilty—but, okay, here goes. Amy's about to have surgery."

"Yes," Gail urged.

"It will correct her—imperfection, if all goes well."

"Which it will."

"Then Amy will ... she'll get ... *adopted*, Gail. Hasn't the thought crossed your mind?"

"Oh!" Gail turned her back on her bread board to face Elizabeth. "No, I hadn't thought that far ahead."

"She'll leave and you'll leave and our whole perfect life will be over!"

"Now, just a minute," Gail went back to kneading, then she divided the bread dough and put it in a couple of bread pans, put a dish towel over them to rise. She came over and sat opposite Elizabeth. "Of course we want—whatever the future holds, for Amy to be made whole and to be well."

"Yes," Elizabeth agreed.

"So this was a river we'd have to cross sooner or later. Look, Elizabeth, even if Amy is adopted, you'll get another foster child, and I'll stay here. As long as you want me."

"It was such a challenge getting Amy—I can't imagine repeating that experience."

"Don't worry, Pet. It'll never be that tough again. The first time you had to be approved and checked into, and observed. Now you could probably get several kids, if you wanted."

"But I don't want any other kids. I want Amy. I feel like ... like she's mine! I mean, particularly. There's a special bond between Amy and me. How can you so casually suggest us shifting our affection to some other child?"

"It's not casual," Gail protested. "It's just—the facts of life. If Amy is adopted into a wonderful home with wonderful people, then ...."

"She *has* a wonderful home with wonderful people. *I* want to adopt Amy."

"Then you'd better have a talk with Mrs. Vargas," Gail said quietly.

Elizabeth's face and shoulders relaxed. "Do you think I can tell her I want to adopt Amy?"

"What are your chances if you don't?"

136 ~ Thea Thomas

"You're right." She reached over and squeezed Gail's hand. "You're so awesome. Would you believe I've been afraid to even talk with *you*? I was afraid it'd sound like I hoped the operation wouldn't go well for Amy. Which, of course, couldn't be farther from the truth. I just can't stand the thought of losing her. So I *must* talk with Mrs. Vargas."

"But don't forget to be calm."

"Yes, yes, I'll practice. I'll practice with you, you can be Mrs. Vargas."

Elizabeth practiced with Gail for several days what she would say to Mrs. Vargas, and she practiced, above all else, how she would remain calm, no matter what the outcome.

*   *

A week later she found herself sitting in Mrs. Vargas' waiting area for her appointment, nervous as an understudy taking on the lead at a premier performance. But she also felt confident. Why would anyone deny Amy's perfect home for her, least of all, Mrs. Vargas?

Finally the office door opened. "Hello, Elizabeth," she said. "It's lovely to see you. Please, come in." Mrs. Vargas ushered her into her office and gestured to a chair opposite a huge desk.

Glancing around, Elizabeth took in the walls covered in photos of children of every color and description. "You ought to have wallpaper made of your walls," Elizabeth suggested.

Mrs. Vargas looked around, then chuckled. "What a wonderful idea! It escaped me how full my walls have become. I simply stick up the next picture when

137 ~ Amethyst Dream

I have another child to work with. But you're right, they're beautiful, my rainbow children walls."

"Very, very beautiful," Elizabeth agreed.

Mrs. Vargas focussed her attention on Elizabeth. "But tell me about you—is there a problem?"

"Oh no! I mean yes, that is, things as they are, are perfect." Elizabeth relaxed in the warm presence of Mrs. Vargas. "I ... I want to adopt Amy," she blurted. Boy, she thought, I sure didn't rehearse that!

Unruffled, Mrs. Vargas nodded thoughtfully, quiet for a moment. "Are you sure you know what you're saying?"

"Yes. I've been thinking about it ever since Amy came into my life. At first it was a kind of fantasy. But now—now I can't imagine life without her. I mean, it simply feels like she's my daughter, and that I'm her mother.

"I was also concerned that I'd lose Gail as well, but she assures me she'll stay on, whether for Amy or some other child. Although that made me relieved and happy, it doesn't change how I feel about Amy. And Amy so very much loves and trusts Gail and me. We're a family. All we need now is documentation. In short, what can I do to expedite adopting Amy?"

"I'd hate to lose you as a foster parent," Mrs. Vargas said. "Foster homes where I feel comfortable about the environment and the motive of the people are *extremely* hard to come by. But apart from that, there *is* another problem."

"Oh?" Elizabeth asked. "What is that?"

"Married people have a higher priority for adopting than single people."

"Really? You mean, I'm good enough to be a foster parent, but not good enough to be a real parent?" Elizabeth curled her finger nails into her palms. Stay calm, she told herself. Stay calm. "I've already given Amy a good home. My being married wouldn't make it better.""

"Infallible logic," Mrs. Vargas agreed. "I'm just telling you the standards I'm subject to in this particular organization. When the adoption committee makes adoptive decisions, married people come before single people, given everything else being equal, and babies, of course, are the most adoptable."

"After Amy's surgery, she'll be—highly adoptable."

Mrs. Vargas agreed. "Assuming everything goes well."

"Of course everything will go well," Elizabeth could feel tears threatening. "Of course everything will."

Mrs. Vargas smiled at Elizabeth. "Foster parents often form strong attachments to a child, Elizabeth. It's the hardest part of foster parenting. Some people just aren't cut out for it. I hope you'll be tough enough to deal with it when the time comes. Let me say again that your home is an excellent foster home. You and Gail make a wonderful team."

Elizabeth nodded, feeling far away. She wanted to be alone. "But I don't consider foster parenting a 'job.' Loving Amy has been the most fulfilling experience of my life." She stood and reached her hand across Mrs. Vargas' desk. "Thanks for hearing me out."

"You're welcome," Mrs. Vargas returned Elizabeth's firm handshake. "So, let's see," she glanced down at a calendar on her desk, "it looks like Amy goes into surgery a week from Thursday. I'll probably see you in the hospital."

Elizabeth nodded and left the office.

When she got home, she recited to Gail the conversation with Mrs. Vargas, but for the first time ever, she didn't feel like listening to Gail's practical logic. She only felt as though her child was soon to be taken from her. She felt silent and protective. After she fed Amy her supper, she took her upstairs and played quietly with her on the bed until they both fell asleep.

The next day at work she let the telephone ring and ring, she couldn't seem to hear it. And she'd been there for two hours without even saying hello to Marsalis.

He came to the door of his office. "Elizabeth, *Elizabeth!*"

She looked up.

"I'd like to speak with you."

She dragged herself into his office.

"For heavens sake, Elizabeth, what's wrong with you?"

"Nothing Marsalis. I—I've just got a lot on my mind." She didn't even see him, her eyes focussed somewhere beyond the far wall.

"Well, what?"

She heard his exasperation. "Oh, Marsalis, you're not the only person living and breathing. There are others of us out here, and sometimes we have problems."

Marsalis softened. "I'm sorry, Liz. I don't express myself very well, but that doesn't mean I don't have sincere feelings for you. Please, talk to me."

For some reason, Elizabeth let the gates open and poured out the whole story—how she was sure she was about to lose Amy because she wasn't married, and how unfair it seemed. How devastated she would be to have Amy taken from her.

Marsalis glided around his desk and took both her hands in his.

"Lizzie, is that all?" he asked softly.

"Is that all? I guess you don't have any idea what Amy means to me."

"Yes, I do, I can see it. And I have the solution to your problem. I've been trying to get closer to you, but you've been so busy with the baby ... and ... everything. But now—Elizabeth ...." he raised her left hand to his lips and kissed her ring finger, "this is a terrible environment for this question, and I hesitate to ask it, but under the circumstances ... do you think ... would you could consider marrying me?"

Elizabeth looked up at Marsalis, completely stunned. *"Marry you?"* she whispered, trying to understand if she'd heard correctly.

"Yes."

"But ... but ...."

"But what? This is not the setting I had in mind, and, yes, it's sudden, but, it's what I've been wanting to ask you for some time."

"But, Marsalis, do you really want to be married, and with a child and—and—everything?"

Marsalis hesitated for a moment, then he let his guard down. "I've never known a woman like you, Elizabeth. You make everyone around you comfortable and happy. I've watched you work with clients, and in the most natural way, you're aware of their needs and intuitively fulfill their wishes. You get people into the home they desire.

"I have to work so hard to do that. I'll never meet a woman who has more of everything I could ever hope to find in one person. Sweet, charming, smart, beautiful ...." He kissed her fingertips. "The beautiful child ... ahm ...."

"Amy?"

"Yes, Amy, is adorable. And you have what's-her-name to help. Everyone can be made perfectly happy with one little word from you."

"You mean, 'yes'?"

"I mean yes."

"I have to think," Elizabeth breathed deeply, feeling confused and a bit faint. "Frankly, Marsalis, you seem like ... like someone who would never marry."

"You're wrong, Elizabeth. Maybe I seem like that because I've built up a wall. It's true, I've believed I'd never meet a woman who could possibly touch my heart. But—you *have*. Besides all your amazing attributes, you *understand me*. I think sometimes I don't even understand myself—but you do. Can't you see how everything would be perfect if you just said 'yes'?"

Amy's dear little face came to mind. This *would* be the perfect solution to everything. She'd never seen Marsalis with his guard down. It was so compelling, so reassuring, so attractive. "Yes," she whispered, "I will marry you."

Marsalis leaned over and kissed her. For the first time, Elizabeth allowed herself to relax and kiss him in return. For the first time, she felt they could have a real, true future together.

Chapter XVII

That afternoon, after Marsalis had gone out to show some homes, Elizabeth sat at her desk vacillating between calling Gail and telling her about the engagement, and arguing with herself that it would be better to tell her in person.

Peter, in his jogging togs, jogged into the office. Edna gave him her usual disapproving over-her-glasses look. For once it amused Elizabeth.

"Hi," Peter said, pulling up a chair and leaning it against her desk as was his habit.

"Hi," Elizabeth returned, fairly bursting with the news, but not wanting Edna to hear.

"I came by to cheer you up, but you appear quite cheerful already. I've been a bit worried about you. Gail said you were really down."

"Oh she did, did she? She was only supposed to tell you Amy seems to be coming down with a cold."

"She did tell me that. I hope our little Angel is better. But Gail also said you were depressed, but that she couldn't talk to me about it, or you'd be angry."

"I would have been upset, if I'd known. But not today!"

"No," Peter agreed, "today you're exceedingly cheerful. Why the big mood change?"

"Because ...." Elizabeth glanced at Edna and then motioned Peter to follow her into Marsalis's office. She closed the door.

"I've been very depressed the last couple days because Mrs. Vargas told me I was unlikely to succeed in adopting Amy—which I want more than anything in life—because I'm not married. I've been miserable. Until this morning."

"Until this morning?"

"Yes. When I told Marsalis the whole story, he proposed."

Peter's mouth fell open. "Marsalis asked you to *marry* him?"

"Yes!" The thrill of the words voiced by someone else, making it very real, swept over her. "Oh, Peter, I'm so elated, it's the solution to everything."

Peter studied Elizabeth for a moment, then he finally said, "So—you accepted."

"I accepted. Now I can adopt Amy without complication."

"That's the only reason you're marrying Marsalis?"

"Well, of course not. I just ... I never imagined he felt the way he does about me. When he asked me to marry him, I was stunned. I argued—I told him I didn't think he was the marrying kind. He told me I'm the only woman who has touched his heart. That he's been trying to ask me to marry him for some while, but I've been so preoccupied with Amy, the time didn't seem right."

"Well then, Elizabeth," Peter said quietly, "I'm happy if you're happy. I hope this marriage provides everything you want and need. No one deserves it more than you."

He stood and hugged Elizabeth. This was the first time they'd ever hugged and Elizabeth was stunned to find herself thinking how good his body felt. She pulled away from him, shy and flustered—after all, she was almost a married woman.

Peter had a little frown between his brows.

"Thank you Peter. I'll need your friendship more now than ever."

"How's that?" Peter asked. "You won't need—or want—me around at all."

"Oh no, Peter, you're my dear friend, I need you in my life. And Amy and Gail need you too."

"Uncle Beetie, that's me," Peter said quietly.

"That's right!" Elizabeth said cheerfully, opening Marsalis's office door and edging back to her desk.

After Peter left, a strange and discomfiting sense of loss washed over Elizabeth. Then she realized that no matter what she wanted to believe, Marsalis would never let Peter have the same place in her life that he had, until now, occupied, never mind that their relationship was entirely platonic.

Peter must have realized that immediately, which was why he became so quiet.

She couldn't deny that she'd miss Peter's friendship. But Amy's welfare came first.

She left the office at four. Marsalis had not come back, but he'd called and arranged to take her out to

dinner. She wanted to get home and tell Gail everything before he arrived.

Gail and Amy were playing with blocks strewn
over the living room floor when she walked through
the door.

"Oh-oh!" Gail said. "Caught in the act! You're
early. I intended to have the place tidied up before
you got home."

"It doesn't matter." Elizabeth picked her way
among the blocks and swooped Amy up, Amy giggling. "I have big news."

"Big, *happy* news, apparently," Gail observed,
gathering up the blocks.

"Don't do that right now. Undivided attention,
please!"

"I can pick up blocks and listen," Gail said, continuing to clean up.

"Okay," Elizabeth said. "I'm getting married."

Gail stopped picking up blocks. "*WHAT?!*"

"I thought you could listen and work."

"You dropped a bomb. Did I hear what I thought
I heard?"

"If you heard me say I'm getting married, you
heard correctly."

"To whom? Peter! He called this morning, but I
told him you'd already gone to work."

"No, not Peter. You just can't let go of that notion,
can you?"

"Not readily."

"Marsalis, of course."

"Oh."

"'Oh'? Geez, Gail, how about 'that's great'?"

"Well, certainly I hope you'll be very happy." Gail became quiet.

"We'll *all* be very happy. Just because you like Peter better than Marsalis doesn't mean he's someone I should marry, now does it?

"If you'd seen how sensitive and responsive Marsalis was this morning, I know your opinion of him would change. I had no intention of telling him anything about the situation with Amy. But he insisted. He took me into his office and got the whole story out of me. He was so sweet and so romantic."

Elizabeth stood cuddling Amy. "He said he'd been wanting to get closer to me, he said that, although asking me to marry him was very sudden, he has wanted to for a while.

"Oh, come on Gail," Elizabeth coaxed, "be happy for me! He may not be as verbal as Peter, but he is sweet and caring in his own way. Give us all a chance, Gail. Be on my side."

Gail shook her head. "It's not part of my job specification to approve or disapprove people's marital partners. Although I can't help how I feel. I wonder what Peter will have to say about this?"

"He came in this afternoon and I told him. He was shocked, he seemed depressed, sort of, too. But I realized that was because he understood more quickly than I did that our friendship will change, of course. I'm sorry about that too. But Amy comes first. Don't you, Baby-face?" Elizabeth snuggled Amy close to her. "Just think, Gail, we're bound to succeed in adopting Amy now."

"And that's the reason you're marrying Marsalis."

"You and Peter own the same recording, I see," Elizabeth said. "As I told Peter, I never had an idea that Marsalis wanted to marry me. Or anyone! But of course that's not the only reason I'm marrying him. We've been dating since we met. He's so sweet when he lets his guard down.

"And, frankly, Gail, he needs me more than Peter needs me, even if Peter were interested in me in that way, which he's not. Peter is so secure, so sure of himself. Marsalis, for all his cool facade, is fragile and needs love and attention."

"Maybe Peter is strong and would make a much better life-partner than Marsalis who is selfish and demanding," Gail observed. "I don't care how gorgeous Marsalis is, *I* wouldn't marry him."

"Lucky you!" Elizabeth exclaimed. "You don't have to, I am. But you're still leaving out one fairly significant point. Marsalis asked me to marry him. Peter didn't."

Gail nodded. "That's true."

"So please, please like him. I want us to live in harmony."

"I do too, of course," Gail agreed. "I have every intention of keeping disharmony as far from me as possible."

"Good! Marsalis is taking me out to dinner tonight, we have to get all the details worked out. So I hope you don't mind if I abandon you two to get ready."

"Go, Sleeping Beauty, leave us to our blocks, we're fine. Aren't we, Amy-Pet?"

"Hah!" Amy agreed, as Elizabeth handed her back to Gail.

Running upstairs she wondered why Gail called her Sleeping Beauty. She'd have to remember to ask.

When Marsalis came that evening, he had two bouquets of flowers, one for Elizabeth and one for Gail. He was polite and quiet and went out of his way to make conversation with Gail. As Elizabeth came down the stairs, she winked at Gail as if to say, "See how good he can be?"

"Has Elizabeth told you the big news?" Marsalis asked Gail when Elizabeth came up alongside him.

"Yes. But it still hasn't quite sunken in yet."

Marsalis laughed congenially, flashing his brilliant teeth. "I guess we all feel that way!" He turned to Elizabeth. "You look lovely, my dear."

"Thanks, Marsalis." She'd worn another of her mother's outfits, a dark blue velvet dress with a fitted bodice and gored skirt and a wide off-white lace collar.

"Shall we go?" he asked.

Elizabeth nodded. "Don't wait up for us," she called back to Gail.

*　　*

The next morning, actually, it was almost noon, Elizabeth dragged herself downstairs and joined Gail and Amy, who were playing out on the patio.

"Good morning you two," she called cheerily, pulling her bathrobe tight around her.

"Good afternoon," Gail answered.

"Bet!" Amy exclaimed.

"Amy!" Elizabeth answered.

"So—tell me everything," Gail insisted.

Elizabeth held up her ring finger. "Can you believe he actually ran out and bought a diamond yesterday afternoon?"

"Kinda small," Gail appraised.

"I didn't expect *anything* on such short notice. I'll bet you wouldn't be so critical if Peter had given it to me."

"Peter wouldn't give you such a microscopic stone."

"Please, Gail stop criticizing my ring," Elizabeth said, walking to the edge of the patio, facing the lake, with her back to Gail. "Please stop trying to take the energy out of my happiness. What's the matter with you, anyway?"

"I'm sorry, Lizzie," Gail apologized, sounding sincerely contrite. "You're right, it's rude to criticize someone's engagement ring. If you're really happy, then of course I'm happy for you."

"Well, I *am* happy. Elated. Except that you're making me very worried about how we will all live together in peace under one roof if you're so completely unable to approve of Marsalis."

"I'll adjust."

"You'd better step up your clock," Elizabeth turned to face Gail. "We're getting married next Saturday, and we're asking you and Peter to be our witnesses."

"Next Saturday!" Gail jumped to her feet. "Are you ... are you absolutely certain you want to move that fast?"

"Of course. As long as we've agreed to marry, it may as well be right away."

Gail shook her head. "Okay, I won't say anything more, I hope, after this. But I would be irresponsible if I didn't say that my instincts and experience tell me this is not a wise decision, although I'll support you as much as I can. Now I've said it, and I'm done. So! I guess, as you say, I'll have to adjust rather quickly."

"Please do," Elizabeth nodded. "Now let me change the subject."

"Okay."

"Why did you call me 'Sleeping Beauty' last night?"

"Because the true prince hasn't kissed you yet."

Elizabeth laughed. "Really, Gail, you're *too* romantic. If my true prince hasn't kissed me yet, well then, I guess he just isn't going to. But let me tell you about last evening ...."

"Wait!" Gail interjected. "Amy will be in the hospital. How can you get married with Amy in the hospital?"

"I've thought it all through, and I realized it's the *best* time. When she comes back on Monday, Marsalis will be moved in and everything will be homelike for her. There'll be three of us to take care of her and to love her. When Mrs. Vargas comes over, she'll see the perfect environment for Amy to be adopted into. Marsalis and I discussed all of this last night."

"Maybe I've misjudged him. I hope I've misjudged him."

Elizabeth grinned from ear to ear. "Now, *those* are the words I've been waiting to hear!" The phone rang and she dashed inside to get it. Seeing Peter's name on the caller ID, she excitedly answered the call. "Hi, Peter!"

But he didn't respond. Instead, there was a noisy crackling on the line.

"Peter?"

"Hello, Elizabeth?"

"Yes."

"What's up?" Peter said, sounding puzzled.

"*You* called *me*," Elizabeth said, completely mystified.

"No. You called me."

"No, I didn't. I was out on the patio with Gail and Amy, the phone rang, I ran inside, saw your name on the caller ID, answered the phone and said, 'hi, Peter.' There was an awful crackling on the line, and then you finally said, 'Hello Elizabeth.'"

"Hmmm," Peter mused, sounding even more puzzled. "I was on the front porch plotting my new novel, when I hear the phone ring. I ran inside and answered it, and before I said anything, I heard you say, 'Peter.'"

"Okay," Elizabeth said. "*Not too strange.*"

"Well, completely strange!" Peter said. "But, I confess, I was *thinking* about calling you."

"And what were you going to say to me in this imagined phone conversation?"

Peter didn't say anything for a few moments. Then he said softly, "I was going to tell you not to marry Marsalis. I'm sitting on the porch swing, on a beautiful sunny day, and I'm thinking I would tell you not to marry Marsalis. And then, Elizabeth ...."

Peter stopped talking. Elizabeth sensed he was about to say something else she didn't want to hear.

He took a deep breath, then continued softly. "I'm thinking I would tell you not to marry Marsalis, when the shadowy figure of an elderly man passed me and ... and walked *through* the front door. Moments later, the phone rang. I was—I mean I *am*—very shaken up."

"*Grandfather*," Elizabeth whispered, then paused. "You *said* you wanted to live in a haunted house."

"I ... I was wrong. I didn't know what I was saying."

Emotions flowed through Elizabeth, one after another from shock, to irritation, to disbelief, to knowing, back to irritation. She didn't want to be angry, and certainly not with Peter—*nor Grandfather!*—but her mother-tiger instincts roared to the surface, and all she could think of was protecting Amy. "Well, Peter—and, I guess, Grandfather, too—I *am* marrying Marsalis. If you really feel so strongly, Peter, perhaps you don't want to be one of our witnesses."

"I will be witness, Elizabeth. I said I would, and I will. And, truly, I would never have said what I've just said to you except for this strange sequence of events. I may be thinking it, but I would have kept it to myself. What you do is your business. But, since that gate has been opened, I *do* feel I must go on record as saying I believe it's not what's best for you."

Elizabeth sighed deeply, releasing her irritation. How could she be angry with Peter? He simply stated his opinion, and she needed to respect him for it. It probably wasn't easy. "Everything will be fine, Peter.

Marsalis is a completely different person since I said I'd marry him. You'll see."

"What about this ... this *visitation?*"

"I don't know, Peter. I don't know. Maybe Grandfather is giving me his blessing."

Peter paused for a long, long moment. "Perhaps ...." he finally said in a cautious and dubious tone.

"We'll talk more about it later, Peter. But right now I left Gail out on the patio with Amy—we're in the middle of our making plans ...."

"Oh. Sure. We'll talk later. Bye, Elizabeth."

A strange pathos ran through Elizabeth as she put down the phone. She gathered herself for a few moments before returning to the patio.

"Who was it?" Gail asked.

"Peter."

"Oh? Anything interesting?"

"No," Elizabeth answered, picking Amy up. "Just, sort of recapping I guess." She started making funny faces, which caused Amy to giggle uncontrollably. She felt Gail giving her a hard study.

She set her mental heels in, resolving to ignore everything that did not have to do with the shortest, quickest, route to becoming Amy's legal mother.

Chapter XVIII

The next week was a tsunami of activity. It wasn't the way Elizabeth had ever envisioned her wedding. But then, she asked herself, had she ever actually envisioned her wedding? Had she ever seriously believed she *would* get married? No, she answered her silent question. She had not.

The wedding would be very, very small, and she was just fine with that. She had no relatives to speak of who would miss this event in her life. Except, *maybe*, her mother, where ever she was. Not even Martha knew where her mother was.

Martha! Elizabeth hadn't talked with her in days. She must invite Martha to the wedding. But, Elizabeth reasoned, Martha was always so busy, she probably wouldn't come anyway, and she set the thought aside, She set out with Gail and Amy in tow, focused on shopping for a dress.

After the better part of a day going from shop to shop, she finally found a mid-calf length antique white dress with a delicate lace bodice, an empire waist and three-quarter length sleeves. Very plain, understated, sophisticated.

"Absolutely lovely," Gail pronounced, holding Amy, the two of them smiling at her image in the three-way mirror. That was good enough for Elizabeth. She was quite through and then some with the shopping expedition.

All she could really focus on was the fact that Amy would be in the hospital when she wore this dress to become a married woman. Yes, she'd love to be able to spend time fantasizing about her life with Marsalis. But ... she couldn't. She couldn't take her mind off Amy—*in the hospital*.

Marsalis can wait a couple months while Amy recuperates, she thought, and while we get adoption proceedings in motion. Then I'll give him undivided attention.

*   *

The dreaded day of Amy's surgery was soon upon them. She had Gail drive to the hospital, while she sat in the back next to Amy in her car seat, patting her and cooing to her, making faces and the two of them giggling. Holding back her tears. Holding back her fears.

Elizabeth was so grateful to see Mrs. Vargas waiting for them when they got there. She trusted Mrs. Vargas with all her heart. She knew she'd make everything all right.

"Hi Elizabeth, Gail, little Amy," Mrs. Vargas said cheerily as she came up to them, patting Amy's hand. "I've filled out all the paperwork."

She took in Elizabeth's expression, which, Elizabeth surmised, must bear a resemblance to the proverbial deer-in-headlights. "It'll be all right, Elizabeth. Calm, positive energy is best, yes?"

Elizabeth nodded, wordlessly. Then a blur of events occurred transpired as Amy was taken from her, then Gail led her to a waiting area.

The three of them sat waiting, waiting, speaking little. Elizabeth knew she ought to take the opportunity to tell Mrs. Vargas about the wedding—*only two days distant!*—but she couldn't put her mind on it.

She didn't want to talk. She wanted only to focus on Amy.

Finally a surgical nurse came out and reported that all had gone perfectly, and Amy would soon be in the recovery area. The three of them heaved a sigh of relief.

Before long, they stood by Amy, her black curls tousled about her angelic, beautiful face. Elizabeth couldn't believe the dreaded event was over.

She couldn't remember anything since she walked into the hospital—she felt as though she'd been swimming in murky water, with sounds and forms coming toward her, then moving away.

But now all her senses popped on as if a switch had been thrown.

Elizabeth turned to Gail and Mrs. Vargas. "She's all right!" she exclaimed.

They both nodded, grinning.

"Did I tell you I'm getting married Saturday?"

"Gail mentioned it."

"I'm sorry I didn't say anything earlier. My mind was on Amy." Elizabeth imagined she looked as guilty as she felt.

"Mrs. Vargas smiled. "I understand, Elizabeth. We've all had our minds on Amy."

"What did Gail tell you?"

"She said that Marsalis—remember I met him briefly?—asked you to marry him."

"That's right, you did meet him. I'm afraid he didn't make a very good impression."

"As I recall, he hadn't been told about Amy."

"Yes, it was all quite a shock for him." She paused, then charged forward. "I suppose this is a bit premature, but I'd like to put a little bug in your ear. Marsalis and are hoping to be able to adopt Amy."

"Yes, Gail hinted at that little bug."

"Oh! She did, did she?" Elizabeth grinned at Gail. If anyone could help pave the way for this adoption, it would be Gail. "What do you think, Mrs. Vargas?"

"Let's see how everything sorts out. But, Elizabeth dear, isn't it biting off quite a lot to be dealing with Amy, who will need undivided attention when she gets home, and a new husband, who is likely to think he deserves a lot of attention as well?"

"Marsalis understands completely. He's going to *help* with Amy. After a while, when Amy is good as new, we'll go off for a few days. We're adults, we can be patient."

"But shouldn't you postpone the wedding in that case?"

"He and I agreed it would be best to get married while Amy is in the hospital, and then he can become settled in the home before Amy comes home. For me and for Gail and for Marsalis, Amy comes first."

"I'm glad you all feel that way," Mrs. Vargas said. "But let me caution you, Elizabeth, not to make a major life decision based on whether you'll get to adopt Amy or not. It still may not happen."

Elizabeth bit her lip. Why did Mrs. Vargas have to say that to her *now?* "Then Marsalis and I will have one another," she answered quietly.

Mrs. Vargas nodded. "Yes, of course. Well, I must be off. I'll talk to you both later." She smiled down at Amy then left.

"Why did she have to say that?" Elizabeth asked Gail.

"She's not trying to hurt you, Pet. She's just stating facts and keeping you apprised of reality."

Elizabeth collected herself. "Yes, she does keep doing that with me. *Ooh!* Sometimes I'm a brat!"

Gail chuckled and put a comforting arm around Elizabeth's shoulders. "At least you're aware of it. And you're a sweet brat."

Chapter XIX

Before she knew it, it was Saturday afternoon. Elizabeth was somberly putting on her wedding dress. She could hear commotion downstairs as Gail organized the living room. Surely the doorbell had rung too many times for the three people who were coming, but she couldn't give it any thought, she was so nervous. Yes, she wanted to *be* married, but right now she was equally certain that she didn't want to *get* married.

She'd done very little planning. She bought her dress and called the pastor. Marsalis had gotten the marriage license. Now it dawned on her that she should have given thought to some sort of reception, if only for the four of them. Five if the pastor stayed.

And she certainly hadn't given any thought to music, although music suddenly welled up the stairs. She looked at her watch. 1:58. Well, two o'clock was when she said she'd do it, so she might as well do it, she told herself. She started down the stairs. Halfway down, Gail scurried up the stairs and handed Elizabeth a bouquet of antique-white tea roses and baby's breath.

"Ralph is going to give you away," she leaned over and whispered.

On the landing below stood Ralph in a tuxedo, freshly shaved and hair combed back. Elizabeth hardly recognized him. As she descended toward him, he smiled up at her. She was so touched, she thought she'd start to cry then and there.

Of course Ralph was the perfect person to give her away, she realized, since he'd been the closest person to Grandfather besides herself, the last twenty years of his life.

But the notion of being given away had not crossed Elizabeth's mind!

When she reached the landing, Ralph extended his arm and Elizabeth took his elbow. She turned toward the living room and was amazed to see it filled with people.

"What ...." she whispered, turning to Gail, who had scampered away to her place as matron of honor.

The chords of the wedding march burst forth and everyone, already standing, turned to watch Elizabeth walk the fifteen feet across the living room to the pastor.

Peter stood beside Marsalis, both of them gorgeous in tuxedos. Marsalis stood puffed up and proud, as though playing the lead role in one of the world's greatest films.

Then she heard herself repeating words after the pastor, after which Marsalis did the same. It could well have been a grocery list, she felt so removed, she didn't know what she said, she didn't hear what Marsalis said. They exchanged rings.

Then the pastor said, "I now pronounce you husband and wife."

Those words she heard.

Marsalis leaned down and kissed her gently.

She was married.

Elizabeth tried to pull herself back into reality, but she felt disembodied. She turned to sort out *who all these people were!*

She saw Martha with a man she didn't know, a chubby lady at a synthesizer keyboard producing the music, which continued on now with the likes of *Moon River* and other romantic songs. Ralph, Gail, Peter, the pastor, Marsalis, of course, and two men and a woman Elizabeth didn't know.

Well, that was not really so many people, she reasoned, but it had sure looked like a crowd when she came down the stairs expecting to see only Gail, Peter, Marsalis and the pastor.

In the dining room, a beautiful cake caught Elizabeth's eye. Peter opened a bottle of champagne.

"A toast to the new wedded couple," he said.

Everyone grabbed a glass. "A toast!" they all cried.

"May your marriage be happy and your lives be long," Peter proclaimed.

Everyone agreed noisily, and general mayhem ensued, while Martha insisted Elizabeth cut the cake.

"Oh, thank you, everyone, for being here! I didn't expect ... I didn't expect it!" Elizabeth's voice quavered.

"We love you too," Martha said. "Now, cut the cake so I can put my photographer to work!"

Marty, the man with Martha, continued firing away with a battery of cameras on his person as if they were automatic weapons.

Marsalis introduced the mystery guests as Jim and Joe Johnston, brothers, and Joanna, Joe's wife. He introduced them as his oldest and best friends, although Elizabeth had never heard Marsalis mention them before.

"Friends, we might add," Joe said to Elizabeth, smiling, "who've just lost a bet that the number-one-confirmed-bachelor would never get married!"

Elizabeth laughed. "I hope you didn't lose too much! I wouldn't want you to dislike me from the outset!"

"*We like you,*" Jim insisted.

"Yes," Joanna agreed. "When you walked into the room, Jim leaned over and asked me how Marsalis snagged a woman with so much class."

"I did," Jim nodded. "How has our Marsalis suddenly become so clever?"

"Okay!" Marsalis laughed. "Enough abuse. Let's mingle, shall we, dear?" He swept Elizabeth away from his friends, joining Peter, who was talking with Martha.

"Thanks pal for being my best man," Marsalis said. "I would have had Jim, but I couldn't even find him until yesterday."

"The pleasure was mine," Peter said. "Now I believe I get to kiss the bride." Peter leaned over and kissed Elizabeth on the cheek. She smiled up at him, certain that she fulfilled the blushing part of being a bride.

As Peter moved back from her, saying something about how beautiful she looked, she caught a glimpse of Marsalis, giving Peter a stormy look.

Marsalis turned abruptly to Martha. "And who might this stunning woman be?"

"I don't know about 'stunning,' but I'm Martha, an old, *old* friend of Elizabeth and her mother."

"Her mother!" Marsalis exclaimed. "I thought her mother was someone who virtually didn't exist."

"Very well expressed," Martha agreed. "She *virtually* doesn't exist. Which is her loss today!" Martha took Elizabeth's hands. "You look radiant, fantastic, beautiful, Lizzie-girl."

'Thank you, Martha. Oh, Martha, I feel so guilty not inviting you. I *thought* we weren't going to have anyone. How did you find out?"

"Gail invited me."

"I couldn't be happier! Between you and Ralph ..." Ralph was standing alone behind Martha and Elizabeth reached a hand to him and brought him into the group. "I'm just so touched that you were here for me. Thank you."

"It makes me happier to get to see you on this day, Miss Elizabeth, than you can imagine," Ralph said shyly.

"How about some dance music?" Marsalis said to the woman at the keyboard.

They all partied and ate cake and *hors d'oeuvres* and drank champagne until dark. But, suddenly, as if on cue, everyone left, and the house emptied as she and Marsalis stood at the door, saying goodnight to Gail and Peter, the last to leave.

Gail, wrapped in a shawl with a bulging shoulder bag slung over her shoulder, gave Elizabeth a hug. "I'm staying at my mother's this weekend. I'll see you Monday when we go pick up Amy."

"All right," Elizabeth nodded. "And you'll visit her tomorrow?"

"You know I will," Gail assured her.

"I'll be there, too, of course. Thank you, Gail, thank you for ... for everything. I don't know how you did it, but you made today so, *so special*. I just love you for it. Oh, wait a minute." Elizabeth ran into the dining room, grabbed up her corsage and scurried back to the front door. She pressed it into Gail's already full hands. "I believe you're next in line!"

Gail giggled. "Ah, to feel like a girl again!"

They waved goodnight to one another, then Elizabeth closed the door upon her previous life. Now a married woman, she was at home alone for the first time with—how strange it sounded in her mind—her husband.

Chapter XX

Monday morning, after Marsalis left for work and while Elizabeth waited for Gail to come home so they could get Amy, Elizabeth reflected on her weekend.

The wedding, which now she got to savor for the first moment, had been wonderful. People she loved had shown her how much they loved her in return. She'd never felt such warmth in her life.

But from the moment she saw the nasty look Marsalis directed at Peter when he so platonically kissed her on her cheek until now, she wondered what she had done to her life.

Marsalis's behavior that first weekend, the posing and strutting, the sexual aggression, the lack of sweetness—the lack, it seemed to her, of thinking of her as even a person—had her in a state of shock.

Was this to be her married life? Gail and Peter and Mrs. Vargas and yes, even Grandfather, if that had been him beyond the edge of the three dimensions, all suggesting caution. They were right.

But she would not let anyone know.

More than once that weekend Peter's soft kiss on the cheek and his hug the previous week came to her. She wished with all her heart that she had never experienced that soft touch, that emotional sweetness. What could she to do about it anyway? Go on comparing Peter's sensitivity to Marsalis's brutish behavior for the rest of her life? She desperately hoped not.

She had to keep the truth, the sad, dark, truth, about her marriage secret. She had to maintain an exterior that implied, "Oh yes, we're happy, we're close, we're the perfect couple." Perhaps this weird, possessive, machismo attitude of Marsalis's would disappear. Surely it would after they established a routine.

But, for the moment, she'd been profoundly relieved when he said that morning he was going to the office.

She could only imagine how many women, throughout time, had given themselves in marriage, or even worse, had been *given* in marriage by family, believing in love and sharing and togetherness, only to discover that the man had no more intention of sharing or becoming friends than flying to Alpha Centauri, which, if he did, would be a huge relief, she mused.

She silently philosophized with herself that it was peculiar indeed that many societies believed it the height of morality to give women in marriage with the expectation that they surrender their bodies without argument, but that prostitutes, who at least *chose* to give their bodies, were considered immoral. And what *that* seemed to be saying, Elizabeth thought, was that women were immoral if they had a will of their own.

This was a new line of thinking for Elizabeth, and she thought about how she had become a different person over the weekend. She wondered if Gail would notice, and, if so, if she'd comment on it.

But right now, all she longed for was to hold Amy, to give her love, to tell her everything would be all right. *And to mean it.*

Finally she heard Gail's car in the driveway, then she came into the kitchen through the garage.

Elizabeth hurried into the kitchen. "Finally! Let's go get Amy!"

Gail looked her up and down. "Can't we girl-talk for a few minutes?"

"No. I mean, let's talk in the car. Really, I only have one thing on my mind and that is to get Amy home. Poor baby! What does she think of us, leaving her there for days on end?"

"Okay, okay," Gail conceded, seeing Elizabeth's urgency was not to be deflected. "Let's go. You got everything you need?"

"Sure," Elizabeth said, "I've been ready and waiting for an hour."

Another blurred whirl of events passed while getting Amy checked out of the hospital. Gail, filling the gaps as always, chatted with Mrs. Vargas, while Elizabeth, with Amy back in her arms, had nothing to say to anyone. Amy was in her arms. That's all that mattered.

When the three of them arrived home, Amy, trussed up and hardly able to move, was conspicuously delighted to be home.

"Bet!" she crowed, "Gao!"

Bet and Gao smothered her in affection and new toys that each had surreptitiously been buying with abandon while Amy was in the hospital.

They laughed at each other's indulgence, as the two identical, *huge*, fuzzy-stuffed elephants they had gotten surfaced, Amy's immediate favorites. "*Lfat! Lfat!*" she squealed, hugging giant elephant in each arm, completely blocking her from view.

"I don't know when you had time to get all of that, planning your wedding and everything else," Gail said to Elizabeth.

"Me! I didn't do any planning. What about *you*? Not only did you manage to get a pile of toys as big as mine, but you found Martha, and asked Ralph to give me away, and got food and a cake and music for the wedding. And kept it all a secret. Oh! Thank you again, dear Gail, ever so much, from the very depths of my heart."

"Yes, Pet, You're welcome. You've thanked me more than enough."

"Not possible. I can't thank you too much."

"The only thanks I want, is for you to be happy."

"I'm happy," Elizabeth said, "if Amy's happy. Are you happy Amy-Pet?"

Amy looked at Elizabeth. "Bet home!" she crowed.

Gail and Elizabeth looked at each other, eyebrows raised.

"Yes, yes," Gail said, "all my pets are home."

"A new word!" Elizabeth applauded. "And what a good word ... *home.*"

All afternoon they played. The three of them were lying on the floor giggling when Marsalis came through the door late in the afternoon.

Stepping into the living room he gave them an undisguised look of disgust, then growled, "Where's dinner?"

Elizabeth got up and dutifully went over to kiss him on the cheek. "It's a bit early for dinner, dear."

"I don't even see any evidence of it materializing," he groused.

"Well, don't worry. By dinner time, there'll be dinner," Elizabeth assured him. She looked over her shoulder at Gail, crossing her eyes in exasperation.

"I want to talk to you." Marsalis turned and retreated upstairs.

She shrugged at Gail. "Guess I'd better go see what the lord and master wants."

She went upstairs, wondering how she would be able to keep up the illusion that she was happily married. In the bedroom she closed the door behind her.

"How was your day?" she asked.

"Never mind my day, which, by the way, was pretty worthless. Look, we just got married and I don't feel like coming home to this house full of people."

"It's not a house full of people, Marsalis. It's Gail and Amy. They live here. They're family. *How* can you be so callous? Don't you care about Amy? We just brought her home from the hospital. Couldn't you at least ask about her?"

"I can see with my own two eyes that she's fine. But you and me, how are we supposed to get to know one another with them around all the time?"

171 ~ Amethyst Dream

Elizabeth felt her pulse quicken. Was she angry—or frightened? Or both? "Marsalis, Amy is the center of this family. You and I discussed this at great length. Amy comes first. You agreed."

"Well, I didn't know it was going to be like this. I want us to have time together alone. Like this weekend. Wasn't this weekend wonderful?"

Elizabeth chose to ignore the question. But she marveled at the complete difference two people could perceive the same event. "We'll have time alone together when Amy has recouped and, hopefully, the adoption is proceeding. We'll go away somewhere. But in the meantime, have some compassion! Please don't make me regret what I've done!"

Marsalis's expression, even his body language changed. He took his hands off his hips and sat down on the bed. "I'm sorry, Liz," he said quietly. "I'm just stressed. That office is getting on my nerves. The whole business is getting on my nerves! I wanted to come home to you all day." He patted the bed. "Come and sit by your mean old Marsalis."

Elizabeth sat by him and he put his arm around her shoulders. "I'm glad Amy's home and that she's okay. This is what we wanted, to see her home. So now, you and I should be able to get away. Gail is more than capable of taking care of Amy."

"That's not the point, Marsalis. I want to be *here*, I want Amy to know I'm here, I want her to see that I'm taking care of her. I wish you would want to become close to her, too."

"Well, sure, of course. I understand that. But if we went to Hawaii for just a week, Amy wouldn't even notice it."

"Hawaii?" Elizabeth asked, surprised. "This is the first I've heard about Hawaii."

"I love Hawaii," Marsalis said.

"I don't want to go so far away," Elizabeth answered. "We can lie on a beach here."

"I want to go to Hawaii, everyone knows it's romantic. And I want to go this weekend."

"No, Marsalis. I won't go this weekend. Why put us at odds when we discussed that we would go somewhere in a month or so? And I definitely had some place closer in mind, like, perhaps, Lake Tahoe."

"Come on," Marsalis said, convincingly, "you have to compromise somewhere. You can't have everything your way."

Utterly vexed, Elizabeth remained silent. Things that they'd agreed on a week ago she was called self-ish for expecting.

She began to see that she had two children; Amy, brave and good-natured, and Marsalis, spoiled and ill-mannered. In the light of *that* appraisal, perhaps he did need more of her attention than Amy.

"Marsalis, let's just both think about this for a while. I'm going down to start dinner."

"I thought that was Gail's job."

"Not in the least. She cooks because she likes it and when and if she wants to. Which, true, is most of the time. But since Amy needs undivided atten-tion now, Gail will be attending to her. *That's* her job. She's a nanny, not a cook."

Elizabeth went downstairs and found Gail already in the kitchen, heating Amy's food and washing vegetables. Amy's play pen stood in the kitchen door-way where Amy sat, happily cooing.

Elizabeth joined Gail and shrugged and sighed. "Hungry men! Everything I've ever heard is true. But who would think he'd want dinner at four?" She started cutting up vegetables.

"Yeah," Gail agreed. "It's enough to make you think the honeymoon's over."

Elizabeth giggled. "Even when you're funny, you're wise."

Marsalis didn't bother to come downstairs until he was called to dinner.

Conversation was nearly nonexistent during dinner. Elizabeth sensed that everyone was simply exhausted and they all agreed to retire as soon as the table was cleared.

"Let's let Amy sleep in my room tonight," Gail suggested.

"Oh!" Elizabeth was torn. They'd moved Amy's crib into the room beside the master bedroom. Yet Elizabeth hated for Amy to sleep in a room alone her first night home, when she'd slept in Elizabeth's room before she went to the hospital.

"I don't know," Elizabeth said. "I don't want to start that habit. But, you're right, I don't want her to sleep in a room by herself tonight."

"Why did you fix up that room for her if you weren't going to have her sleep in it?" Marsalis asked.

"Well, whatever you decide," Gail said calmly. "I'm sure she'll sleep through the night, she's so exhausted."

"Yes," Elizabeth said, hesitating. "Well, let's try putting her in her room."

Gail carefully picked Amy up and carried her upstairs, followed by Elizabeth and Marsalis. She went into Amy's room and Elizabeth followed her, while Marsalis went on into the master bedroom.

Gail put Amy in the crib, and she did not wake up. Then Gail turned on Amy's new carousel night light.

Elizabeth patted Amy's cheek and bid Gail good night.

It was three in the morning when Amy began shrieking at the top of her lungs. Elizabeth ran into Amy's room, and Gail dashed up the stairs and was right behind her. They picked Amy up, cuddling and reassuring her.

Elizabeth had never heard Amy shriek like that and she was pale and crying herself, as Gail comforted them both.

Marsalis stumbled into Amy's room, looking stormy. "What the *HELL*," he growled.

"*Shhh*, Marsalis, please, you'll scare her more," Elizabeth begged quietly.

"Make her be quiet."

"We're trying. She's really frightened."

"Bet's home," Gail cooed. "Bet's home."

But Amy refused to become calm.

"Maybe she's in pain," Elizabeth suggested.

"I'll get her medication." Gail hurried downstairs and back up.

Marsalis looked at the three of them as if it was all out of his control. "Oh, I can't stand it!" he finally seethed. He turned and went into the bedroom. He came out a minute later, dressed, buttoning his shirt.

"Marsalis!" Elizabeth called. "Where are you going?"

"I still have a month's lease on my place. I'm going to get some rest." He stormed down the stairs.

"Marsalis, please, don't," Elizabeth begged as the door slammed.

Gail laid a hand on Elizabeth's arm. "Let him go. You've got to give him time to adjust. It's too much all at once. At least you know where he's going."

Elizabeth nodded. "You're right."

Amy quieted down.

"You're absolutely right. He's upset about other things as well. He wants to go to Hawaii this weekend, just the two of us, and I told him no. I don't know where he came up with that idea, we discussed all of this last week. But I guess he either thought it would be all right, or thought he could manipulate me. We'll work it out."

"Of course you will," Gail agreed.

"I'll take her to bed with me," Elizabeth said, taking Amy.

"What if Marsalis comes back?"

"I don't think he will tonight," Elizabeth surmised.

Elizabeth was right. She lay awake all night watching Amy sleep peacefully beside her.

Chapter XXI

The next day Elizabeth fought an urge to call Marsalis, but she didn't. And he didn't call her. But he came home after work with an arm full of spring flowers, and a stuffed rabbit for Amy.

Dinner was somewhat quiet and uncomfortable, but after dinner, Marsalis got down on the carpet and played with Amy. Elizabeth and Gail exchanged a surprised and meaningful look, then got on the floor with them and they all played. Everything was going perfectly until Elizabeth and Gail got up to get juice for Amy and beverages for themselves and Marsalis.

A moment after they were in the kitchen, Amy started to protest.

"No, Beetie," she said. "No, *Beetie!*"

Elizabeth and Gail came back into the living room.

Marsalis was sitting with his back against the fireplace mantle, having moved away from Amy.

"What's the matter with her?" he asked. "I haven't lifted a finger. Why is she telling me not to beat her?"

Gail and Elizabeth broke out laughing. Elizabeth picked up Amy and pointed to Marsalis. "No, Beetie," Amy said again.

"Beetie, is Peter," Gail explained. "She's saying that you're not Peter."

"Well I know I'm not Peter," Marsalis growled.

"I guess she's just a one-man sort of girl," Gail laughed. She patted Marsalis's arm and looked at Amy. "This is Marsalis. Marsalis is nice, Pet, see? Nice Marsalis."

Elizabeth joined Gail and Marsalis on the floor. "Nice Marsalis," she agreed, patting him.

Amy looked from Gail to Elizabeth then back to Marsalis. "No Beetie," she maintained.

"No," Gail agreed. "Not Peter. This is Marsalis."

"Be nice to Marsalis," Elizabeth said. "See, Marsalis brought you the pretty rabbit?" Elizabeth handed the new stuffed animal to Amy.

Amy nodded cautiously. "Marsa-Bet."

Elizabeth and Gail chuckled. "Yes," Gail said, "Marsalis-Pet." Elizabeth and Gail continued to pat Marsalis.

"Well," Marsalis said, drinking up the attention. "I guess I could get used to this!"

After that, Elizabeth's whole world seemed to calm down. She agreed with Marsalis to go to Hawaii in three weeks.

The next week Elizabeth invited Mrs. Vargas over for dinner, who commented on Amy, recouping ahead of schedule.

"This is a lovely picture," Mrs. Vargas said when they retired to the living room after dinner. Elizabeth, sitting on the sofa, cuddled Amy. Marsalis sat next to her with his arm around her, making faces at Amy, making her giggle. Gail relaxed in the rocking chair by a crackling fire. "I'm so happy to see Amy at the center of this charming family. I believe we can begin processing the adoption paperwork next week, if that's suitable for everyone."

"Oh! Mrs. Vargas," Elizabeth exclaimed, "it's suitable. It's more than suitable, it's wonderful."

"Finally!" Marsalis agreed.

Gail nodded and smiled serenely.

Elizabeth remained in a wonderful frame of mind the day before she and Marsalis left for Hawaii. She still didn't want to go and could hardly bear the thought of being away from Amy for even a day, let alone a week. But she'd told Marsalis they would go and she was not about to upset the delicate balance by reneging.

While she packed, the doorbell rang and she heard Gail open the front door.

"Peter, hi! What a sight for sore eyes! *Elizabeth*," Gail yelled up the stairs, "Peter's here."

Elizabeth came to the landing. "Well, hi there, stranger. I've got to get some packing done. I'll be down in a few minutes."

"Don't rush," Peter said. "Sorry I didn't call, I had to do some business in this area and thought I'd stop by to take a peek at Amy."

"Good! Play with her, she'll be so delighted to see Beetie. I'll be right down." She went back into her room, listening as Peter and Gail move through the house and out onto the patio. With the house quiet and Elizabeth's windows open, she heard every word between Peter and Gail.

"She's packing?" Peter asked.

"Yes," Gail answered. "Would you like something?"

"Oh, maybe a glass of water," he said. "Hi Amy! Oh look at you, beautiful, happy girl!"

"*Beetie!*" Amy chortled.

Elizabeth smiled. Her little darling still had a warm spot in her heart for "Beetie."

"Where's she going?" Peter called toward the kitchen.

"Hawaii," Gail called back, then returned to the patio. "For a week. She doesn't think I know she doesn't want to go, but I know she doesn't want to go."

Really? Then why is she going?"

"Because that Marsalis insists."

'*That*' Marsalis? Elizabeth's eyebrow went up in surprise.

"Hmm," Peter said. "Oh yes, Amy-Pet, cute elephants!"

"Lfat, lfat," Amy chimed.

"Their very first weekend he threw a big temper tantrum because she wouldn't go to Hawaii," Gail stage whispered. "So she agreed to go as soon as Amy was a bit recouped. For pity's sake, she's got two children."

"Hmm," Peter said again, showing interested but not commenting.

"Here's the punch line," Gail went on, "she's paying for it."

"How do you know that?" Peter asked.

"Because at dinner a couple of nights ago he candidly asked her for her VISA card to give to the travel agent. Can you believe it?"

There was a silence. Elizabeth imagined a shrug from Peter.

"Well, as far as I'm concerned," Gail said, "she clearly married the wrong man."

"Really?" Peter asked. "Who would you have had her marry?"

"*You*, of course. Why didn't you ask her?"

"Well, Gail," Peter sounded uncomfortable.

Elizabeth thought she'd die of embarrassed on the spot, greatly relieved that no one could see her discomfort. Gail was *incorrigible!*

"Elizabeth and I were hardly—an item."

"It was just a matter of time," Gail answered in her maternal, matter-of-fact voice.

"She was always very taken with Marsalis," Peter said. "You can't blame her. He's a very good-looking guy."

"Sure, sure, he makes Valentino look like a shoe-shine boy. But let me tell you, Peter, he's a text book case of beauty being only skin deep. He's so spoiled, and insecure at the same time. It's only because she's such a good mother to Amy that I went along with the whole thing.

"Let me tell you something else, 'Beetie,' It's not that Elizabeth wasn't attracted to you, she was just star-struck."

"Oh, come on Gail. She's never even read one of my books. How could she be star-struck?"

"Doesn't matter. She told me she was awed by you."

"Really?" There was such a long pause that Elizabeth had to fight the urge to peek out the window even as her embarrassment mounted.

"It looks like I was in the running without knowing there was a race," he finally said. "I mean, she—I would have ... that is, there's not much anyone can do about it now, is there? We might all just as well close these thoughts away. I value Elizabeth's friendship and I think it's best to concentrate on that now."

Upstairs, Elizabeth sat on the edge of the bed, contemplating what Peter had just said—and what he didn't say—could have meant for the unfolding of her, of *their*, futures. Then she hid the conversation away. She was married to Marsalis, she would make it work.

She closed the locks on her luggage and her heart. Then she went down to the patio, all smiles and hugs, and indulged in a lovely hour of chit-chat with her three favorite people.

After Peter left, Elizabeth asked Gail if she had an extra copy of one of Peter's books she could borrow. "I've been meaning to start reading his work, but it has just gotten away from me. I'm sure I'll have a chance to get some reading done on this trip since Marsalis's already said he wants to laze around on the beach most of the time."

"Sure, Pet. I've been waiting for you to ask!" Gail went into her room and brought Elizabeth *After the Year Before the Millennium*. "When you come back you'll be able to join us when we have one of our literary discussions," she teased.

Elizabeth made a face at her and put the book in her purse. Now she was packed and as ready to go as she could be.

Chapter XXII

When Gail drove them to the airport the next day, Amy seemed to realize that something she wouldn't like was about to happen and she began crying the moment they walked into the terminal.

After they checked in they stood in line at a restaurant for a bite of lunch before going to the terminal, but Amy continued to whimper and cry, making the saddest face ever. Elizabeth looked at Gail and Amy. "You'd better go," she said. "She's so unhappy, there's no point in making her hate the airport, and I can't bear to see her so sad."

"Yeah," Marsalis growled under his breath. "Plus it's just *annoying*."

Gail nodded to Elizabeth. "Say bye-by, Amy," she said.

Elizabeth took Amy and kissed and hugged her. "Don't cry, baby. I'll be back before you miss me."

"No, Bet, no. No bye-bye!"

"Say bye-bye to Marsalis, sweetheart."

Marsalis patted her on the shoulder. "Bye-bye, Amy. Be a good girl." Then he turned away.

Elizabeth handed her back to Gail. "Call Peter and the three of you do something together. She'd like that."

"Okay, I will. Travel safely." Gail kissed Elizabeth on the cheek, then walked away.

Elizabeth felt tears sting her eyes. Boy, am I having fun now, she thought as she waved to Amy, her little hand reaching out to her, as she cried over Gail's shoulder.

A few hours later she and Marsalis landed in the hustling and bustling Honolulu airport.

If only we could have gone somewhere peaceful and quiet, Elizabeth thought. I could perhaps enjoy myself some if we stayed in a remote place. But here we are, in Waikiki, in a big boring hotel where every room is a stale replica of a million others around the world, when one might as well have gone to the same hotel that's only two miles from home.

But when they got into the room, it was filled with yellow and white tea roses, by the bed, on the dresser, on the table, even in the bathroom and out on the lanai.

The room, fragrant with rose perfume, cheered Elizabeth considerably.

"Did you get the roses?" Elizabeth asked, picking one of them from a vase.

"You'd better believe it," Marsalis said, checking out the closet space. "Nothing's too good for my girl!" he continued, with his back to her.

"Thank you, Marsalis. That was very sweet." She drank them in for a moment, then started to unpack.

After relaxing, they walked out into the evening and found a charming Italian restaurant where they had dinner. Then Marsalis insisted they walk among the street vendors.

"Isn't this fun?" he asked.

"It's—interesting." She looked at her watch. It was one a.m. at home. Too late to call. Marsalis wouldn't let her call when they first arrived, insisting that she give Gail and Amy a chance to get adjusted to her not being there.

Fine, Elizabeth thought, so how long will it take *me* to get adjusted to not being there?

Although the street vendors had beautiful jewelry and art objects, she only had eyes for things that Amy might like. She resolved to come shopping some time without Marsalis. He'd already said he wanted to lie out in the sun all day anyway. Boring, and something her fair skin did not find agreeable beyond a few minutes. Thank goodness she'd brought Peter's book.

Still, the prospect of the whole week stretched before her as boring, boring, boring.

Why? she wondered. Because Marsalis is boring, she answered. What a shock! She didn't realize she thought he was boring until she was faced with being stuck alone with him day in and day out. She'd been infatuated with him—well, his beauty—at first sight. She had tried to gain his approval from the outset, and she saw now that that was not so different from her life with Grandfather. Maybe that's why being with Marsalis seemed like the right thing to do. It was familiar. It was what she knew.

In the midst of the crowded vendors' stalls, she looked around for him. He'd wandered to a showcase of men's gold watches.

Come on Elizabeth, she reprimanded herself, every-one was interesting in *some* way. I have to give Marsalis a chance. For one thing, he loved her, at least that's what he said. In any event, he was dependent on her, always looking for her approval. For another thing, well, there was that bit about having gotten *married*.

There must be something they could discover that they were both interested in, that would make Marsalis more interesting to her. She hoped.

How much she'd changed in the last month! Before the wedding it would have been impossible to imagine Marsalis ever seeming boring. But she'd known nothing of married life. She'd been bogglingly naive.

Lately, all the little criticisms Gail had made of Marsalis before the wedding came to her, and they made more and more sense. To Gail's credit, how-ever, she'd not said a negative word about him to her since the wedding.

Well, Elizabeth advised herself, you made your bed.

Marsalis looked around and caught her eye, then motioned her to come over to him. "Can you believe these prices on the gold? How can they sell this stuff so cheap?"

Elizabeth shrugged. "I don't know."

"It's even cheaper than at the swap meet. And the styling is better. Look at these, European looking. Classy."

Elizabeth nodded absently. She was not inter-ested in watches or gold. "Yes. Attractive," she said for the sake of agreeability. She noticed a unicyclist riding down the side of the road, considerably more interesting than the watches.

"Okay," Marsalis said, "let's look at something you're interested in."

Elizabeth returned her attention to him, surprised. She couldn't recall him ever making any reference to something she might be interested in. "Me? I enjoy people watching. I'm perfectly content to float around like a little bubble, relaxed and unhurried."

Marsalis chuckled and took her hand. "Cone on then, little bubble. Let's find some ice-cream."

After enjoying some delicious gelato, they meandered back to the hotel and sat at the outdoor seating of the hotel bar, watching a stunning sunset bathe the ocean in a frenzy of fuchsia, orange, gold, and pink, then fade to an intense and velvety indigo.

Marsalis drank too much, stumbled a bit and slurred his words when they walked back to the room. He flopped himself down on the bed and fell directly into a deep, loud snoring, sleep.

Elizabeth was glad for the California king-sized bed, where she curled up on the other edge and read Peter's book until the wee hours. Although she didn't understand most of the science in the book, it really didn't matter as the characters lives were so engaging.

She had to agree with Gail. Peter was a fantastic writer. She'd soon finish the book, and the bulk of the week would stretch boringly out before her. But maybe she'd find a bookstore the next day and get another of Peter's books!

She finally fell asleep at two a.m, the equivalent of staying up all night to her internal clock, given the time difference. Marsalis woke her at seven. "Come on, girl. Get up, we gotta go bake ourselves in the sun! I can't believe you let me sleep all night in my clothes."

Elizabeth shrugged."You seemed quite comfortable." She didn't say anything about how she felt that he drank himself into a stupor.

At least I have Peter's book, she reminded her self with quiet, internal glee.

When they got settled among the row of baking humans, she opened the book.

"What's that?" Marsalis asked.

"Well, gee, Marsalis," Elizabeth teased, "it looks quite a lot like a book."

"You won't be much company with your face in a book," he complained.

"My goodness, if you think of something to say, just talk. It's only a book, not a wall."

"What's it called?"

Elizabeth held up the book.

"*After the Year Before the Millennium*," he read. "By Kim McCorky. It looks like science fiction."

"It is."

"You don't seem like someone who would read science fiction."

"As rule, I'm not. But I was curious about this book because Kin McCorky is Peter."

"Really? That book was written by Peter?"

"Um-hum," Elizabeth answered. "Gail has all his books. She let me borrow this one."

"Seems like you could have gotten a new book at the airport."

"I *could* have gotten a new book at the airport. But I wanted to read *this* book."

Sullen, Marsalis dropped the conversation. Elizabeth read until she felt scorched. "I've gotta get out of the sun," she said to Marsalis an hour later. "I can't put enough sunscreen on to block it, and it's making me feel light-headed."

Marsalis nodded, lethargic and half-asleep.

Delighted to be alone in the cool, shaded, room, Elizabeth dialed home, anxious to hear Amy's little voice.

"It's about time you called," Gail launched in. "Amy and I have been worried sick. Why didn't you call when you got there?"

"Marsalis wouldn't let me. He said I must allow you and Amy to adjust to my not being there. So— are you adjusted?"

"Of course not. We miss you! But ... are you having a good time?"

"I'm so bored! The only thing that's saving me is reading Peter's book, which, by the way, I love. I just wish I had the rest of his books with me. I could read them all this week. I want to be home. How can I stay here another whole six days?"

Gail was quiet for a few moments. "Hang in there. Take in some cultural experiences. Go to museums. You'll be mad at yourself if you don't. Hawaii's history is rich and interesting. Go exploring and see the water falls, the plants and the birds. Don't stay in that westernized city the whole time."

"Oh, Gail! Of course, you're absolutely right! Okay, boss, I'll do it." Elizabeth sighed a huge, relieved, sigh. As always, Gail made her feel much better. "What's Amy doing?"

"Taking her nap."

"I guess it's about that time," she said, disappointed to not get to hear her precious, little voice. "Well, give her my love when she wakes up."

"You know I will."

"I don't know when I'll get to call again. Maybe Marsalis is right, maybe I shouldn't call. I mean, I feel so lonely and depressed now."

"Dear, dear—it's not that bad," Gail consoled. "You're in paradise, get the best out of it. We'll see you soon. I'll call you if there's anything you need to know, so don't worry about the home front. Relax. Take care of yourself. And ... have some fun."

"Okay. Love you. Bye-bye." Elizabeth hung up and stepped out on the lanai. The water sparkled, the sky was clear. Beauty met her eyes in every direction.

"I *am* in paradise," she said to herself. "I should be clever enough to enjoy it."

She went downstairs to the front desk where they had row upon row of flyers on the sights and events that the surrounding area had to offer. She took one of each, went back to the room and studied them.

Two hours later she was almost finished going over them and making notes when Marsalis came back to the room, brown as a nut. Elizabeth wondered how much darker he could possibly get.

"You'll never get a tan hanging out in the room," he said.

"Once again, Marsalis, I don't tan. I'm lily-white or red. Right now, I'm rather more red than I'm comfortable with."

"Why bother to come to Hawaii then?" he asked.

"*Awk!* My question, exactly. It wasn't my idea to come here."

"I see," Marsalis said.

"But," she said cheerily, shuffling through her brochures, "as long as I'm here, I might as well get everything out of the experience I can get."

"That's the spirit."

"I'd like to book us for a Luau tonight. There's a nice one at the hotel next door. How does that sound?"

"Fine. That sounds fine."

"Then I thought tomorrow we could rent a car and drive around the island. Do you know it only takes a couple hours to drive around the entire periphery of the island?"

"Really?"

"Yes. There's a botanical garden on the opposite side of the island." She held the flyer in front of him. "I thought it'd be interesting to see that. Then the next day we could go to a museum." She held up another brochure. "Then I thought we could look into visiting one of the other islands. Maybe even stay over a night."

"You've been doing a lot of—thinking, it sounds like."

"Sure," Elizabeth said. "I'm trying to make this trip interesting."

"I'm not interested in 'interesting.' I run around enough when I'm working. This is a break for me.

Besides, with all that running around, when will I get my tan?"

"It looks to me like you've gotten it. How much darker do you intend to get?"

"This? This is nothing!" Marsalis posed in front of the mirror, one way, then another. "You wait and see, you won't believe how dark I can get. I'll tell you what, I don't mind if you plan things in the evening, but I really don't want to run around during the day."

"Okay." Elizabeth stacked the brochures together, feeling the spirit draining out of the fun she had worked to build up. Then a shift occurred inside herself, and she cheered up. "You won't mind if I check these things out on my own?"

Marsalis shrugged, clearly in love with the mirror. "I suppose not, but I can't imagine how you could face going back home without a Hawaiian tan."

"The same way I face every day of my life without any bit of tan. I'm more inclined to wonder how we'll get closer to one another if we don't spend time together."

"It's not my idea to be apart, with you running around all day," Marsalis retorted.

"On some other hand," Elizabeth pointed out, "you don't seem to care that too much sun makes me ill, and that lying around all day doing nothing bores me to tears."

"I care, but I can't do anything to change you, now can I?"

Elizabeth was so amazed by his candid insistence that she was the only one who should change, that she snapped her mouth shut, while her realization of his total oblivion of her as a person finally hit home.

"I'm going to take a shower." Marsalis headed into the bathroom. "Then I want to take a nap."

"What about lunch?" Elizabeth asked.

"I had lunch downstairs."

Elizabeth frowned. "Alone? You didn't invite me?" She heard the shower start. "That's just odd," she said to herself.

She stepped out onto the lanai with her handful of brochures. She *would* enjoy herself no matter how much Marsalis crossed her at every turn. And, by the way, she reminded herself, *I'm* was paying for this trip. She bent over the roses on the table to drink their fragrance—including even these roses he bought for me.

"Thank you, Elizabeth," she said aloud, sarcastically. "Thank you for the lovely roses. Oh, you're most welcome!" she answered.

However, again unpredictably, that night at the luau Marsalis was sweet and attentive, fun and funny. Elizabeth reprimanded herself for expecting Marsalis to want to do exactly what she wanted to do. After all, they were two different people. If he wanted to relax and tan himself, why shouldn't he?

Anyway, there was a real advantage in going to places like museums and botanical gardens alone. She could indulge in her love of loitering as much as she wanted.

For the next two days Marsalis went out to the beach in the morning while Elizabeth explored the island's rich, wonderful, and fascinating culture and nature. Then the two of them got together for a luau at a different location each evening. It was bit like heaven Elizabeth decided. It would have been *entirely* like heaven if Amy and Gail were with them.

In the evening she chatted about all the things she'd learned and seen during the day, and Marsalis half-listened, asking an occasional question, but mostly just content to see and be seen.

Elizabeth reasoned that she'd been alone with her own company for most of her life. She'd never expected her grandfather to share in her fun, what little she'd been able to come up with. He did not believe in 'fun,' he told her many times.

On the fourth morning, Elizabeth woke at five a.m., unable to return to sleep. She looked around for Peter's book. She hadn't finished it yet, with the busy schedule she'd kept for herself taking in all the sights, but she couldn't find it.

That's strange, she thought, I saw it right here on my bedside table yesterday afternoon. It has to be here somewhere.

She didn't want to wake Marsalis by stirring around looking for the book, so she quietly slipped into her jeans and sweatshirt, jotted a note to Marsalis that she was going for a walk, and hiked to Diamond Head Park in the brisk morning breeze, the ocean inhaling and exhaling off to her right. The morning light was glorious and she felt herself breathing in and out with the ocean, right down to her toes.

The entire scene was beguiling and peaceful, and at that moment Elizabeth was really, truly, happy to be in Hawaii. *Finally*. The smell of the very air was new to her—fresh, salty sea, brisk, going right through her body as if she were a filter, welcoming her to the islands, in this moment before the city geared up and exhaust contaminated the environment.

Suddenly, that animate energy she'd heard people mention when they talked about Hawaii, entered her. A strong, feminine, demanding-yet-compassionate, irrepressible vitality.

If she had come here for no reason other than to experience this energy, *it was enough*. She knew she would always, from this moment forward, have it to tap into.

She also had a troubled sense that she would need it.

She passed a homeless person here and there—as if anyone living in paradise could be considered homeless—stirring awake from a bench, or shuffling about, getting ready for the day's panhandling. They gave her studied looks. She had the impression they were veterans at their chosen profession, knowing that early morning joggers and walkers rarely had money on them.

Later in the morning she would take a bus tour of Waikiki and the Pearl Harbor war memorial. As always, she'd invited Marsalis, but, predictably, he shrugged and said, "Enjoy yourself."

The tour would pick her up at eight a.m. in front of the hotel. By the time she got back from her hike to and from Diamond Head, she only had a moment to run up to the room and grab her purse. Marsalis was gone. Out baking himself already, no doubt. She grabbed a sweet roll, an apple and a carton of almond milk from the restaurant and hurried out to the street, where the tour bus picked her up. After a fascinating four-and-a-half hour tour of the city, and a somewhat sad visit to the Pearl Harbor war memorial—why couldn't everyone just get along? she wondered—the tour bus dropped her off at her hotel.

She decided to go straight to the beach to find Marsalis. She wanted to share tidbits she'd learned about the mix of cultures, she wanted to talk about how curious and ironic it seemed to stand at the Pearl Harbor war memorial, thinking sadly about the young American men who had lost their lives to prevent the Japanese from taking Hawaii, while the balance of the tour had been about how the Japanese were buying up Hawaii as fast as money could change hands. How much more civilized was money as means of acquisition than weapons, she thought.

Marsalis probably wouldn't find her chatter very interesting, but she wanted to talk about it, even so.

As she scurried through the lobby of the hotel on her way to the beach, she saw Marsalis with his back to her, standing in the doorway of the restaurant, talking with a girl with a waist-length mane of tawny, honey-colored hair, his fingers entwined in a couple of her tawny locks. The girl looked up at him with spellbound admiration. Elizabeth had no desire to see the look he gave her in return.

She backed around the corner, then hurried up to their room.

She paced up and down. Was what she just saw really incriminating? Women found Marsalis irresistible, she knew. She knew that just from watching the waitresses when she and Marsalis went out to dinner. But that fact didn't justify his returning the adulation by standing around with his fingers stuck in a stranger's hair in broad daylight. She felt humiliated.

She stormed inwardly. And why, she wondered, didn't she just approach him when she saw him, instead of running away as if *she* was guilty?

Because, she answered, she was afraid. Her instincts told her to approach him then and there. But she was so furious, that she didn't want to embarrass herself in public. She would wait until he came to the room. Whenever he remembered that his new wife waited for him in their honeymoon suite.

Apparently Marsalis was not able to enjoy himself with his own company, she thought sarcastically. Apparently he had to be with someone all the time.

Well, this line of reasoning is not making me calm, she reasoned.

She decided to take a hot bath. A long, hot bubble bath always helped melt problems. She gratefully remembered Peter's book. A hot bath and a good book would let her mind relax. But she tore the room apart looking for the book and it simply wasn't there. Not under the bed nor in the bed nor on the bed nor in the end tables nor in the dresser. Not in the closet, not in the bathroom, not on the lanai, not on the table, not on the floor, not in the luggage.

It was gone.

She hated to think where it was, but then, she knew where it was. Marsalis had thrown it away.

When Marsalis finally came to the room two hours later, she was outwardly calm, dressed for dinner.

"Let's stay in the hotel for dinner," she said.

"Okay by me," Marsalis answered cheerfully, starting his shower.

At dinner Elizabeth was civil, if quiet. She remembered that she ordered a Cobb salad, but she had no idea if it came, or if she ate it, or if it was good.

After the waiter poured their after dinner coffee, Elizabeth asked quietly, "Where is my book, that is, Gail's book."

Marsalis gave her one of his why-do-you-bother-me-with-your-silly-little-problems looks. "I don't know where your book is."

"I believe you do," Elizabeth said. "Just give it back, Marsalis. It's not my book. Gail let me borrow it in good faith, trusting that I wouldn't harm it. And Peter signed it for her. It's very wrong for you to do anything with it.""

"Don't blame me, Elizabeth, if you can't take care of things you're responsible for!"

"I've changed our return reservations to the first flight in the morning," Elizabeth said.

Marsalis, looking like a gorgeous native with his dark skin and pale floral shirt, had returned to smiling and looking at the people around him. Suddenly the dark vein on the left side of his forehead surfaced.

"What do you mean, Elizabeth? Over a *book*? Are you completely crazy?" His voice became low, but his temper seethed. "I'll be nice about this and pretend you didn't say that. I won't let you put me in a bad mood over a *stupid* thing like a bad book!"

"*You* won't let *me* ... oh boy, Marsalis. You don't know the meaning of 'bad mood.' You should have been me for the last few hours."

198 ~ Thea Thomas

"What are you babbling about? What's gotten into you?"

"The sight of you fawning over some strange girl with more hair than a wig-maker and your fingers wound up in it—that's what's gotten into me."

Marsalis's angry expression changed ever so slightly.

"Oh for pity's sake! You react like this to *that*? Sweetheart, she's irrelevant, she's so—nothing! Just a little girl who found me irresistible." Marsalis chuckled.

"What's funny?" Elizabeth asked, feeling cold. "You had your fingers in her hair. In broad daylight."

"Oh! Well! I'm a flirt, I'm the first to admit it. But it's harmless, believe me. You think I'd do anything to risk losing you?" He reached over and grabbed her hand. "Be realistic, Elizabeth, she's just a little girl. You're a woman! There's no comparison."

"And this woman is telling you that she's changed the return flight reservations to tomorrow morning. You've managed to take away any joy I may have had in this trip, up, down, and backwards. I'm going home, I want to be with Amy and Gail. I don't want to have to wonder what you're doing in the lobby."

Marsalis chuckled again. "Well, gee, Elizabeth, there's lobby's everywhere."

"That awareness has not escaped me, Marsalis. But at least at home I don't have to go downstairs and see it. I'm going home. I'd get on a plane this minute if one was available."

Marsalis gave up on his forced joviality. "I don't want to leave, and certainly not for such a stupid reason."

"As you please, Marsalis. But it goes without saying that you can charge your room and room service and meals and your return flight to *your* VISA. It does seem more appropriate, doesn't it, since you're the person who wants to be here? Please be aware that I've closed the credit card account you've been using with wild abandon."

Neither of them spoke while they finished their coffee, after which they rose and went to the room without a word.

Elizabeth packed her things while Marsalis stood out on the lanai, then she went to bed.

Still not speaking, Marsalis came in and packed. He neither spoke to her nor touched her.

Early the next morning Elizabeth went out into the hall looking for the housekeeper. She found her in the other wing.

"Excuse me."

"Yes, miss?"

"Did you clean the rooms on this floor yesterday?"

"Yes, miss."

"Did you happen to find a book in room 7114, a book called *After the Year Before the Millennium*?"

"Ahm, yes, miss." The woman became uncomfortable.

"Do you happen to have it?"

"Yes, I do. I was going to read it. But I didn't take it. It was in the trash. People sometimes throw books in the trash."

"I *know* you didn't take it," Elizabeth reassured her. "I wouldn't even ask for it back, but it belongs to a friend of mine and the author—the author is a friend of hers, and he inscribed it to her. That book really means a lot to her."

"Certainly, miss. I saw the note in it from the author. I thought it was strange to throw it away. Here." The woman pulled the book out from under a package of paper towels and handed it to Elizabeth.

"Oh! Thank you! Thank you *so much.*" Elizabeth took the book gratefully and handed the woman a twenty dollar bill. "Please buy a copy for yourself. It really is a very good book. I wonder if you happen to remember which trash it was in?"

"Let me see—oh yes, the right side of the bed. I remember because there was sand on the carpet on that side of the bed. It was in the trash under newspapers."

Marsalis's side of the bed. No mistake about it, he threw it in the trash. Elizabeth nodded. "Thank you again."

Back in the room Elizabeth slipped the book into her suitcase while Marsalis slept.

A couple of hours later when they silently went down to check out, Elizabeth stifled a gasp when she looked at the pages long and very steep bill, but said nothing. Some lessons, she told herself, were expensive.

Finally they were at the airport. Until they got back to Orange County, a monosyllable was a long conversation between them.

As their plane came into the airport, Elizabeth turned to Marsalis. "I expect you to keep up a pleasant front. I don't want Gail to see this tension, to say nothing of being unpleasant around Amy."

Marsalis took her hand. "I'm sorry the trip wasn't much fun for you. I get caught up in things. I was caught up in being in Hawaii. I'm a kid sometimes."

Elizabeth melted ever so slightly, but she refused to show it. "Yes, you are. But now you're a married kid, so start growing up!"

"Okay, Elizabeth, I will," Marsalis said contritely.

One of his better acts, Elizabeth thought.

Elizabeth was never happier to see anyone than when she saw Gail holding Amy at the gate. The way Gail grinned and Amy wriggled, the feeling was clearly mutual. When they came together, the three of them hugged and laughed, while people flowed around them.

"Oh! I feel like I've been gone a year!" Elizabeth exclaimed.

"It seems like that to us, too!" Gail agreed. "I was so glad when you called and said the two of you had decided to come home early." She turned to Marsalis. "Come on you bronzed god, let's go home."

Chapter XXIII

After Hawaii, Elizabeth had to think seriously about whether she ought to continue this sham of a marriage. She had believed, until now, that she could give Amy the best home possible. However, if Marsalis continually upset their entire environment, then perhaps it simply wasn't the best home for Amy.

However, he appeared somewhat changed after they returned. He was quieter and seemed less ego-centric. Maybe he really was finally internalizing the fact that he was married, and dealing with what that meant in terms of life style, Elizabeth hoped.

She resolved to be as patient and sweet as she could possibly be. Now, back in the bosom of home, she seemed able to rationalize all of Marsalis's indiscretions. The flirtation with the girl didn't register as nearly significant as it had far from home.

And throwing away Peter's book was simply another manifestation of his adolescent jealousy.

After all, she knew nothing if she didn't know how important Marsalis's notion of his image, right or wrong, was to him. That meant he had to continue to be attractive to other women, while there was to be *no* competition for her attention, even in the form of a paperback book.

A few days after they came back from Hawaii, Mrs. Vargas joined them for dinner.

"Good news," she said after the salad and before the main course, "your adoption of Amy is moving along smoothly."

Elizabeth almost broke into tears. Marsalis took Elizabeth's hand and kissed her fingers.

"Congratulations, Mom," he said.

Gail and Mrs. Vargas smiled approvingly and the moment etched itself on Elizabeth's mind. It was one of those cherished events in her life she knew she'd never forget—the moment she learned she was about to become a mother.

Smiling, she said, "This moment will only be surpassed when I'm told that the adoption is finalized!"

*   *

That moment came a mere three months later, when their lives had settled into a comfortable routine. Mrs. Vargas called from her office to give Elizabeth the news.

"I assumed you'd want to know as soon as I knew," Mrs. Vargas said.

"Oh! Mrs. Vargas!" Elizabeth sat down on the floor in front of Amy's play pen, looking at Amy with a new intensity. *Her daughter!*

"Are you still there?"

"What's wrong?" Gail asked, worried.

"Yes," Elizabeth answered Mrs. Vargas, "I'm still here." She looked up at Gail, "I'm a mother."

"Oh, Lizzie!" Gail ran over and hugged her. "Congratulations! Thank you Mrs. V.," Gail called towards the receiver.

"It's certain?" Elizabeth asked, disbelief creeping into her voice.

"The signed and stamped paperwork is right here in my hands."

"I just ... I have to tell Marsalis! Thank you, thank you, thank you, Mrs. Vargas."

"And thank you for providing a good home for a deserving little person."

"Yes, she is!"

When Elizabeth called Marsalis, he said that was wonderful news and he was happy for her. But he had that same flat affect he'd had about everything lately, as though everything was equally unimportant.

"We'll have to celebrate," she said, hoping to stir him up to show some enthusiasm.

"If you want, but it's no surprise to me, it's been a foregone conclusion all along, hasn't it?"

"Not necessarily," Elizabeth said. "If I'd thought it was a foregone conclusion, I could have saved myself a lot of worry."

"And so you should have."

Elizabeth wouldn't let Marsalis's passive mood dampen her relishing the newness of motherhood. Amy was really and truly her daughter now! The biggest immediate challenge Elizabeth had was to teach Amy to call her mommy.

A pleasant task indeed. Euphoria washed over Elizabeth. If anyone had asked, she would have said life was pretty nearly perfect.

Chapter XXIV

Elizabeth hurried to the telephone. "Hello?"
"Hi, Elizabeth, it's Peter. I'd like to see you."

"I'd love to see you too. Why don't you come over for dinner tonight? Amy and Gail miss you."

"I miss them too. Is Amy calling you mommy yet?"

"Yes, she is. She seems to think it's terribly amusing that all of a sudden 'Bet' is 'Mommy.' She teases us by mixing it all up, calling me 'Bet-Mommy' and calling herself 'Amy-Mommy' and Gail is 'Gao-Mommy. I guess for the moment 'mommy' has become a last name.

"So, anyway, why not come over early, say, five-ish?"

"I'd love to, Elizabeth," Peter answered. "But right now I'd like you to come over here. Just you. I have—something rather strange to show you."

"Strange? What do you mean, Peter?"

"I can't go into it over the phone."

"Honestly, Peter, this isn't like you."

He was silent, so she gave in. "Okay, I suppose you mean for me to come directly?"

"That would be good, yes."

"How mysterious! I'll be there as soon as I can get there."

Elizabeth hung up. Something told her not to tell Gail where she was going, and why. Not that she knew why. She got her purse and went downstairs. "I'm going out for a bit, Gail. Hold down the fort."

"Huh?" Gail pulled her head out of the freezer.

"I've got to, uhh, go get some materials for the baby's rug—I'm going to finish that thing now, or know the reason why. I'm tired of seeing it hung up in there two-thirds done."

"Oh," Gail nodded. "Okay. That's good."

"Amy go!" Amy said seeing Elizabeth's purse on her shoulder and her keys in hand.

"You stay and help Gail, Baby-face. Gail needs you. Mommy will be back in a little while."

"*Amy go with Mommy!*"

"Finally!" Gail said.

"Yes, what a clever girl, to call me Mommy when you know I'm going off without you." Elizabeth went over to Amy and picked her up and kissed her. "You little blackmailer, you! This time you have to help Gail. Next time Mommy will take Amy shopping. When it's more important, okay?"

Storm clouds gathered on Amy's little forehead and rain threatened, but Elizabeth handed her to Gail and Gail showed her the inside of the freezer, talking to her importantly.

"Now, Miss Amy, what would you do to organize a messy freezer like this one?"

Elizabeth sidled out the back door and into the garage.

What, she wondered on her drive to Peter's, did he have on his mind, and why did he have to sound so mysterious? He was typically very transparent.

She parked in the driveway when she arrived. Peter stood in the back doorway, waiting for her.

"This better be good! It's the first time I've ever lied to Gail and Amy and I hope you'll vindicate me." She said, half-joking. She smiled up at Peter as she climbed the four steps into the back porch.

Peter wasn't smiling.

"Peter, what ...."

"Follow me, Elizabeth."

He led her through the house to his library. He pointed to the desk. Precisely in the center of the desk stood a tube of lipstick.

"Is that yours?" he asked.

Elizabeth gave Peter and odd look. "What sort of inquisition is this?" She picked up the lipstick, looking it over, puzzlement on her face.

"Frankly," Peter went on, "it doesn't seem like your color. It's too dark, but since you're the only woman who has lived here in many years ...."

"Yes, Peter, it's mine. That is, you're exactly right, it's too dark for me. It was the first lipstick I ever bought in my life. I bought it just shortly before you and I switched houses. And right after I bought it, it disappeared. It was peculiar, because I only had it and a compact in the medicine chest in the upstairs bathroom and right after I bought it, it was gone. I figured it rolled away somewhere, although I couldn't find it. Then I dismissed it because it wasn't a good color for me anyway.

"So where did you find the silly thing and why did I have to drive twelve miles to see it?"

"I found 'the silly thing' exactly where you picked it up. I haven't touched it. It just ... appeared there."

209 ~ Amethyst Dream

Elizabeth frowned. "Just appeared?"

"That isn't all, Elizabeth," Peter went on. "When I came in and saw it on the desk I—I wish I could say I fell asleep, but I didn't. I went into another state of consciousness. This room sort of faded and became like it was when you showed me the house. It was a very odd sensation. The room, like it is now, was here, but it was faded, as if there was too much light. The previous room was superimposed on it, it looked like a solarized photograph.

"And you, Elizabeth, came running into the room, transparent and in slow motion. You answered the phone. It had been ringing, but I didn't realize it until you answered it. It was Marsalis."

Goose flesh jumped up on Elizabeth's skin, she wrapped her hands around her arms.

"I don't know how I knew it was Marsalis. I couldn't hear him, I didn't see him. I just knew it was him. He asked you something. You hesitated. You were weighing something in your mind. Then you said yes.

"At that instant I had an image of a small mirror, like in a compact, breaking. And then the room returned to normal and the light in the room returned to normal and everything was normal. Except the lipstick was still there."

Elizabeth grabbed Peter's hand and pulled him to the kitchen. She sat at the kitchen table, shaken.

"When did this happen?" she asked.

Peter put water in the tea pot. "Just before I called you. That is, it happened, then I sat there for a while, waiting to see if anything else would happen. Then I called you."

Elizabeth breathed deeply. "You just described, in detail, the first time Marsalis asked me out. The day you looked at this house, after you left, he called. And, well, that's what happened, including the fact of finding my compact mirror broken, in the bathroom sink."

"What does it mean?" Peter asked.

Elizabeth, mystified, shaken, shrugged. "You tell me, you're the writer."

"I write science fiction, I don't write about actual occult phenomena."

"The odd thing is that it's not just some old ectoplasmic film clip that replays itself harmlessly," Elizabeth said, "like they say the probable explanation for ghosts is. It's my grandfather, trying to communicate something ever since almost a year ago when that lipstick disappeared and the mirror broke."

They exchanged a mystified look.

"Rationally, scientifically, realistically, I don't believe it," Peter said. "Emotionally, psychologically, or I guess I should say, parapsychologically—it happened. And here's physical evidence. So, I must believe it. I'm wondering if the vision is because of something that's in the past, or something that's pending. I don't know. I was hoping you had an idea."

Elizabeth shook her head, deep in thought. "I don't. But I feel very—odd."

"You're not alone," Peter agreed.

"Come home with me for dinner," Elizabeth coaxed.

"I don't mind if I do. Maybe I'll think more objectively at some distance. Besides, I miss Amy. I mean, *your daughter*."

"Oh, yes. She'll love to see Beetie."

"Marsalis won't mind?"

"He doesn't seem to mind much of anything lately. He's so passive and disinterested. I don't think we should mention any of this. Not even to Gail."

"Of course not. That's why I had you come over here, alone."

* *

"Look who I found," Elizabeth called when she and Peter returned.

Amy and Gail had finished cleaning the freezer and were watching cartoons when Elizabeth brought Peter in.

"Beetie!" Amy and Gail both called out. Amy struggled out of Gail's grasp and toddled over to Peter.

A look of happy amazement spread over his face. *Amy! Baby!* He caught her up and held her tight. "You're walking!"

"Amy-Bet walk!" she squealed.

"You didn't tell me," he said to Elizabeth.

"I didn't? Shame on me! I have this problem with her, she does so many amazing things one right after another, I can hardly keep track."

"How's my Amy?" Peter asked.

"Beetie!" Amy screeched, flinging her arms around his neck again.

"What an incredible, adorable bundle," Beetie said softly, burying his face in her curls and inhaling.

"And what an incredible, adorable bundle you are," Gail said, coming over to Peter and getting her hug too.

212 ~ Thea Thomas

Elizabeth grinned at the pretty picture they made, although for a moment the thought stole across her heart that she wished this picture was the rule, not the exception.

"Come over here," Gail ordered her. "You're not too good for us! Come over here and get your group hug."

Elizabeth shrugged and ambled over, "If ya gotta get hugged, ya gotta get hugged!"

During dinner Marsalis remained in his recently acquired aloof attitude. Elizabeth was prepared for some nasty response to Peter's presence, and she had warned Peter of the possibility, but it seemed that even Peter no longer riled him.

During dessert, when everyone but Marsalis was laughing, he came out of himself long enough to address Elizabeth. "I'm going to look at some property tomorrow in San Diego. I won't be back until late."

"San Diego? Why San Diego?" Elizabeth asked, surprised.

"Because there's a great deal on some property there."

"Oh," Elizabeth didn't want the happy mood of the moment to be disrupted. "Well, that sounds interesting. Drive carefully."

Marsalis nodded and said nothing further. A few minutes later he excused himself and went upstairs.

"Marsalis is really checked out," Peter said later when Elizabeth walked him to his car. "What do you suppose is eating him?"

"I don't know. At first I thought he was simply becoming adjusted to married life. But he seems to go deeper and deeper into himself. I have no idea who he is anymore."

213 ~ Amethyst Dream

"How can you live like that?"

"I'm okay," Elizabeth reassured. "I have Amy and Gail. I have your friendship. I have my work, which I enjoy. That's another thing, he gets nothing out of work. No satisfaction, no happiness, no pleasure. I think he hates it. And, just between the two of us, he's not very good at it. Since I've gotten my license, I've outsold him three to one, and I put in half as many hours.

"That's why his going to San Diego tomorrow takes me completely by surprise. He never shows that much interest in work."

"Maybe he's trying to become interested," Peter suggested.

"I hope you're right. But it would be very much out of his recent character."

They came up to Peter's '56. "The old jalopy looks great," Elizabeth complimented.

"Doesn't it? Not only do I love this car, but, in view of recent events, I don't want to do anything to upset whoever might be observing me at my new home."

"You sure bought a package, didn't you? You've gotten yourself embroiled in something you'd probably prefer not to be bothered with."

"Not true, Elizabeth. I don't think that that vision, or whatever it was, would have happened to me if I didn't care about you. And I do care what happens to you."

Elizabeth nodded. "I know you do. Thank you, Peter. I know."

214 ~ Thea Thomas

Chapter XXV

The next night Marsalis solved the problem of getting home late by not coming home at all.

"Do you suppose I should be worried?" Elizabeth asked Gail after they'd put Amy to bed. She looked up at the clock. "Eleven-thirty. Now, to me, that's late. That's very late to not even call. And when I call him, it just rings through to his answering service."

Gail looked up from her needlework of embroidering a pillow slip for Amy with little ducks and flowers and nodded.

"Should I worry? Should I get angry?"

Gail shook her head. "Either of those choices will only take a toll on you. My gut feeling is, he's just fine." Then she added something under her breath.

"What's that?"

"I said, he's just fine."

"No, I mean that last part."

"I said, 'the louse.'"

"Oh." Elizabeth was perusing a carpet-making supplies catalog and she returned her attention to it. "So you think he's up to no good."

"Who knows?"

"Maybe he really is in some sort of trouble."

"Maybe."

"Well, I think I'll go to bed," Elizabeth yawned. "I guess there's no point in losing sleep over him."

"That's wise. Sleep tight."

Elizabeth woke in the middle of a bad dream that she couldn't remember, trying to figure out why she woke up, when she heard Amy whimper. She turned on her bedside light, noticed that it was four a.m. and no Marsalis. She hurried in to Amy.

"Shh, Baby. *Shhh*. Everything is all right. Mommy's here. You were having a dream."

But instead of relaxing and drifting back to sleep, Amy sat up.

"Mommy here."

"Yes, I'm here, Amy."

"No. Not Bet-Mommy."

"What, sweetheart? Do you want Gail?"

"Not Gao. Not Bet-Mommy. Mommy, *there!*" Amy pointed into the corner of the room.

Gail came through the door and Elizabeth practically jumped out of her skin.

"What's going on?" Gail came up and patted Amy on the back. "Did I scare you?" she asked Elizabeth.

"Yes. Half to death."

"Sorry."

"Mommy *there*, Gao." Amy continued pointing into the corner.

"What's she saying?"

"I believe she had a baby dream about her natural mother," Elizabeth said.

216 ~ Thea Thomas

"Really?! Oh dear, who would have thought she'd have any memory of her?"

Elizabeth picked Amy up. "It doesn't look like we're going to be blessed with Marsalis's presence tonight, so I guess I'll just take her to bed with me. It'll be daylight in a couple of hours."

"Okay. Sleep tight, you two."

Elizabeth wondered how many more weird things were about to happen as she tucked the blankets around Amy and they both fell rapidly to sleep.

The bedroom door slammed and Amy jumped. Elizabeth opened her eyes sleepily to see Marsalis scowling over them. She looked at the clock. It was nine-thirty in the morning.

"What's the brat doing in my bed?"

"*Shhh*, Marsalis. Don't talk so loud and don't be so rude. She had a nightmare."

"I'll be loud," he said, raising his voice. "And I'll be rude, too, if I feel like it."

Elizabeth woke up fully now, realizing Marsalis was, at nine-thirty a.m., drunk. She picked up Amy and took her to her crib.

When she returned to their room, Marsalis sat on the edge of the bed, looking at the carpet between his shoes.

She closed the bedroom door.

"Where have you been all night?" she whispered. "And why are you drunk in the morning?"

"Leave me alone!" he growled.

"I mean it, Marsalis. I want to know where you were."

"San Diego."

"So you told me. But you also told me you would be home late. This is beyond late, Marsalis. You're late for *work.*"

"I'm not going to that hell hole anymore. I hate that office. I don't have to work, I've got a rich wife. Why should I work?"

He kicked off his shoes and rolled over, unconscious before he even stretched out.

"Why should you go to work?" Elizabeth answered her un-hearing husband. "I'll tell you why, because I don't want you around here all the time, for one thing. And I don't want to have to wonder where you are if you aren't here the rest of the time. That's why you have to keep working."

She struggled him out of his shirt. There was a business card in his pocket. "Michelle Stone—San Diego Coast Real Estate."

"Well, at least it looks like he started out legit, in San Diego, with a real estate agent." She took the shirt downstairs to the laundry, and showed the business card to Gail.

"Should I look into this?"

"It depends on what you're prepared to find out," Gail advised.

"Yes. Well. I guess I won't really know that until, perhaps, the damage is done. On the other hand, how much upset does this household have to tolerate?"

"Also a valid point," Gail agreed.

"There he is, passed out, drunk, after being out all night. He says he refuses to work any longer. So what am I supposed to do with him all day around here?"

"Something tells me that's not likely to be a problem."

Elizabeth shook her head. "I suppose I'd better call Edna and tell her his highness won't be in." She dialed the office. "Hello, Edna, this is Elizabeth. Marsalis won't be in the office today."

"So what's new? He wasn't in yesterday, and he ran in and out of the door the day before. But you might remind him that he has a couple of closings that he's going to completely lose if he doesn't do some work."

"Really? Why don't I know about this?"

"How should I know? You're the one married to him."

"That's right, Edna. I believe I'll come in and see if I can organize things a bit."

After she hung up, she turned to Gail. "He's got closings he's about to lose. He's falling apart before our very eyes. I'm going to the office. I hope he stays unconscious for the rest of the day."

When Elizabeth got to work, she went into Marsalis's office and closed the door. She ended up spending the day on the telephone trying to appease a slew of buyers and sellers and other real estate agents.

When she felt she had everything as much under control as she could get it, she pulled out Michelle's business card and dialed the number.

"Hello, yes, I'd like to talk with someone regarding a real estate deal I heard of from a friend."

"What was the property?"

"That's what I don't know. This agent talked with my friend and my friend told me it was a great deal.

Or so his friend, this agent's name was Marsalis I think he said, told him. Up here in Orange County."

"Oh, yes, I remember Marsalis," the voice on the telephone said.

Women always do, Elizabeth wanted to say. But she kept it to herself.

"You'll want to talk with Michelle Stone. One moment please."

Directly a kittenish voice came on the line. "Michelle Stone speaking."

Elizabeth went through her little speech again. Michelle sounded a bit surprised. "I believe Marsalis is interested in the property for himself. He sure wasted no time talking about it to other people. I mean, he just looked at the condo yesterday and he, ahm, left San Diego this morning."

Elizabeth shook her head. Well, this was all the information she needed. That she hoped she wouldn't hear.

"Yes," Elizabeth answered. "My friend just called me. See, I've been looking for a place in San Diego. Apparently my friend got the impression from this Marsalis that there were other condos available there."

"I could check into it," Michelle said sweetly. "If you'll give me your number, I'll get back with you this evening."

Might as well go all the way, Elizabeth thought. She gave Michelle the home number. "But please don't call before six."

Elizabeth was gambling that Marsalis had not given Michelle his home number.

"All right. And who am I speaking with?"

"Ask for Gail," Elizabeth said. "I'm looking forward to your call."

That evening while they were finishing dinner the telephone rang. Elizabeth got up and answered it.

"It's for you, Marsalis."

Marsalis went across the room and took the receiver.

"Hello? Ahm ... no, of course I'm not Gail."

Elizabeth studied him while he talked. He turned and gave her a peculiar look, then looked away. "How'd you get this number? Yes, it's Marsalis. Gail did?" He looked at Gail.

Gail, confused, gave him a lost look in return.

"Yes, go ahead and give me the details," he said, not writing anything down. "I'll talk with you later. After I discuss this with Gail. Bye."

He hung up and came back to the table, his brows lowered and eyes narrowed.

"Gail," Elizabeth said, "why don't you take Amy out get a gelato?"

Gail looked at Elizabeth quizzically. "Are you sure?"

"Quite sure. Never mind clearing the table."

"Well, if you're certain." Gail stood and took Amy out of her high chair. "Come on, baby, let's go get a goodie." She put a little jacket on her. "We'll be back soon. Okay?"

"That's fine, Gail," Elizabeth agreed.

After they'd left, Elizabeth turned to Marsalis. "Suppose you tell me the significance of Michelle in your life."

"She's a real estate agent, with some really special deals on some remarkable property. My God, Elizabeth, this jealousy thing of yours has got to stop. It's absolutely impossible to live with."

"Are you telling me I'm wrong about this woman?"

"That all depends on what sort of delusion you've worked up about her."

"The 'delusion' that you spent last night with her."

"Yes," Marsalis nodded vehemently, "that's about what I expected of you."

"Why are you looking to buy a condo in San Diego?"

"What makes you think I'm buying a condo, just because I talked with another agent about some property?"

"Because that's what she told me."

"She did not."

"Marsalis, she told me that you were looking for a condo for yourself. She also, inadvertently, I'll admit, told me you spent the night with her."

"That's the most ludicrous thing I've ever heard. What woman would tell a wife that she'd spent the night with her husband?"

"She didn't know she was talking with a wife. She thought she was talking with a potential client. But she was very puzzled how I knew about the property through a third party a short time after you left her. And she couldn't understand why you would be advertising a property that you wanted for yourself.

"You know what's strange?" Elizabeth went on, "I feel sympathy for her. I know you didn't tell her you're married. And the poor thing's no doubt ga-ga over you. Like women always are—at first."

"So you've put it all together, have you?" Marsalis sneered.

"I guess I have," Elizabeth said calmly, although her heart raced. She'd hoped desperately that somehow Marsalis would tell her something to convince her that she was wrong. But she could see that was not to be the case.

"Marsalis, I want you out of this house. I want you out of my life as well, but we'll start with first things first. I loved you, that is, I tried to love you. But you just wouldn't let it happen. It seems you can't recognize love. However, I'm not about to lose any more of my life over you."

"Just calm down, Elizabeth. I'm not going anywhere. Not permanently, anyway. You're my wife, this is my home and I'm not leaving. Besides, aren't you afraid of losing your precious Amy?"

"Not anymore, no. Even if they were to take her away from me because of you, it would be better than if she is to be around any more of your influence. You don't care about her at all. Now, please, just go pack and *get out.*"

"You would actually kick me out on the street?" Marsalis tried to put on a wounded look. "Where would you have me go?"

"San Diego was good enough for you last night. Michelle must be dying of curiosity about what's going on. Who Gail is, for instance."

Elizabeth started clearing the table. "I've found myself wondering all day, how many times, how many women you've been involved with since I've been with you. Goodness, Marsalis, you're very sloppy about it, aren't you? I guess you think I'm remarkably stupid. Or desperate. But I'm neither."

"Stop clearing the table!" Marsalis shouted.

Elizabeth ignored him and carried a stack of plates into the kitchen. She returned and piled up another stack.

"I said, stop doing that!" Marsalis rushed toward her, slapping the dishes from her hands. They went flying, crashing into the wall and floor. Then he hit her in the face so hard she crumpled to her knees, broken china cutting into her left knee and right hand.

Shocked, she tried to stand, blood ran from her hand and oozed through her slashed jeans.

Gail came in the back door.

"Oh my God! What's going on?" she cried.

"Don't let Amy see ..." Elizabeth said.

"I can't stand this!" Marsalis yelled, bolting from the house. He ran outside and jumped in his car, tires squealing for a block.

"It's too late," Gail said. "She's already seen. We have to get you to the hospital."

Gail hurriedly grabbed towels and made compresses on Elizabeth's hand and knee after checking to make sure there was no china bit in them.

"What happened?" she asked while she administered to Elizabeth. Amy stood by, eyes as round as little moons, trembling.

"It's all right, Amy," Elizabeth said. "Mommy's okay. I just fell down and got an owie. We're going to go for a little ride, so why don't you go find a cuddle toy to take?"

Amy toddled to her pile of stuffed creatures and hugged her her two elephants close.

"I faced him about this Michelle person. He didn't deny it. Then I started clearing the table and he told me to quit. But I didn't and he knocked the dishes out of my hands and ... I slipped and fell on them. Can you believe he was actually willing to go so far as to buy a condo so that he could go down there and play without distraction? No doubt with my money, too."

"Awful, awful," Gail hissed. "Poor Elizabeth! What an awful man!"

"Even so, Gail, even now, I feel sorry for him. Because he doesn't know what's he's doing. He simply doesn't have a conscience. He's not all right."

"All the more reason to be frightened of him, Elizabeth! Who knows what he'll do next?"

Amy came back to Elizabeth and cuddled up against her, an elephant's ear in her mouth.

"I'll feel sorry for him," Elizabeth said, putting her left arm around Amy. "But I will not tolerate him frightening my daughter."

While they waited in the emergency room at the hospital, Gail looked at Elizabeth in the light. "Look at that, a black eye! He hit you in the face?"

"A black eye?" Elizabeth asked, surprised. "Really? How can I go to work with a black eye? Does it look very bad?"

"It's going to be a real work of art, from the looks of it. Poor girl, you must have one heck of a headache."

"Well, I do, now that you mention it. I was too preoccupied with the pain in my hand and knee—and heart—to notice it."

Gail jumped up and, with Amy on her hip, got an ice pack and some aspirin and a glass of water from the nurses and brought them back to Elizabeth. "We have to tell the police. You can't let him hit you."

"Oh dear. No, Gail. Please, let's not. I mean, I'm just not ready to try and sort out anything more right now. The police will take hours. And I really *so* just want to go to sleep."

Gail acquiesced, but not happily.

They returned late from the hospital, Amy in Gail's arms, sound asleep, Elizabeth stitched and bandaged, leaning on Gail on the other side. They entered cautiously, but there was no sign of Marsalis.

"I wonder if I can impose on you to call a locksmith," Elizabeth said. "I want the locks changed right now."

"I'm in complete agreement." Gail called a twenty-four hour locksmith. "He'll be here in an hour."

"I hope Marsalis doesn't come back before then."

"If he does, I *will* call the police," Gail said. "And, again we should anyway."

"If we have to, yes. But for now, I'd rather not. If Marsalis comes now, then yes."

Gail nodded.

"Oh, Gail!" Elizabeth started to cry. "I just can't take any more. So much has been going on. You don't even know what all ...."

"Don't worry, Pet. You don't have to tell me things I already have a good idea about. Don't worry. We'll get him out of your life."

"I feel horrible about putting poor little Amy through this."

"She'll be all right. She knows we love her."

"I have several appointments tomorrow. Marsalis has fouled up on three major closings. How can I have meetings with a black eye? I don't even know if I can drive with my hand like this. Honestly, Gail, a black eye is not businesslike."

Gail tried to chuckle. "Rather much of an understatement, yes? You could say you were in an automobile accident. Really, Elizabeth, just don't go to work tomorrow."

"Black eyes get worse looking for a few days instead of better, don't they?"

"If blacker is worse, then usually they do, yes."

Elizabeth sighed, resigned. "Where *is* that locksmith? Even with all this excitement, I don't feel I can stay awake."

"It's shock and stress, Lizzie. Go to bed, I'll take care of the locksmith."

"I feel guilty, but I just don't think I can go on." Elizabeth got out her VISA card and handed it to Gail. "Give the locksmith this. I think Amy should sleep in your room tonight." Elizabeth glanced in the living room where they had put Amy down in her play pen, asleep. "I'm going to sleep in the guest room."

"Okay," Gail agreed. "I'll clean up the broken china and put some of Marsalis's things in a box and set it outside, just in case he comes back and tries to use that for an excuse to get in."

"Good thinking, Gail. Thanks. Good night."

"Good night, Lizzie-girl."

*   *

The next morning Elizabeth called Edna at the office. She knew there was some chance that Marsalis would be there, but she doubted it.

"Edna, it's Elizabeth. Listen, I need to postpone all the appointments I made for today. I had a little accident last night and I'm indisposed. I'd be terribly relieved and grateful if you could help me."

"You don't sound good," Edna said. That was the nicest thing she'd ever said to Elizabeth. "Couldn't Marsalis at least try to handle a couple of the more urgent meetings? After all, they are all *his* closings. And I use the word 'closings' optimistically."

"Oh. If he's there, perhaps he could take care of ...."

"No, he's not. You don't know he's not here?" Edna was silent for a moment. "I was just saying that maybe you could have him take care of a couple of the meetings."

"I don't think he can be counted on today, Edna. If you'd organize meetings with those people for me on Monday, I'd really appreciate it. Please tell them I was in an accident."

"Okay, Elizabeth, I'll do what I can."

Elizabeth was surprised at Edna's unantici-pated civil attitude toward her. At least that was a bit of relief on an otherwise horrible and distressing day. Maybe Edna had learned more about Marsalis recently than even Elizabeth knew. She had to take his calls, write his messages, and at times, perhaps even know where he was.

With the way Edna had carried the torch for Marsalis, Elizabeth could see that her previous animosity toward Elizabeth, whom she saw as an interloper, might turn to sympathy.

Now the physical pain really began to set in. Her whole body felt swollen and cut and bruised, instead of just in three distinct locations. She stayed in bed for two days, hoping to be recovered by Monday.

Every time she fell asleep, she awoke with a start with the horrible vision of Marsalis moving on her. The ghastly anger contorting his face, the clear determination to do her harm. All she'd done was try to love him, try to find the place in him where love lived and coax it out of him. But it was not to be found.

He made it obvious that he didn't trust her, or anyone. Which was surely because he was completely untrustworthy himself, she concluded. She felt like a failure because she could not get through his barrier, even though she knew that was an unfair judgement on herself. Marsalis's problems were a lot longer in the making than a year of her efforts to turn them around could repair.

During the weekend Elizabeth was as occupied with healing psychologically as physically, but she knew she would have both kinds of scars. She pondered what sorts of painful experiences Gail must have had to have strong, instinctive, negative reactions to Marsalis, practically on sight.

She wondered if she would now develop the same kind of psychic sonar.

Oh! She exclaimed to herself, why couldn't everyone just be nice? Wasn't life hard enough? Look at poor beautiful Amy, born with a defect, without a natural father who would claim her, and then she lost her mother. Weren't all the things one could not do anything about quite enough, without people going out of their way to harm and hurt one another?

She looked at her bandaged hand, a result of not wanting her husband to philander.

No, she said inwardly. I reject this treatment, I won't tolerate ever again being treated like this.

Never again.

I claim my right to be a happy person, to expect good things in my life, to be respected. I resolve here and now to never let anyone belittle, abuse, or demean me. Every person has the right to expect happiness and joy and peace in life. I'm laying claim to that human birthright.

When she came out of her bedroom Monday morning, she felt like a completely different person.

Chapter XXVI

"No sound nor sight of Marsalis for three days," Gail said when Elizabeth came down for breakfast. "That's a good sign."

"Umm," Elizabeth nodded. "I'm cautious to develop a sense of false security."

"I agree. But we have to be able to live in peace."

"We will, Gail. I just hope and pray what has happened doesn't scar Amy."

Gail shook her head. "We won't let it."

"I'm coming home as soon as I can. I have to get through these meetings. How does my black eye look? I keep vacillating between, 'it's hardly noticeable' to 'good grief, what makes me think I can go out in public looking like this?'"

"Well, it's kind of between the two," Gail assessed. "The swelling has gone down, and that's good. At least your face is its natural shape. But even with your make up it *is* black and you can expect people to ask or to stare. It might be a good idea to come up with a little story."

"I've got a little story, all right! Call me if anything happens."

Edna gave a whistle when Elizabeth walked into the office. "Boy! You weren't kidding when you said you were in an accident! How are you?"

"I'm okay. That is, I'm better. I hope I can get through these meetings quickly, with as little conflict as possible."

"Good luck. Some of these people are really irate."

"I don't blame them, the way they've been song-and-danced."

Elizabeth went into Marsalis's office, marveling at the change in Edna. She had figured out that something was wrong. Or maybe it was just her curiosity that made her nice.

Later that afternoon Elizabeth was in the middle of her third meeting. Everything had gone very smoothly and all the clients expressed sympathy for her accident. She told herself that she'd have to remember to get herself beaten up whenever she wanted strangers to be nice to her, ha, ha.

Right then Edna called on the intercom. "Gail's on the telephone. I told her this wasn't a good time to disturb you, but she insists it's an emergency."

"Thank you, Edna. Excuse me a moment." Elizabeth's heart raced like bee's wings as she picked up the phone. She took a deep breath. "Hello, Gail ...."

"Marsalis just took Amy."

"Oh my God! Did you call the police?"

"Yes."

"I'll be right there." Elizabeth hung up and leaped from her chair. She looked at her clients blankly.

"Ahh, excuse me, I have to leave. My—my baby has been kidnapped." She ran from the office. "Edna ... it's ... Amy's been kidnapped. Cancel everything."

Before Edna could say a word, Elizabeth was out the door, running to her car.

Stay calm, she told herself. But questions flew through her mind. How did Marsalis get in the house? What would he do with Amy? What was going on in his confused, and, Elizabeth feared, dangerous mind? Why would he take Amy when he didn't even care about her? He had no idea how to take care of her.

Pulling into the driveway she didn't wait for the garage door to open. She jumped from the car and ducked under the garage door as it slowly slid up. *"Gail! Gail!"*

"Here I am."

"Why aren't the police here?"

"They're on their way. Sit down, Elizabeth. Look at you, you're white as snow."

Gail made Elizabeth sit on the sofa. A siren could be heard.

"There they are," Gail said.

"How did he get in?"

"He must have been watching the house very closely. I was doing the laundry, so, since I was going in and out the back door into the garage, I left the door unlocked. I ran upstairs to check out Amy's room for stray laundry. "I heard a 'clunk,' but I thought it was the washer changing cycles.

But when I came down the stairs, I saw the front door standing open. I couldn't believe it! I flew downstairs. Amy was gone from her play pen. I ran outside, and then I heard Marsalis's car, but I couldn't see it. He was gone."

There was a resounding knock at the door. Gail got up and answered it. She showed a policeman and a policewoman into the living room.

"But how did he get in," Elizabeth beseeched Gail.

"The garage door opener," Gail answered. "We forgot about his garage door opener."

"This is Officer Timms," the policeman said. "And I'm Officer Avery. There's been a kidnapping?"

"Yes," Gail and Elizabeth said together.

Elizabeth and Gail followed the police around while they figured out what Marsalis must have done. He'd apparently been spying on them from the lake side of the house. As soon as Gail went upstairs, he ran around to the front of the garage, opened the garage door with his opener, ran through the kitchen and dining room, picked Amy up from her play pen in the living room and dashed through the front door.

He'd parked his car in front of the neighbor's house which was blocked from view by a row of evergreens.

"And what is this person's relationship to the child?" Officer Timms asked.

"He and I are her adoptive parents," Elizabeth answered.

"Really?" Officer Timms responded. "What then is his motive, in your opinion, for kidnapping?"

"He and I are estranged, but I don't know why he'd take her," Elizabeth said, beginning to tremble. The police woman had hit on Elizabeth's greatest fear. "He's never been particularly attached to her. But I couldn't imagine how anyone could be anything less than completely in love with Amy. His ... his character has completely changed lately. He's become so withdrawn and just ... odd.

"Lately I've felt like I have no idea who he is. Last Thursday night he attacked me when I told him I'd found out about his involvement with another woman. I told him to get out. He hit me, then left. We had the locks changed."

"Hence the black eye," Officer Avery said. "So it looks like it's either a blackmail or revenge action," he continued. "You'll hear from him. He'll try to make a bargain with you, just go along with whatever he says. Be sweet and unflappable no matter how much you have to fake it. The important thing is to get the child back."

"Yes, yes," Elizabeth agreed. "I'll do anything!"

"Don't let him make you angry," Officer Timms admonished. "Don't let him push your buttons, which, of course, he's sure he has the power to do now."

Elizabeth nodded. She began to feel a bit hopeful. These people were so reasonable, so sure, she felt they *must* know how to get stolen children back to heartbroken, anxious mothers.

"Do you mind if we tap your telephone?"

"No, please, do anything," Elizabeth urged. "How long will it take to get her back?"

Officers Timms and Avery looked at Elizabeth sympathetically. "We don't know. The sooner, the better."

"Come on," Gail said to Elizabeth. "Let's let them do their work."

Elizabeth followed Gail into the kitchen, feeling empty, lost and frightened.

Gail made her sit down, then she put on the tea kettle. "I feel so guilty," she said quietly. "Why didn't I sense him lurking around? I don't know what's wrong with me."

Elizabeth took in Gail's tragic expression. "Don't Gail, please! How can you blame yourself? We both forgot about his garage door opener. If Marsalis was so determined to take Amy, I don't think either of us could have done anything to keep him from it. It's my fault for not calling the police the other night. I am not blaming you, Gail."

"I was afraid you'd be angry with me, and rightly so."

"It won't help if a wedge is driven between us, will it? I need you now more than ever."

Gail nodded. She went into the living room and asked the officers if they'd care for anything, and they both agreed a cup of decaf would be nice.

Then Officer Timms went out to the garage and dusted for prints.

"Of course, his prints are all over the house," Elizabeth pointed out.

"But these are fresh and hopefully unmarred. We also need pictures of him and the child and some article of clothing of each. Something we can familiarize the dogs with."

"Oh, yes. I'll get them," Elizabeth said, her heart sinking. The dogs. It sounded so frightening, so violent.

"The box outside the front door is Marsalis's stuff," Gail said. "He didn't even bother to pick it up. Shouldn't you be out looking for him before he gets too far away?"

236 ~ Thea Thomas

"We've already got an Amber Alert out," Officer Avery assured.

After the police left, Elizabeth and Gail went into the living room to brainstorm where Marsalis might be.

"Maybe he's on his way to the condo in San Diego," Gail hypothesized. "Maybe you should call that Michelle person and see if she knows of his whereabouts."

"But if she's in with him she'll simply lie. If she's not, she'll tell the truth, but I'll still think she's lying." Elizabeth paused, thinking. "I don't think he'd go there now, anyway. Not after I found out everything about the condo."

They spent the rest of the evening writing down what Marsalis might say when he contacted them, and putting down the responses that hopefully would not anger him. Anything to get Amy back in their arms.

At midnight, Elizabeth couldn't stand it any longer. She called the police station, asking for Officer Timms.

"She works the day shift," the desk clerk answered.

"I'm sorry," Elizabeth apologized. "How stupid of me. She seemed so competent, I guess I thought she'd work around the clock. I wonder if there's someone else there who could apprise me of the status of the Amy Antonella kidnapping?"

"Just a moment, please."

A few seconds later an irritable voice came on the line. "May I help you?" he barked.

"I hope so," Elizabeth answered. "I was wondering what's the status of the Amy Antonella kidnapping."

There was a pause. "Officers Timms and Avery are assigned to that case."

"Yes, I know. But I was wondering what is being done now."

"There's an Amber Alert out on the alleged perpetrator."

"Alleged!"

"Until convicted otherwise, ma'am," the exasperated voice replied.

"I'm sorry to bore you, but my little baby is out there in the night. Without her food, without her blankie. She's recently had surgery, she needs particular attention. I hate to think that she's only being looked for during the day shift. I hate to think that I'm sitting in a warm house, waiting anxiously to hear from the law enforcement agency, and they're not even looking for her."

The voice on the other end softened. "I'm sorry, ma'am. She and the kidnapper are being looked for. I assure you, anyone driving a red Corvette today had a less than peaceful day. As a matter of fact, we busted a drug dealer we've been trying nail, in the process of looking for your daughter."

"I see. Well, thank you," Elizabeth said quietly. "I know, you're doing everything possible." She hung up and turned to Gail.

"They won't find Marsalis. He doesn't want to be found and he won't be found. It's up to me. And he's certainly not driving that Corvette around, advertising himself." She turned and headed for the stairs. "I'm going to bed to think. Good-night, Gail."

Elizabeth sank onto her bed and sank into an even darker despair. She'd known Marsalis was changing lately, but she hadn't bothered to figure out what was wrong with him. She'd given all her attention to Amy and now *he* had Amy. That, he probably reasoned, would teach her a lesson.

She only blamed herself. When she thought about Amy, out there in the night crying for her, Elizabeth felt she would crawl right out of her skin. She couldn't stand it, she just couldn't stand it! How could she even stay in this bed, comfortable and warm? But where could she go to look for Marsalis? She could only pray with all her heart that he would not take out his anger or revenge, or whatever it was he was feeling, on little Amy, defenseless and trusting.

Even Amy had never warmed up to Marsalis. No one in Elizabeth's life had liked Marsalis. Why, in heaven's name had she? It wasn't, in point of fact, his physical beauty, which, in any case, she'd learned was too perfect to be interesting. And his own love for his good looks was unattractive in the extreme.

No, after they were married and she'd gotten to know him better, she'd fallen for his need to be loved. He refused to talk about his childhood or his parents, who had been quite old when they'd had him, and were now both dead. Elizabeth had never been able to learn from him what were the holes in his nurturing.

But they were there. After a while she hadn't needed him to tell her stories of childhood neglect.

She intuited them.

Somewhere among these thoughts, she drifted into a half-sleep, only to jump awake when the telephone rang. It rang twice, she grabbed it, but no one was there.

Frustrated, she went downstairs. It was dark and Gail was apparently asleep in her room, no light coming from under her closed door.

Elizabeth's hand and knee throbbed. She really needed to get some sleep if her body was to heal. She went back upstairs, into the bathroom and switched on the light. She'd forgotten about her black eye all day, and she was curious to see what it looked like.

She gasped. It had gotten much worse. The left side of her face was purple to her jaw bone and the inside of her eye and down along her nose was ... *black*, there was no other word for it. It seemed to be more swollen than in the morning. She went back to bed. Three-thirty a.m. Had Marsalis called and let the telephone ring twice, just to harass her? Who else would call at three-thirty a.m.?

Chapter XXVII

Three hours later, she dragged herself downstairs. Gail was in the kitchen making breakfast.

"I can't eat anything, Gail, thanks."

"You have to, Elizabeth. I insist. Look at you! Your black eye is worse, you look peaked, and you'll eat something if I have to force feed you."

"Did you hear the phone ring last night?"

"No."

"About three-fifteen. It rang twice, I picked it up, but there was just a dial tone."

"I can't imagine I would sleep through the phone ringing," Gail said, bringing Elizabeth some toast. "I think you're over-wrought. You wish so much that it'd ring."

Elizabeth shook her head. "No, it rang. Right by my ear. Should I call the police?"

"Let's wait until we're sure Timms and Avery are there. You know they'll call you the instant they know anything."

"I suppose. I guess Marsalis thinks it'll prove his point by calling and letting the phone right twice. From now on, if the phone even makes a peep, grab it."

"Okay." Gail gave Elizabeth a worried look, but she didn't say anything more.

"I think I'll try calling Michelle." Elizabeth got Michelle's number out of her purse and dialed.

"Hi, Michelle, this is Gail ... the person who called you the other day about the condo Marsalis was interested in?"

"I don't understand what went on," Michelle's kitten voice said. "I called with the information you asked for and first thing I know, I'm talking with Marsalis. Do you live with Marsalis?"

"Well, yes. I have a little confession to make. You see, I'm his housekeeper. I didn't hear about the condo through a friend, Marsalis had chatted with me about it. And it sounded like what I've been looking for. But you know, I didn't want to tell him I'm thinking about leaving. It just so happens that I've been thinking about moving to San Diego. So the other night when his girlfriend answered the phone ...."

"His girlfriend?"

"Yes. Anyway, when she answered the phone and you asked for me, Mr. Antonella just went and took the phone from her. He's like that sometimes. Sometimes he won't even let me take my own calls."

"His girl friend," Michelle said again.

"Yes," Elizabeth-as-Gail answered. "Yes. She lives here too."

"Really!" Michelle said with disgust.

"Anyway, the reason I'm calling is to get the information you had for me. Is there another condo available?"

"Yes. Two, in fact. A one bedroom and a two bedroom."

"I suppose Mr. Antonella was looking at the two bedroom."

"Yes, but this unit I'm talking about is a different one."

"Oh, good," Elizabeth said. "I hope it's not too close to the one he's interested in. I mean, if we both happened to move into the same complex, I wouldn't want to be bumping into him."

"No. They're not at all adjacent. The two bedroom available is—let's see, number 410 and the one Marsalis is considering is 37."

"I see. Well, could you give me the address? I might sneak down and take a peek today or tomorrow. If I like what I see, I'll give you a call."

Michelle gave her the address and said she hoped she'd see something she liked.

"I'm wondering," Elizabeth said to Michelle, as if a last thought, "if you've seen Marsalis yesterday or today? I haven't seen him, not that it's that unusual, he has a way of disappearing for days sometimes. But I'd be embarrassed to run into him down there— if I do happen to get away today."

"No," Michelle answered. "I haven't seen or heard anything of him. He's about to lose his condo. Among other things," she added quietly. "You might want to go by 37 too since it might be available after

243 ~ Amethyst Dream

all. In which case you really wouldn't have any worry about running into him."

"Wouldn't that be nice?" Elizabeth said. "Thanks so much, Michelle. You've been a great help."

She hung up and turned to Gail. "I don't think he's down there at all. That poor girl has sure been duped."

"Well," Gail said with disgust, "she's not the only poor girl who's been duped."

"Yes, I remember who the other poor girl is, and I don't even need to look in the mirror to be reminded."

The telephone rang under Elizabeth's hand, Peter's name came up on the caller ID. "Peter!"

"Elizabeth, what is going on there?"

"Oh, Peter, you won't believe it. Wait, how do you know something's going on?"

"Because a thin old man with high cheek bones, a long, thin nose and a shock of white hair, appeared on the front stairway last night and told me."

Elizabeth collapsed onto the couch. "Grandfather!"

"Yes. Clear as day, even more defined than the day he walked through the front door when I was on the porch."

"What did he say?"

"He said that I should 'tell Elizabeth to listen and watch, to not be afraid.' He said someone is trying to reach you. That you must keep your mind open. Then he said an odd thing. He said it was best that you have the amethyst."

"Not *the* amethyst, Peter," Elizabeth said. "Amethyst ... that's Amy's real name. Oh, Peter! Marsalis kidnapped Amy yesterday."

"What do you mean,"kidnapped?'"

"I mean, he broke into the house and stole her. Last Thursday night, I faced Marsalis with evidence that he was having an affair. He attacked me and I kicked him out."

"Why didn't you call me? Are you all right?"

"I'm cut up and I have a black eye."

"You called the police?"

"Only after he took Amy. I should have when he attacked me. I had no idea he'd go this far."

"What have the police done?"

"They don't know anything more this morning than they did yesterday afternoon." Suddenly Elizabeth couldn't stand the sound of those bleak words. How hopeless it all seemed, and how helpless she felt. She began to cry.

"Don't cry, Elizabeth, please don't cry," Peter said. "I'll be there in a few minutes and we'll figure out where Marsalis is."

"Don't cry, Pet," Gail said, patting Elizabeth's shoulder. "You don't want to lose your energy."

"You're right," Elizabeth acknowledged, collecting herself, "both of you. But I feel I need to cry! Oh, Peter, did you happen to call about three a.m. last night and let it ring only twice?"

"No, Elizabeth. However, that was when your grandfather appeared to me. I wanted to call you immediately, but I waited until this morning. I thought I should see if the—visitation seemed as real in the daylight as it did in the middle of the night. It does. You should have the police tap your phone."

"They already have."

245 ~ Amethyst Dream

"Good! I'm on my way, I'll be there soon." He hung up.

Elizabeth turned to Gail. "He's coming."

"I'll make some more breakfast," Gail said. "In the meantime, perhaps you'd fill me in on what's all this talk about your grandfather?"

The telephone rang again. Elizabeth grabbed it before one ring was finished.

"Mrs. Antonella? This is officer Timms. I just got on duty and got your message from last night. I'm calling to let you know that nothing concrete has turned up yet, but we're working on it."

"Thank you, Officer Timms. I guess I don't need to tell you how anxious I am. Also, do you have any record of my phone ringing last night, about three-fifteen?"

"Just a sec." Officer Timms came back directly. "No. Why?"

"The phone rang twice, but when I picked it up, there was just a dial tone."

"The equipment won't register a non-connection."

"I see," Elizabeth said. "Well, thanks again." She hung up and turned to Gail. "The equipment doesn't register a non-connection."

Gail nodded. "If someone wants to reach you, they'll call again, won't they?"

"I suppose."

The phone rang yet again under Elizabeth's hand. She grabbed it up. "Hello? Oh! Mrs. Vargas!" She exchanged a look of dismay with Gail.

"Hello Elizabeth. I'm in China, working on some international adoptions. I've just received an Amber Alert about Amy."

"Marsalis took her. We—we've had a falling out. His behavior has become so erratic and—anyway, he took her yesterday."

"Have you heard anything?"

"No. And I'm just ...."

"I understand, Elizabeth. I've worked with kidnappings before. I have a remarkable team, and I'll get them on it immediately. I'll be back in a couple of days. Right now, I must get off the phone as my plane is about to take off. Stay strong. For Amy's sake, you must stay strong."

"I will Mrs. Vargas. Thank you, I will." She hung up and turned to Gail. "I completely forgot about her in all this madness."

"That's understandable," Gail comforted. "What did she say?"

"She's in China, working on some international adoptions and got an Amber alert about Amy. With the world so small, why can't we find Marsalis? She said she's had to deal with kidnappings before and she'll put her team on finding Amy."

"That's excellent," Gail said. "Her people are amazing."

A few moments later, Peter arrived. Elizabeth told him about the conversation with Mrs. Vargas and he then filled Gail in on the paranormal events occurring at the old house.

The three of them began brainstorming, trying to outguess Marsalis. But they only realized that, between the three of them, they knew very little about him, and were incapable of conjecturing where he might hide out.

"Well, you two," Elizabeth said in the middle of the afternoon when it seemed that they had covered more ground about Marsalis than possible and still had gotten nowhere, "I can't endure sitting around here any longer. The police haven't called, Marsalis hasn't called, and it's late afternoon. Soon it'll be night again. I cannot endure another night like last night.

"This is what I think we ought to do. Peter, I think you should go home in case any clues manifest. Gail, you stay here and answer the landline phone. I'm going to go driving. Call my cell if *anything* happens."

"What will driving accomplish?" Gail asked. "You're not going to just run into him."

"You never know. Anyway, I can't even think anymore, sitting here. At least if I'm in motion, I can think."

Gail shrugged. "Whatever you feel is best, dear."

"I need to be alone and I need to be in motion, or I think I'll go crazy."

"Go, go with our blessing," Peter said. "But *please* be careful."

Peter left, and Gail walked out to the garage with Elizabeth. "You're in an extremely distracted frame of mind, you really must be very attentive and careful."

"Don't worry Gail, just stay close to the phone."

Chapter XXIII

Elizabeth started out crisscrossing the neighborhood, driving up one street and down the next. She knew this was no way to find Marsalis, but she felt that, at least, she was doing more than just sitting around the house, tense and unable to think.

Up and down and back and forth she drove, getting farther and farther from home. She got a call from Gail. Officer Timms had called to say that nothing had turned up.

Dusk was falling and with it, the horrible dread stole over Elizabeth. Amy was out here, somewhere, a second night. How could she possibly endure another night without her baby? It felt like ages since she'd seen her.

Elizabeth wanted to scream. She couldn't recall ever having felt like screaming in her life. But she didn't scream. She inhaled deeply several times and continued driving.

She would not allow Marsalis to have this power over her. Everything he'd done was about showing her he had the power to make her do his will. He didn't see that he had attacked and injured her, he only saw that she had humiliated him by telling him to get out. She had hurt his pride, his fragile, sensitive, sick pride. He'd returned his hurt by hurting her where she was most vulnerable.

Marsalis only wanted Amy as a pawn. Elizabeth knew he'd have a slew of demands of her if she ever wanted to see Amy again. Why hadn't he called?

A fog settled on the night. Elizabeth hadn't even noticed it, and suddenly there it hung, dense and dreamlike. No traffic at all. Elizabeth looked at the car clock. "Goodness!" she exclaimed. It was midnight— it had been three hours since she'd called Gail. How had the time slipped away from her?

She looked around. She didn't know where she was, nothing was recognizable in the dense fog. The intermittent street lights made pools of light below them, the fog capturing their light. Everything was eerily light and dark at the same time. Elizabeth looked for a street sign to give her some bearing.

She came to an intersection and stopped at the red light. It felt absurd to sit patiently at a red light when there was not one other car anywhere.

Finally the light changed. As Elizabeth went through the intersection, still peering into the fog for street signs which remained oddly absent, she noticed a white sedan coming through the intersection facing her.

It came out of nowhere. A plain white car. The driver stared at her. Elizabeth couldn't make out if it was a man or a woman. The person had short dark hair and large dark-rimmed glasses. Light reflected off the glasses and Elizabeth couldn't see the person's eyes, but she could feel the eyes on her. Then the driver waved at her, trying to make her stop.

Elizabeth's car filled with an electrical charge and the frail hairs on her forearms stood up. A spiky feeling crept up the back of her neck, and she tasted metal.

She slammed her foot onto the accelerator, racing to the next intersection, she glanced in the rear view mirror—the white sedan made a U-turn in the road and followed her!

Elizabeth turned left, speeding past houses that suddenly looked familiar. She saw that she was now close to home. Accelerating dangerously, she began pressing the garage door opener from two blocks away, driving madly. She tore into her driveway and through the open garage door.

As the garage door clanked shut, she peered out into the night, into the suddenly fog-less street.

No vehicle could be seen.

Elizabeth stumbled into the house. Gail came rushing out of her room, tying her bathrobe around her.

"What's wrong," she cried, flipping on the light. "I could hear a car burning rubber for blocks. Except I didn't know it was you until you practically drove through the garage."

"I was followed. The fog was so thick and a car just came out of the fog." Elizabeth gasped for air and grabbed onto the kitchen counter. "It came out of the fog—the driver was staring at me and waving. I couldn't find any street signs, I didn't know where I was because of the fog.

"The car made a U-turn and started to follow me. I don't know why I was so terrified. The inside of my car was charged with electricity. I tore through the stop sign and suddenly I recognized where I was. I was right here! Close to home, after all that driving around."

Gail led Elizabeth into the living room and planted her on the sofa. "I think, Elizabeth, you've overextended yourself. You're too stressed and pushing too hard," she said calmly. "There hasn't been any fog tonight. And I very much doubt someone was chasing you. It was probably some poor lost individual who's been driving around for hours.

"You know how confusing these residential streets can be. You're probably the only other person they saw in an hour, in the middle of the night like this. Calm down, Lizzie. I haven't heard from you in hours. I've been worried sick."

"I know. I'm sorry. But that's another thing. I don't know what happened, I was driving around and all of a sudden, three hours had gone by and there was this fog. I tell you, Gail, I ran into this pocket of fog, dense and white as wedding cake. A white car came out of the fog and the driver looked at me, but I couldn't see the person's *eyes*, light was reflecting off his or her glasses, and it made my skin crawl."

"What light, if the fog was so dense?"

Elizabeth stopped, mouth open. "That's it! Something bothered me at the first moment, but I was so preoccupied with the fog and the car. That's what really scared me. Where did the light reflecting off the glasses come from? I had just noticed, before I saw that car, that the fog had the light from the street lamps all sort of captured. Oh, Gail ...." Elizabeth shivered.

Gail took the comforter off the back of the sofa and wrapped it around Elizabeth. "Do you want me to make a fire?" she asked.

"No. I'm fine ... I'm better. Did anyone call?"

"No. I mean, just Peter, once, to see if you'd come back. Nothing else unusual has happened there. The police didn't call, Marsalis didn't call."

The telephone rang. Both Elizabeth and Gail jumped. Gail grabbed the receiver.

"Hello?" A look of dismay and disgust crossed her face. She handed the receiver to Elizabeth. "Speak of the devil! Keep him talking!" she whispered.

"Hello?" Elizabeth said into the receiver. She began to shiver again.

"I'll bet you're sorry you kicked me out, aren't you?"

Elizabeth took a deep breath. "Yes, Marsalis. I am," she said sweetly.

"Yeah, well, your con act won't work with me. I can see right through that saccharin voice."

"What do you want?"

Marsalis started laughing. Elizabeth had never heard him so gleeful. "Oh, I'll tell you what I want. Piece by bit. But not without the pleasure of watching you crumble. And you can be sure I'm watching you."

"Okay, Marsalis. Watch me crumble and fall apart. But think about Amy. She's a child, an innocent baby. Why hurt her when it's me you want to punish?"

"Sometimes kids find themselves in the path of trouble," Marsalis philosophized. "That's life."

"But, Marsalis, I'll do anything you say, anything you want. Just bring Amy back. Let Gail have her. You and I can work out our problems. But don't let a baby suffer. Are you taking care of her, Marsalis? Are you feeding her? Keeping her warm? Are you doing her therapy?"

"Did you ever, for half a minute, care about me like that?"

"Of course I did, Marsalis. I loved you!"

"Loved. Past tense. That's the key."

A dial tone resounded in Elizabeth's ear. She looked at Gail, and her shivering became almost convulsive.

"Oh, Gail, Gail, *I CAN'T STAND IT!* He wants to break me. I'm broken. I'm broken! He didn't tell me anything about Amy."

Gail picked up the telephone and called the police. Yes, they'd traced the call. It came from El Toro Road. But of course by the time a squad car got there, Marsalis was long gone.

"I'll make us some hot cocoa," Gail said, "it'll help you relax."

They sat silently by the cold fireplace, sipping the hot cocoa. Slowly Elizabeth felt a warmth steal through her aching heart and limbs as if she'd had a couple of stiff shots of brandy. Maybe Gail did put a bit of brandy in the cocoa, Elizabeth thought. She hated to think that she could slip into such a relaxed state with all that was going on. But maybe her mind and body were just giving way.

"Thank you, Gail. I'm going to try to sleep, now." She dragged herself up to bed.

She awoke with a start when the telephone rang. She was sure it had only rung once. She snatched it up.

"Hello?"

There was crackling and snapping on the line like a bad international connection. "Hello?" Elizabeth said again, raising her voice.

Far, far away and faintly, Elizabeth heard a voice.

"What? I can't hear you. Please, speak louder!"

The voice repeated itself. This time through the echoing popping sounds, she thought she heard it say, "I want to help you."

"You want to help me? Yes, how?"

"I ... want ... to ... help ... you," came again.

"Yes," Elizabeth said. "Yes, yes!" She didn't know what else she could say to encourage the distant voice.

Again the voice repeated itself, but more faintly, "I ... want ... to ... help ..." And it faded away.

Grandfather, and someone in a white sedan, and now a woman's voice at some great distance were all trying to reach her, to tell her something, to help her. Why, oh, why had she run away from the white car? Why hadn't she understood, as Grandfather had told Peter, that someone was trying to get in touch with her?

How silly her fears seemed when compared to the formidable powers persevering to contact her. She saw that she had to let go of even her instinctive fears if she hoped to have her precious daughter in her arms again.

Chapter XXIX

The next morning she woke before Gail. She went downstairs and out onto the patio, watching the lake, letting her thoughts reflect off its rippling surface.

She had been considering calling Martha, and the thought had led to much deeper thoughts. What did it mean that she wanted to talk with Martha about the present, horrible problem? Martha was her friend, of course, and would want to know what was happening in Elizabeth's life.

But, Elizabeth asked herself, what did she expect to get from Martha? Martha, by her own admission, was not very fond of children, so her sympathy would be general. Why disrupt Martha's very busy life with something she would be unable to do anything about?

Elizabeth suddenly realized that Martha, despite however much she had thought of her as a girl friend, was a surrogate mother. Elizabeth was always inclined to go to Martha when she had a problem, like she probably would have gone to her mother—if she was around.

Now she saw that she didn't need a surrogate mother, or even a real one. She was a mother now, and she had every bit of character fiber she needed to develop her own strength. She would tell Martha, sometime, about this period in her life, but afterwards, and as a friend only, without any expectations of her.

To be honest, she had to admit that the weaning was significantly assisted by the presence of Gail in her life. Still, she felt as if she and Gail were more equals, even if Gail knew more about some things than Martha and her mother put together.

"Who called last night?" Gail asked, coming out onto the patio.

Elizabeth jumped. "You startled me! You heard the phone ring this time?"

"Yes, I did. It rang about three-fifteen, the same time that you said it rang the night before."

"It sounded like a bad international connection." Elizabeth stood up and went to the edge of the patio, leaning against the low fence, the fence she'd had built for Amy. "There was a great deal of static and noise on the line. Then, very far away, a woman said, 'I want to help you.' She repeated it several times. Finally her voice faded away to nothing."

"Did you call the police to see what kind of follow-up they were able to do on it?"

"No. I'll do that now." She went in and called, then returned to Gail on the patio. "They said it *was* like an international connection, except they couldn't trace it to any country. They said they only heard my end of the conversation."

Elizabeth tried to force herself to eat breakfast, but she couldn't. She went upstairs to change and to get ready for her day of driving.

She moved around as if in a trance. Her intention was to go into her bedroom, but she found herself in her rug room, standing in front of the loom with the very nearly finished baby carpet. She stood staring at the little pastel rug, wondering why she'd come in here, when, slowly, the carpet changed from soft pink and blue and yellow and green to tans and browns and dark greens. Instead of the dainty little cottage and meadow, she saw two gigantic fir trees on either side of a rustic cabin. Three steps. Gravel path. Up, on a hill.

She stared intently at the image, as it slowly morphed. She felt faint and reached out for the wall. The moment she touched it, the bright sunshiny room came back and the sweet pastel rug hung before her on its loom.

She went to her room, sat on the edge of the bed and put her head in her hands. Her heart was palpitating but she wouldn't let that interfere with the image she just saw—she wanted to burn it into her mind's eye. She didn't know what it meant, but she knew it would become clear to her. She pulled on jeans and a sweatshirt and went back downstairs.

"I'm going," she told Gail. "Keep me posted."

"I will."

Elizabeth drove farther and farther away from home. She drove up and down El Toro Road, but no matter where she looked, nothing made her feel she was closer to Amy.

She went home for an hour after dusk, touched base with Gail, then got back in her car.

She drove back to El Toro Road, winding in the hills among the housing, willing the dense fog to return. This time, she would not run away. Glancing at the car clock she saw it was nearly midnight. Then as she drove around a city park, the palpable fog came up off the grassy plateau of the park and practically walked toward her. She drove slowly, noticing that there was no fog at all among the houses across the street.

The fog stole across the road. Elizabeth stopped at a stop sign, glancing in her rear view mirror. Coming toward her through the fog was a white sedan. Elizabeth refused to give in to the fear.

The car pulled up slowly on her right side. Elizabeth peered into it, but she only saw an unclear shadow of the person with short dark hair and wearing large, dark-framed glasses. The car pulled away from the stop sign and drove into the fog.

Elizabeth followed. Unlike the night before, the driver seemed to pay no attention to her. They returned to El Toro Road and the white sedan turned right, toward the Santiago Mountains. Elizabeth followed.

The farther they went, the denser and whiter the fog became. The white sedan drove faster and faster, but Elizabeth kept following its red tail lights. She careened at sixty around curves that the small car ahead seemed to be taking in a leisurely fashion.

Suddenly, instantly, the car ahead disappeared, in the night, in the fog.

Elizabeth slowed down and looked around. The fog was stealthily lifting and she saw she was just a few feet from the Silverado Canyon turnoff. She had no idea what she should do, where she should go. Disappointed, exhausted beyond evaluating anything, she turned around and headed for home.

*   *

"Peter just called. He wants you to call him the minute you get home," Gail said when Elizabeth walked through the door.

"Oh? Did something ...."

"No. He said no. He just wants to hear your voice."

"He wants to make sure that I'm still in one piece—which I'm not sure I am." She dialed Peter's number. "Hi. It's me."

"Elizabeth," Peter said, concern in his voice, "Gail tells me you're driving all over the place and ...."

"And that I'm acting a little cuckoo? Yes, it's true. But the ... whoever it is, has been visible to me two nights now. I won't let go. No one has any information. Do you?"

"No. Nothing has happened here."

"So, whether I'm crazy or not, I'm still the only one with any sort of lead. I think I'm hanging on pretty well, given ... everything."

"I think so too, Elizabeth," Peter said. "But please, *please* don't do anything to endanger yourself. If you don't get a good night's sleep tonight, you should let Gail or me go driving with you tomorrow. It's only logical. You won't help Amy if you get hurt, or even if you're at such a low energy level you can't function well."

She knew Peter was right. "Okay, I'll try to be reasonable tomorrow."

"Do you want me to come over?"

"Thanks Peter, but, no, not right now. I'm exhausted. And I don't want to diffuse the energy."

"Okay, but I'm coming over tomorrow. Gail invited me for dinner."

"That's good. We'll see you then."

The next morning Gail and Elizabeth were sitting at the breakfast table after a quiet night. Neither Marsalis nor the mystery person had telephoned.

The front doorbell rang. Elizabeth jumped up and met Mrs. Vargas at the door. Tearfully, she ushered her into the kitchen.

Mrs Vargas now saw the other side of Elizabeth's face, and her still swollen, purple eye socket. "Did Marsalis do that to you?"

"Yes. I told him that we were through and that he had to leave. For revenge, I guess, he kidnapped Amy. I've been driving around, hour after hour, looking for him."

Mrs. Vargas' expression became very sad. "I'm very disappointed."

"Don't be disappointed in Elizabeth," Gail defended. "She's turned herself inside out to be Amy's mother. If you'd just let her adopt Amy in the first place when you saw the three of us were a perfect family, instead of making Elizabeth feel she had no alternative but to marry the first person who asked, this would never have happened.

"Look at her!" Gail went on, heated. "Beaten, abused, stitches in her hand and knee, sleepless, worried, and traumatized, and see how calm and rational she is? She's amazing.""Oh, Gail," Elizabeth protested, "don't upset Mrs. Vargas."

"No, no," Mrs. Vargas said. "I'm glad to hear her testimonial, I trust Gail's instincts."

"If you must be disappointed in someone," Gail continued, "be disappointed in me. I'm the one who left the door from the house to the garage unlocked and forgot that Marsalis had a garage door opener, which is how he got his hands on Amy. Elizabeth was at work expecting that I keep up my end of protecting Amy."

Mrs. Vargas nodded. "Unfortunate. Unfortunate all around."

Elizabeth told Mrs. Vargas about the events of the previous days. She trussed up her courage and even told her about the paranormal events Peter had been experiencing.

"When my grandfather, or who, or whatever it was, told Peter that Amy's real name is Amethyst, which Peter did not know, it became clear we were getting help from another dimension—that something spectacular was happening. Knowing that Amy is being watched over by those no longer embodied is all that has kept me sane."

"Perhaps," Mrs. Vargas said carefully, "people pick up bits of information from someone they care very much about. That is, I suppose a person as close to you as Peter is, and as sensitive and intelligent as he is, would be able to psychically access Amy's real name and even tie it together with a lucid dream with a man like your grandfather in it. But I don't believe it goes any farther than that."

"A few days ago I would have been pressed to believe even that. I'm just an ordinary person who's greatest desire is to live an ordinary life. But events larger than me have been taking place, and I can't deny them with an explanation of mere sensitivity and dreams." Elizabeth then told Mrs. Vargas about the previous two nights, the dense fog, the white sedan, the driver with short dark hair and large glasses.

Mrs. Vargas became visibly agitated as Elizabeth's story progressed. When she finished, Mrs. Vargas asked, "Where did you get that information?"

"What?" Elizabeth was stunned by Mrs. Vargas' disapproving voice, a tone she had never heard from her.

"Those details, how did you come up with them?"

"Why, just exactly as I said," Elizabeth answered candidly. "The way I told you."

"There is no way that you could know ... let me tell you a story," Mrs. Vargas said, becoming her calm self once again. "One day I got a call from a young mother asking me if I knew of any financial assistance to help her provide medical attention for her infant. I visited her and she told me her story, which no one, besides myself, has ever heard.

"She had wanted nothing more than to have a child, although she had no man in her life. Working second shift as a word processor in a big empty building and living with her mother, there seemed little probability that she would meet someone. Still, she longed for a baby.

"An attractive man left work every day just as she came on to her shift. He noticed her looking at him and one day he asked her to lunch. After a dozen "lunches," she was pregnant. She told him about the pregnancy. The day after she told him, he quit work and disappeared.

"After Amy was born, she took on a second job to support her little family of herself, her mother and Amy. She had to spend a lot of her income on baby sitters and she worked herself into the ground."

Mrs. Vargas paused for a moment. "She loved Amy with all her heart and soul, much as you do. But tragedy struck one night when an unusually dense fog rolled in. She apparently became disoriented in the fog, driving off the road and into a lamp post. She died instantly.

"Amy's grandmother could not afford to provide for her. Without her daughter's income, she had to go on welfare herself. Anyway, she wanted nothing to do with Amy, blaming the poor baby for her mother's untimely death.

"Amy's biological mother had short black hair and wore large, dark-rimmed glasses. She drove a small white sedan."

Chapter XXX

After Mrs. Vargas left, Elizabeth went to her room, exhausted. She fell asleep and immediately began to dream.

She saw the white sedan, and in her dream, she followed it up El Toro Road again. She turned on the car radio—a young woman's voice said, "I chose you to be Amy's new mother because I saw in your heart and soul you would have the same love for Amethyst I have."

The white sedan turned onto the Silverado Canyon Road and Elizabeth followed. The white car disappeared.

Elizabeth woke up, still exhausted. The dream had taken as much out of her as if she'd actually gone through the experience. She got out of bed and prepared for the long night's drive.

She headed directly for Silverado Canyon Road as the sun sank behind her and all the trees glowed, bathed in golds and pinks and oranges, the sky a deepening blue. Birds fluttered about,

Elizabeth watched as a squirrel scampered from a branch of one tree and leapt across to the neighboring tree.

Everything in this idyll was ageless and beautiful—Elizabeth wished with all her being that she could take pleasure in it.

She felt herself moving, suddenly, through the odd, static atmosphere. The interior of the car became charged. She slammed on her brakes as she hurtled headlong into a cabin.

But as she pulled onto the shoulder, gasping with palms sweating, she saw that the cabin was translucent. Dark brown, with a brown shake roof and three steps leading up to the front door. Two gigantic fir trees stood on either side of the cabin—the same cabin that had superimposed itself on the baby carpet.

Now she knew, without a doubt, this was where Marsalis had Amy.

The cabin must be here in the canyon—*somewhere*.

Elizabeth drove the two miles up to the little village of Silverado Canyon. Then she drove the narrow, winding road that snaked among the cabins on the hillside.

But they were all cheek by jowl. None of them had the space around them of the one in her vision. None of them had the giant matching fir trees in front.

She continued up the canyon to the next berg of cabins. They were even more unlikely, as they were not even on a hillside.

Night had fallen and Elizabeth could no longer see to continue her search. She went back down to Lake Forest and home, buying maps of the area at every filling station she passed.

Gail greeted her at the door. "Oh, Lizzie, I'm so glad you're home."

"Why? Has something happened?"

"No. I wish I could say yes, but no. I just mean, you're wearing yourself down to nothing with all this driving around, and you're not accomplishing anything. At least it's only ten o'clock tonight instead of one a.m."

Elizabeth began spreading out the maps on the living room floor.

"What are those for?" Gail asked.

"I'm going to find Amy tomorrow."

"How?"

"From all the information I've been given." She stretched out on the floor and studied all the roads in the Silverado Canyon. Over a hundred years ago, silver mining had been booming in the mountains—there were almost certainly cabins hardly anyone knew about, up in the hills, abandoned. A perfect place for someone to hide.

Elizabeth penciled over three nearly invisible lines—dirt roads, she surmised—on one of the maps, then highlighted them on another, larger map.

She pointed at the three infinitesimal lines. "On one of these roads, that's where Marsalis is hiding Amy. On a hill, in a dark brown cabin with three steps up to the door and two huge fir trees, one on either side of the cabin. That's where my baby is.

"I'm going to bed."

Chapter XXXI

Elizabeth set her alarm for four-thirty. It would be light enough by the time she got to Silverado Canyon to see the almost nonexistent roads and the cabin. She dressed and went quietly down to the garage. As she drove she thought about encountering Marsalis, who was clearly not in his right mind. Perhaps he even had a weapon.

But she couldn't stop now. The police had not found Amy. Amy was *her* responsibility, and she was taking charge.

She put the map she'd folded down to the three obscure roads across the steering wheel, studying it, hoping another vision would come to her. But it did not, and before long she was at the Silverado Canyon turn off.

All three of the roads were far up in the foothills of the mountains. Elizabeth drove through the winding sleeping village of Silverado Canyon as day dawned, fresh and beautiful. But Elizabeth had no mind for nature now. She *knew* she was close to Amy.

Finally she came to the first road and turned onto it, driving on un-drivable terrain, following two barely discernible ruts.

Thick vegetation grew on both sides and in the middle of the ruts. There was not the slightest hint of a building anywhere. The terrain did not look right either, it was too flat. But Elizabeth followed the bumpy ruts until they became completely grown over.

There was no place to turn around, and, she feared she might get stuck. She backed up cautiously until she came to a space wide enough to turn around, then made her way back out to the main road. One road down, two to go. The next road looked a bit more promising, the area was more hilly.

She turned onto it, but had only gone half-a-mile when she came to a sign:

*YOU ARE ENTERING
PRIVATE PROPERTY
NO TRESPASSING —
THIS MEANS YOU!
TRESPASSERS WILL BE SHOT
SURVIVORS PROSECUTED!!*

Elizabeth felt a mixture of amusement and amazement. What kind of mentality was this? Was it a joke, or perhaps—not.

No sign, however, even if it read "Road to Hell" would deflect Elizabeth from her purpose. She drove another half mile, when the biggest, burliest man she'd ever seen in her life came at her in a jeep.

She stopped. He jumped out of his jeep as if he were ready to tear her car limb from bumper.

She tried smiling as he roared up. "What's the matter with you? Are you illiterate?"

Elizabeth was hugely tempted to say, *"Hola, no habla ..."* but she resisted. The man appeared to lack humor. "I stopped and read your most gracious sign. I'm not the enemy, sir. I'm looking for someone who is out here, somewhere." She held her map out the window, pointing at the three highlighted roads. "See? I'm looking for a cabin that's up on a hill, with two huge fir trees on either side of it."

"Well, you won't find it here. I live alone up here and I don't have any shacks like that."

Elizabeth nodded. She extended her hand. "My name's Elizabeth."

The burly man nodded back, but refused to take her hand. "Okay, Elizabeth, now just turn around and get out."

"What I had in mind, that is, I'm hoping you'll let me go on up this road, just to check it out, and give myself peace of mind."

"I'll give you a piece of *my* mind! I told you that what you're looking for isn't up here. Now *BEAT* it."

"Do you know of any place around here that might fit my description?"

"There's a place something like that on the other road you got marked there," he said, poking an index finger the size of a plump hot dog at her map. "But nobody's lived there for years. It's uninhabitable. You can't even drive up to it anymore, it's so overgrown."

"Thank you," Elizabeth said gratefully, throwing her car into reverse. "Maybe you don't like the idea, but you've just done a good deed."

She turned around and charged back to the main road.

The third dirt road was on the opposite side of the main road, and, according to the map, virtually across the street from the one she'd just exited. But she had to drive up and back twice before she found the unmarked ruts.

As soon as she turned onto the nearly invisible road, though, she knew this was it. She drove for nearly a mile with tree branches thwacking her windshield and scratching the finish of the car. Then the trees thinned and she found herself in a meadow. It was flat, full of wild flowers and the tangible presence of small creatures. Ahead she saw another thicket of growth. Elizabeth continued.

These woods were darker and thicker, the road wound up and down bluff-like hills. Then, suddenly, there it was—a clearing with *the* cabin, and the two giant fir trees that had become etched on her mind's eye, taking three-dimensional form in front of her.

Immediately she cut the engine and let her car roll back into the trees until she could not see the cabin. She crept out of the car and stole among the trees, working her way up the steep hill toward the cabin. Her heart pounded—*she knew she was close to Amy!* She practically gasped for air as she climbed the unmercifully steep hill while struggling through the dense, unyielding underbrush.

Finally she reached the small clearing around the cabin. She crept up to the gigantic near fir tree, bigger around than the burly man she'd just left. She peered around, listening attentively. *And there!* Just peeking out from behind the cabin, was the nose of an old Ford pickup truck. So that's what Marsalis had been sneaking around in.

She heard nothing. She would have to steal the remaining distance to the cabin and peek in a window.

She scurried forward, a couple twigs cracking underfoot as she went, making her more nervous than an edgy cat. The windows were all just barely above her eye level. Standing on tip-toe, she peered through a side window.

There, on a ratty, horrible couch, slept Marsalis. Her heart raced even faster, which seemed impossible.

But she didn't see Amy.

Where was Amy? Elizabeth heard a faint crying from another room. *Amy!* Her baby was practically within her grasp.

"Shut up!" Marsalis yelled. "*SHUT UP!*" He didn't move a muscle to see why she was crying.

Elizabeth suddenly knew what it was to have the strength of ten men. She hoisted herself up through the open window and flew to the back of the cabin where she'd heard her baby cry. There she saw her precious baby, trapped in a corner by a pile of boxes and broken furniture, a cage of sorts. In her life, Elizabeth had never felt rage like she felt now.

Marsalis flew into the room and jumped on Elizabeth, knocking her to the floor. "What's the matter with you?

What's the matter with you! NO WOMAN TREATS ME LIKE YOU DID! No woman ever has, and no woman ever will. You're my wife, you belong to me!"

Marsalis's rage and venom turned his perfect features into a frightening, hideous mask. The pulsing vein in his forehead looked as though it would burst then and there.

"Besides," he continued, digging his fingers like talons into her shoulders, "who else would have you, you wimpy little mouse? I married you for financial security. You were crazy to expect me to stay home and play daddy! I knew how to get you back, all I had to do was take the brat!"

Marsalis stopped ranting and looked down at Elizabeth, trapped under him. "Wait a minute, how did you get here?"

He dragged her to her feet, pulled her over to the window and looked out. There was nothing but trees and wild vegetation to be seen.

"*Hah!* All by yourself. Too smart for your own good, aren't you? Well, you're here now. I knew it'd work, just grab the brat and you'd come running. I wanted to let you suffer some more before I told you where to come. I wanted to make sure you'd obey me after you saw I mean what I say!"

All through Marsalis's crazed harangue Amy was screaming at the top of her lungs, "*Mommy! Mommy!*"

"And shut that brat up! I've had all of her noise I can stand!"

Elizabeth's fury was so intense, she'd become calm. "She'd better not be missing one single hair from her head."

"Ha! Ha!" Marsalis said in a forced tone. "Or what? You going to hurt me?" He slapped her. "I think I should make a matching black eye for that other pretty one I created. You still don't know who's boss, do you?"

Elizabeth wretched herself from Marsalis's grasp and ran toward Amy. She grabbed a chair from the pile and swung it at Marsalis. It knocked him into the wall and he looked at her in complete surprise.

"Don't make me angry, Elizabeth," he warned. "I mean it. You've really been making me angry lately. I won't tolerate it!"

Elizabeth grabbed another piece of the makeshift facade blocking her from her baby, and threw that at Marsalis as well. Another box and she had her hand on Amy. Amy clutched onto Elizabeth. *"Mommy! Take Amy."*

"Yes baby, I'm taking you. Don't worry!"

Marsalis lunged at her, and threw her to the floor. She twisted out of his grasp, her eyes and mind only on Amy, who stood reaching through the last chair blocking her from Elizabeth, crying, "Marsa bad. Mommy take Amy. Marsa bad."

Elizabeth couldn't bear the plaintive cry of her baby. Oh yes, Marsa had become very bad, indeed. "Yes, Mommy take Amy." She kicked with all her might at Marsalis's hand grabbing onto her ankle.

"Damn, Elizabeth, that hurts. Will you just stop fighting me?"

She jumped up, leaned over the chair and grabbed Amy, then sidled along the wall. Marsalis slowly stood, clearly disoriented, but not willing to stop. There were three feet between her and the door to the front room. She jumped through the doorway and Marsalis leapt forward, grabbing her shirt.

She wrested herself free and put Amy down. "Outside, Amy! Amy, go outside!"

As Marsalis threw her to the floor she saw Amy toddling toward the front door. Then Marsalis's hands closed around her throat.

"You stupid disobedient bitch! I'm the husband! You have to *OBEY* me!"

Elizabeth saw the color of blood pulsing in her eyes. She couldn't breathe and she felt consciousness ebbing, but she heard Amy crying outside and she refused to let go.

She arched her back and threw Marsalis off balance. They rolled—Elizabeth broke his hold on her throat. She pulled herself through the front door, rolled, then tumbled down the three steps to the ground. Amy was standing on the porch, screaming bloody murder.

Elizabeth reached up and seized her baby, turned and ran down the hill as if all the demons of a hideous hell were on her heels. And one of them was. Marsalis had regained his footing and was fast upon her.

Off in the distance, Elizabeth was vaguely aware of a siren.

Oh, someone was lucky, she thought. Someone else had help rushing to them, while she was out here alone with a mad man, where no one knew where she was. She got to her car and jumped in, berating herself for not turning it around before.

She locked the doors. Marsalis was in front of the car, wielding a log. He raised it towards her windshield. Elizabeth shoved Amy onto the floor. "Stay on the floor baby," she said as she shielded her face with one arm while starting the car. The car leapt alive, and knocked Marsalis over. Elizabeth pulled forward and made a frantic U-turn. She looked in the rear view mirror. Marsalis had picked himself up and ran at her car.

She pulled away.

"It's okay, Amy, baby. We're going to get away. Don't cry anymore."

Just as she came into the clearing of the meadow, a jeep, followed by a police car, followed by a '56 Chevy, roared into the meadow.

Elizabeth stopped and grabbed up Amy. She stumbled from the car, bloody, with torn clothes. Officers Timms and Avery, Peter and Gail, and the burly, surly man from across the road came pouring out of their vehicles.

At that moment Marsalis burst into the clearing, saw all that was before him, then turned and ran back into the woods. The officers went pounding after him on foot.

Peter ran up to Elizabeth, and she and Amy tumbled into his arms while Peter smothered them both in kisses. "Brave Elizabeth, you silly thing, how could you do this by yourself? Don't you know you can count on me?"

Elizabeth nodded, but could say nothing.

The burly man tugged Gail by the hand as they rushed up to them. "Lizzie, girl, Amy!" Gail panted.

"Thank God you're both all right!" She took Amy's little face in her hands and kissed her.

"Gao! Gao!" Amy cried.

"Why didn't you tell me you were trying to nab a kidnapper?" the burly man asked Elizabeth. "If there's one thing I really hate, it's any kind of person who would do any harm to a kid." His terrifying visage melted into cherubic smiles as he patted Amy. "Hi, baby face," he said in a high-pitched voice. "Hi little-angel-pumpkin-darlin'-cutie-cutie."

Amy chortled gleefully.

"How did you find us?" Elizabeth breathed, tearfully.

"Peter came over," Gail began ....

"I went to your place and saw all those maps, and your pencil scratches on these roads. I'm a little bit familiar with these roads—they're not safe." He led Elizabeth to a log and made her sit, then sat beside her.

Gail and the big, burly man sat on the ground beside them.

"And he thought," Gail started ....

"And I also thought you were probably on to something, so I had the police come along."

"Good thing too, or this giant would have done us in," Gail said.

"Hey!" the burly man continued in his falsetto so as not to startle Amy. "You see what kind of crazies come creeping up into these hills. If not for me ...."

"If not for you, we might not have found them yet," Gail nodded at the giant with unabashed approval and admiration.

Chapter XXXII

"That's going to be so adorable," Elizabeth said to Gail.

Gail stopped rocking and held up the yellow bonnet she was crocheting for Amy, the firelight glowing cheerfully on her smiling apple-cheeks.

Elizabeth hugged Amy, a shadow crossed her features.

"What?" Peter asked.

Elizabeth smiled warmly at him. "I can't hide anything from you, can I?"

"Why would you want to?"

"I don't, my darling. It just passed my mind for a fleeting moment how close I came to losing Amy, and, and *everything*, after CPS took her away because of her unfit adoptive father. If not for you and Gail and Mrs. Vargas fighting for me and for Amy, we would not be sitting here together, all cuddly."

"But here we are," Gail said, "happy as a bunch of little clams."

"Yes, here we are!" Elizabeth tickled Amy until she giggled, then pointed at Gail's crochet hook, flashing in the firelight. "Gail is making a pretty-bonnet for pretty-Amy!"

"Pretty Gail!" Amy said.

Peter chuckled. "You sure got that right!" He sat opposite Elizabeth who was holding Amy in the overstuffed chair beside Gail in her rocking chair, the light of the fire playing over them. "You should see the three of you with my eyes! *What* a beautiful sight!"

"I'm so grateful and utterly filled with joy," Elizabeth sighed, exchanging a long and endearing smile with Peter. "Now we should try to fix Gail up."

"Not necessary! I'm content," Gail protested.

"Yes," Peter agreed, unable to stay even eight feet away from them. He came over and sat on the floor by Elizabeth, taking Amy's foot, he counted off the little piggies. "And this little piggy stayed home. Who do you have in mind for her?"

"Well," Elizabeth answered thoughtfully, "I believe Ralph would be perfect. He's hard working, he's interested in everything like Gail is, he's intelligent, he's good looking, and he's already part of the family."

Peter nodded seriously. "Ralph is an excellent choice."

"Who did you have in mind?" Elizabeth asked him.

"I thought that soft-hearted, tough-acting, ruggedly handsome Mike-the-giant would be a good choice. After gallantly leading us and the police to you and helping Gail trudge through the wild brush, it seemed to me I saw a glint of interest there."

"Oh, yes," Elizabeth agreed. "Another very good option."

Gail got into the act. "You two are on the right track. They both have great potential. In fact, I don't think I'd be able to choose between them. Do you think I could indulge in a bit of polyandry?"

"But Gail, you'd be too busy then, and you know we need you. No, I think we'll only allow you one husband." Elizabeth studied the fire. "Sometimes one can be one more than you want."

Peter took Elizabeth's hand and kissed her palm. "You should have married me in the first place."

"Well—*yes*," she agreed. "But it would have helped if you had asked." She leaned over to give him a lingering kiss.

"*Ohhh!*" Amy clapped her hands in delight. "*Mommy-Beetie kiss!*"

The End

Thank You....

For reading Elizabeth and Amethyst's story.

For a free download of the first chapters of my new book, **Porcelain Claws**, go to:

www.subscribepage.com/PorcelainClaws

Even before Cindy saw the mystical hobbledy-knobbily creature tumble across the road and into the woods when she was a little girl, her life had been on a mystical path.

Determined to fulfill her childhood promise to her father to follow her dream to become a photographer, she begins to encounter other dimensions on photoshoots in vacant houses.

When the Porcelain Goddess appears to her, terrifying and beautiful, she grants Cindy a trans-dimensional gift. If Cindy chooses to bring this gift into the three-dimensions, it will open the door to the fulfillment of her long-ago promise, allow her to triumph over the Goddess of Death ... and *change the world forevermore....*

About The Author ....

I live in the greater Portland, Oregon area. I *love* the Great Northwest where the rainy weather, lush green territory, water falls, mountains, charming neighborhoods, the Pacific ocean nearby, along with a strong writing community, make the writing life a dream come true.

You can connect with me at:
Thea@EmersonandTilman.com

I hope to "see" you soon!